Undeniable

Undeniable

Embracing second chances soothes the torment of regret.

NIKKI FREESTONE SORENSEN

"When writing the story of your life,
don't let anyone else hold the pen."

—Harley Davidson

Prologue

This second book in the Peg Series continues the story of my grandmother, Gladys Irene Tarbet and her adventures in Alaska. Like the first book, *Unladylike*, it is based on true events.

Several readers have asked me if Peg's boyfriend, Charlie, is real. He is not. I created Charlie because my grandmother told me she was engaged to a boy who left to fight in WWI, and I needed a reason for her to elope with my grandfather. She was nineteen years old and Ralph fifty-three! When her boyfriend returned, he was so changed that they broke up. Regrettably, I didn't ask her more questions about it. I wrote Charlie as a redhead because my grandmother adored red hair. My sister married a redhead and Peg hoped one of her children would have red hair! None did.

In this book, readers may wonder if Peg really did work as a deputy sheriff during prohibition. She did, and the story of discovering the milkman selling moonshine is true along with many of the other events. I agree with Mark Twain, "Truth is stranger than fiction, but it's because fiction is obliged to stick to possibilities; truth isn't."

I hope you enjoy traveling back in time to Alaska's pioneer era and experiencing my grandmother's "unladylike" life. The series will continue with Peg's daughter, my very **ladylike** mother, and her love story.

Ismailof Island, Alaska
https://upload.wikimedia.org/wikipedia/commons/6/6a/
AKMap-doton-HalibutCove.PNG

CHAPTER 1

Newport, Washington, January 1922

Sturdy workhorses dragged the farm wagon into the yard. Mary froze, stunned when she recognized the inert body in the wagon's bed. She clutched her chest and lunged off the porch. "John?" Springs moaned as her grown son jumped from the wagon with a pained face and clenched fists.

"Mom," his voice cracked as tears fell. His shoulders curled over his chest.

"John?" her question spiraled into a cry. "John!" She leapt to the end of the wagon and strained on tiptoe against the weathered wood. As her hand cupped her husband's chin, she cried, "John, my dar . . .ling." Hefting herself up beside him, she ignored slivers piercing her hands and placed her cheek against his. She stroked his hair and sobbed, "John . . . John . . ."

She awoke with pain in the back of her throat, her lips trembling. Her hand flew to her mouth as nausea hit. *It's been four years. How many times do I have to relive this?* John's heart attack repeated in her mind like a scratched record. Rolling from bed onto shaky legs, she shuffled to the kitchen and noticed a letter on the cupboard. *Mud must have dropped the mail off after I went to bed.* She recognized her daughter's loopy handwriting, carried it to her chair by the fire and tore open the envelope.

Ishmailof Island, Alaska

March 21, 1922

Dear Mom,

Do you think you could come visit us this summer? There are so many things I want to show you. Every day's a new adventure. Yesterday, a whale got caught in the lagoon during low tide. When Ralph shot it, big chunks of blubber flew into the air! But it still didn't leave, and even my resourceful husband didn't know what else to do. After destroying many of our nets, it finally went out with the tide.

Speaking of whales, a whaling boat *The New England* came into the bay last fall. We went onboard and watched eleven Norwegian men work. After we got out to sea, one crawled up into a barrel at the top of the mast to scan the ocean. He shouted, "Whale Ho! Port bow!" Men flew to work. The whale dove but surfaced again a few minutes later. When the gunner fired, a four-foot harpoon trailing rope hurtled out to sea and hit its mark, then men used a winch to reel the whale in. They lashed it to the side, climbed down right on top of it and cut out blubber hunks with huge knives on the ends of long poles. Finally, they lifted big strips of blubber onto the ship. They took the rest to Port Holborn on Kodiak to be rendered out for fertilizer.

We've had trouble with the sea lions getting tangled in our fishing nets. Ralph killed one and rendered it out on the beach. He saved the oil, mixed it with ocher and painted the warehouses, then trimmed them in white. Ralph can fix so many things. He hewed timber and built our own wharf and pilings, even tapered them at both ends. They look as good as mill-planned timbers.

I so want you to come see our darling Peggy. A baby in this country is quite a novelty. Our good friends, Ted and Alice Nutbeem, have no children of their own and love her. Alice will babysit any time. Ted was raised in the Presbyterian Mission in Unalaska because his English father and native mother died. Alice grew up on Unga Island on the Alaskan Peninsula the Nutbeems exploring several islands and saw many redheaded natives on the island of Chichagof. I guess they descended from an Irish priest who lived there in the early days.

If you come, you can meet the Nutbeems
and all the interesting people Ralph and
I know. Alaska draws those with a free spirit.
An Irish man and his native wife came to
the salteries during herring season. The wife
has a hunchback. Poor thing. She brought
her two little girls with her.
    While in Snettisham, we got acquainted
with a Metlakatla Indian couple. The wife
taught me how to make moccasins, so
I made our Peggy some and am working
on another pair. It gives me something to do
now that I'm stuck inside.

Peg paused, wondering whether to unburden herself to her mother, but decided not to.

I am sitting here enjoying the most
beautiful sunset! I love Alaska. The smoke
of the Illiamna volcano across from Cook's
Inlet settles low in the sky and sets it ablaze.
Well, Ralph should be home soon for supper
and Peggy wants nursing.
    Sending all my love to you and the rest
of the family,

Peg

Mary placed the letter in her basket on top of the baby afaghan she'd been crocheting. She lifted herself from the rocker with a little moan, crossed to her picture window and stared at the glittering snow carpeting the landscape. The orchard's naked branches shivered in the wind. *I wonder if Alaska resembles our winter. I think I will go. It's too quiet here with my John gone. It will give me something fun to plan, and I want to meet my new granddaughter!* After crossing to the stove and stuffing in a couple pieces of wood, she pushed up her roll top desk, opened the top drawer and took out a few sheets of stationery. She settled onto the creaking office chair she'd brought from her store and reached for a pen in the desk's cubbyhole.

Newport, Washington

April 11, 1922

Dear Peg,

Everyone here loves hearing about your adventures. I take your letters to the store where the "stove huggers" devour them. Those old men are living through you and can hardly wait for the next installment of your story! They'll love hearing about your whaling experience. I wouldn't be surprised if ol' Svein hasn't been whaling himself.

We had a lovely Christmas, marred only by the deeply felt loss of your dear father. Of course, we missed you too, but we got exciting news. Gene and Marie announced Christmas Day they are expecting a baby in July! Can't wait for your Peggy to meet her same age cousin someday. I guess they can always be pen pals.

The kids here surprised me with a big birthday party on the 17th. They worry about me, but I promise, I am doing fine. Can't believe I'm already sixty-one years old, but my body's starting to remind me. Remember how you didn't like to share your birthday party with Mud, even though his is just the day before yours? Maybe because he teased that he got the first pick of all the presents since his birthday was first!

In this cold weather, your dear brother Wilbur suffers with his arm. I'll never forget the day the railroad car he and Dad were riding in got hit. Just a wonder he still has his arm! But despite our trials, we have been blessed. The ranch and store made a nice profit, so I think I will come to see you this summer! Would it be too late if I waited until after Gene and Marie's baby? I'd prefer to be here, but Marie's mother is coming down from Spokane, so I'm not needed until she leaves. Hope you're all warm and happy.

Love,

Mom

May 7, 1922

Ishmailof Island, Alaska

Dear Mom,

When I opened your letter, I let out a whoop
and Ralph came running into the house
to investigate. Can't wait to hug you.
We're friends with the steamboat captain,
Captain Howell. Next time we run into him,
I'll make sure he knows you're coming
and ask him to take extra good care of
you. President Harding plans on coming
up next summer to drive the Golden Spike
at Nenena. Would you like to go there?
I want to visit Denali National Park in the
same area. Wouldn't it be something if you
came on the same steamship as President
Harding?

The end of April, Ralph took Peggy and
me to visit the Palmers, an old couple who
homesteaded up around Homer. Ralph and
Mr. Palmer wanted to hunt moose, and
I needed to escape the house! I sure love my
little Peggy, but being tied to the house is
killing me. On days Ralph is home, I take
our dog Miko out for a run with the dogsled.

I helped Mrs. Palmer with her chores,

and she loved rocking the baby. Watching her rock Peggy made me think soon you will, too. Ralph shot a giant moose. It took two days to skin and prepare it for their smokehouse. Since we had to leave, the Palmers committed to keep the fire burning until the meat cures. Ralph and I split and stacked wood for them. They begged us to stay longer, but we assured them we'd come back as soon as possible. You'll enjoy them. They're around your age.

On the last night of our visit, the Palmers invited all the couples living in the area over for moose dinner. We furnished the meat, and everyone brought potluck. Mrs. Palmer and I made cake for dessert. Afterwards, we danced in their large barn until midnight. The women passed Peggy around. She's the only baby for miles. When we got home, Ralph mounted the huge antlers on the shed because our little home has no room for them.

When the snow clears, we want to build another woodshed nearby. One problem, a huge basalt rock sits in the way. Remember how Dad and his hired hand used dynamite to remove the granite stone from our orchard?

Mud and I thought it exciting. I'll bet with
all the mining, someone has blasting powder
up here.

I'm marking the days off on our
calendar.

Love to all,

Peg

CHAPTER 2

Ed scraped the mud from his shoes, opened the back door and called, "Ready, Mom?" He noticed two bags inside the door and loaded them into the back of his truck. Mary adjusted her traveling hat in the mirror and scurried out.

"Thanks, Son, for taking time to help me today. I hardly slept for excitement! I kept thinking of one more thing to take to Alaska."

"I could tell by the weight of your bags," Ed teased. "Wish I could go with you. As soon as you can, make sure you contact Peg's friend, Captain What's-his-name?"

"Captain Howell." Mary slipped her gloves off and stuck them in her purse. "I'd better keep these clean for later."

"You think they dress up in Alaska?" Ed doubted.

"You never know. I want to be presentable and not embarrass Peg."

Ed guffawed, "I don't think that's possible, but probably a good idea to take them off before the dusty train station." He gave Mary his hand as she climbed in. Two miles later, they passed a rancher cutting his hay. "Hope this dry weather holds for him," Ed murmured. "Tell me again your itinerary."

"I'll stay with Aunt Hilah's daughter Winnie in Seattle. She'll take me to the ship and help me buy the ticket. Ralph will pick me up in Seldovia."

"And how far is Seldovia from Peg's place?"

"Not sure. Peg said it's 'just a ways south', but just a ways in Alaska might be a long trip!" Enthusiasm spread over her face. "I'll take lots of photos with my new camera." She patted her purse.

Fifteen minutes later, they arrived at the train station. Ed helped her down and removed her suitcases from the back. After placing her bags on the platform, he followed her inside to the stationmaster's counter. "One for Seattle, please."

"Well, Mary," the graying stationmaster peered over the top of his glasses. "Heard you're off to Alaska. Quite an adventure. My Uncle Jim ran off to the Klondike in 1900. Never heard from him again and . . ."

Ed silenced him with a stern frown and added, "Mom's not going there."

Mary bestowed an understanding smile on the man. "Don't worry, Bill. I'm from hardy stock. We've survived a lot of things," she boasted. "My dad came from Ohio in a covered wagon, met and married Mom in Missouri." She stared into space. "Isn't that funny? My dad's name is John and I married a man named John. Guess I should have named one of my sons, John . . ." She shook her head, "but don't worry. I'm strong, too. Did you know I was born the year the Civil War started?"

He handed her the ticket. "You don't say. Guess that makes you what," his brow furrowed he as calculated, "'bout sixty-one?"

"Yes." She took the ticket, snapped open her needlepoint purse and dropped it in.

Outside, the whistle blew. "Come on, Mom." Ed took her elbow, escorted her out and handed her up the stairs of the train to the conductor. His mother appeared small as she climbed aboard. Apprehension filled Ed's heart. *God, please keep her safe. Maybe one of us should be going with her.*

Mary found a seat next to the window and peered out. Ed stood talking with the Martins who'd come to collect their daughter visiting from Spokane. She knocked on the glass and waved. *My son's so handsome, like his father.*

Ed watched until the train turned into a dot on the horizon. *Take good care of her, Peg.*

Mary withdrew an apple from her bag along with a new novel she'd bought for the trip, *One of Ours* by Willa Cather. She read:

"I was staying on his father's farm when the war broke out. We spent the first week hauling wheat to town."

By page ten, she dozed with her head against the seat.

"This way, Aunt Mary," Winnie hurried down Coleman Dock while checking the time on the clock tower. She maneuvered through a group of Suquamish Indians on the waterfront who waited to catch a ride back to Port Madison Reservation. They rushed past the Black Ball Line and found the Canadian Pacific ticket office.

"Oh, Winnifred, see that one!" Mary grasped Winnie's sleeve and pointed to a steamer with black smoke rolling from two stacks. "Isn't this exciting!" Tugboats bustled across the water as a ferry crawled away. A trawler with *Lady Nora* painted in large white letters on its side slid into the dock. People lined up to board a ferry while longshoremen unloaded a freighter.

They passed Sunde and d'Evers Company where the storefront touted anchors, chain, rope, oars, tackle boxes, pitch, tar, paint, sails, canvas, awnings, oiled clothing, fishing supplies and groceries. Mary glanced back. "I wish we had time to check out the store. I'll bet I could learn a thing or two."

At the ticket office, a garrulous fellow with a reddish beard cornered Mary. "Where you ladies headed?" Winnie recognized the type and attempted to guide Mary away from him, but she stopped.

"Alaska."

"Ah, you'll be sailing on *Princess Alice* then. She's a great little pocket liner."

Mary cocked her head. "Pocket liner?"

"Small version of a cruise ship. She has services like a big ocean liner, just not as many. Good food, too."

"You've been on it?"

He raised his chin and his pride vibrated the air. "Sure, several times. Got a business in Seldovia."

"You do? I'm meeting my son-in-law there. What type of business?"

He puffed his chest. "The Seldovia Salmon Company" and held out his hand, "Richard Hunt at your service."

She shook his hand. "Mary Tarbet, nice to meet you, Mr. Hunt. I own a store myself."

His eyes widened slightly. "You do? What type?"

Frowning, Winnie moved closer to Mary and put her arm around her waist. Mary turned to her. "Oh, this is my niece, Winnifred O'Harra. She lives here in Seattle."

"Well, Miss O'Harra, I'd be happy to watch over your aunt on the trip up."

"It's MRS. O'Harra, and believe me, my aunt can take care of herself," she bristled. Mr. Hunt tipped his hat, popped out a gold pocket watch and flipped it open. "See you 'round."

Winnie whispered, "Aunt Mary, you must be careful of such men. When they see an older woman alone, they're usually up to no good. Make sure to keep your purse on your arm. You don't have all your money in it, do you?"

"No, dear. I've been around the block a few times. Don't you worry about me," she opened her purse with a reassuring smile, moving the contents to one side to reveal a little pistol hidden in the bottom. "Peg insisted I bring it."

Winnie gave her a hug. "I should have known! Let's sit until it's time to board." She found a seat by a window, fished a hanky from her bosom and dusted off the bench. Mary sat close to her and patted her knee.

"Oh, dear, I enjoy your company, but you needn't stay. I'm sure you've got things to do, but I'd love to catch up on your family for a few minutes if you've time. How are your girls?" Winnie began recounting her three girls' and their families' news. Before she finished, they heard, "All aboard for Alaska!" Mary sprang forth with excitement. "I guess that's me! She enfolded her niece in her arms. "Thanks for your help, Winnie."

Winnie followed her to the gangway. "Now you be sure to let me know when you're returning, and I'll be here to pick you up. Remember it takes time for the letter to reach me, so write as soon as you decide."

"I will!" Mary scuttled off without thinking to glance back.

CHAPTER 3

As soon as she settled in, Mary went up top. A young woman on deck sat in front of an easel, painting scenery. Mary strolled over and stood a couple of yards behind, watching her progress. Deep in concentration, the artist didn't notice Mary until she stood to stretch. She brushed auburn ear-length hair from a heart-shaped face as her flowered smock billowed in the breeze.

Mary brought her hand to her bosom. "Oh, I hope I didn't disturb you. I found it so fascinating to watch. You have such talent!"

The artist smiled, thanked Mary and held out her hand. "Carol Cummings. Nice to meet you."

"Mary Tarbet from Newport, Washington. I'm on my way to visit my daughter."

"Where does she live?"

"On a little island in Kachemak Bay, but my son in-law is picking me up in Seldovia." Mary turned toward the smell of cigar smoke. Richard Hunt passed behind her. *Is he watching me? How much did he hear? I must be more careful.*

Miss Cummings sensed her distress. "Do you know that man?"

"No, I barely met him in the ticket office. Be careful," Mary warned. "Something's fishy about him. Are you traveling alone?"

"Yes, I've come to paint Alaska's breathtaking landscapes. It's nothing like the South."

"Oh, I love those friendly southern people. You're from the South?"

"Well, the Southwest, Arizona. I wanted to try something new. My boyfriend hated the idea," she shrugged, "but I didn't cave into him." She reached into the pocket of her painter's smock and shook a cigarette from an elegant case. "Care for one? Let's sit down."

"I don't smoke, but I'd enjoy your company." Mary dragged a deck chair to the railing beside the young woman. *She's just a girl. I'd better watch out for her.* "How far are you going?"

"Anchorage. Dad moved there after Mother died." She cupped her hand against the breeze and lit a cigarette. "I think he needed a fresh start, something to clear his head and help him forget. She suffered for a long time, and he insisted on taking care of her until the end." She pursed her lips and blew a stream of smoke. "He acted so spent. I worried he'd go next. Fortunately, his friend recommended he manage one of his new stores."

"What kind of store?"

She flicked ash overboard. "The Piggly Wiggly chain. He'll open one in Anchorage this year."

Mary straightened. "Really? I own a little store myself. You know, regular customers become just like family. I think that might be just the ticket for him." They sat in silence while thick forests and sharp mountains slid past. Mary's stomach growled. "Well, I'm headed to dinner. Care to join me? My daughter's friends with the captain, so I have permission to eat at his table."

She stubbed out her cigarette on the railing. "Sure. I need a break. Let me gather my things."

"Here. I'll help." Mary held her hand out. "You remind me of my daughter some."

She handed Mary her palette. "How so?"

"Independent and adventurous."

"Why, thank you." Miss Cummings gathered her paints and brushes. Mary followed to her room and helped her in. "Thanks, I'll meet you in the dining room."

As soon as Miss Cummings appeared, Mary waved her over. She'd shed her painter's smock and swept in wearing palazzo pants with a long sleeve silk blouse and a red sash belt. Mary felt a little frumpy in comparison and smoothed her hair.

A waiter appeared. "Would you like a drink while you wait?"

"I'll start with a gin rickey," Miss Cummings replied.

"Do you have lemonade?" Mary requested. They studied the menu while waiting for the captain. As they sipped their drinks, he entered and removed his captain's hat. His sun-tanned face set off his full head of white hair and beard. "Evening, ladies." Miss Cummings set down her glass, leaving a red lipstick half-moon on the rim.

"Captain Howell, this is my new friend, Carol Cummings. She's an artist," Mary reached over and patted Miss Cummings's hand. "A good one, too."

He gave her a pleasant smile. "There's ample beauty in Alaska to inspire you." He picked up the menu.

Mary wanted the best thing available. "What do you recommend?"

"Any seafood. It's fresh. Our chef makes a tasty bread pudding for dessert."

"Oh, this is so much fun!" Mary exclaimed.

The captain suppressed a grin. "There's a dance tonight up top under the stars you might enjoy."

Mary sighed, "How romantic! Miss Cummings, you should go."

"I will if you will," she challenged.

"But you're so young and pretty. I'm a grandmother." Something unraveled in her heart. *I miss my John.*

"Never too old for love," the captain's mischievous dark eyes twinkled under his bushy white eyebrows.

Mary blushed. *I guess I'll go. I love to dance.* She raised her glass. "See you there."

In her cabin, Mary dumped her suitcases on her bed. *I didn't think I'd need anything fancy.* She chose a dark wool skirt and dressed it up by pairing it with a creamy silk blouse topped with a detachable crochet collar. *Am I being silly? Seriously, am I going to a dance at my age?*

Just then, Miss Cummings knocked at her door. "Mary, you ready?"

She opened the door and apologized, "I don't know . . . maybe I'll tuck in early. But you go and enjoy yourself." She waved her hand dismissively.

Oh, no you don't! We had a deal. Now let's see your options." The young woman plunged in. "I'm good at putting things together." She scowled at Mary's outfit, then rummaged through her clothes. "This!" She lifted a red blouse with ruffles cascading down the front. "This is romantic. Do you have a flirty skirt that swings when you dance?"

Mary giggled. "'Fraid not."

"Maybe a scarf for your hair or some jewelry. Follow me. I have a suitcase full." Her infectious enthusiasm carried Mary down the hall. Opening the door, she motioned to a chair. "Sit here." She tried several options while Mary sat patiently. Next, she styled her hair. "Well, what do you think?" She thrust Mary a hand mirror.

"My! I do look younger! You're a magician."

Miss Cummings grabbed Mary's hand before she could protest and proceeded toward the stairs. "Let's go!"

Snatches of music floated outside, drawing the women to the dance floor. Mary shivered. "Perhaps I should have brought a coat."

"Once we start dancing, you'll be fine. Come on." Miss Cummings tugged her hand. "I love this song." She sang along, floated onto the dance floor and began dancing.

I'm just wild about Harry
And Harry's wild about me!
The heav'nly blisses of his kisses
Fills me with ecstasy!
He's sweet just like chocolate candy
Or like the honey from the bee.
Oh, I'm just wild about Harry,
And he's just wild about me!

Mary swayed to the music. "The Blue Danube" brought several couples forth to waltz. Someone tapped her back. She turned as Richard Hunt bowed. "May I have this dance?" She hesitated a moment, but thought, *Oh, what can it hurt?* And the man knew how to dance! She closed her eyes and pretended he was her John.

With few females onboard, the two women danced all they wanted. Mary waltzed with the captain, several of the crew and a young man homesick for his mother. She begged off a few songs to catch her breath. Mr. Hunt asked her again. Men waited in line for a chance to dance under the stars with the charming Miss Cummings. After a couple hours, Mary's feet cried for relief. She caught her new friend's eye, waved goodbye and made her way back to her cabin. With a moan, she kicked off her shoes, rubbed her feet and fell back onto the bed. *So far this vacation has surpassed my hopes. I just wish John were here to enjoy it with me.*

After all the exercise and excitement of the trip, Mary slept well. She awoke surprised she'd slept until eight-thirty. *Better hustle if I want breakfast.* The dining room stood almost empty. A rotund, bald waiter handed a menu to a woman about Mary's age.

Mary approached her. "May I sit with you?" The stranger inspected the empty room, then shrugged. "I know there's plenty of room, but I enjoy visiting," Mary explained as she joined the stranger at her table. "Mary Tarbet, nice to meet you."

"Clara Trace." She resumed studying the menu.

"I'm going to visit my daughter. What takes you to Alaska?"

Mrs. Trace bowed her head and said nothing, then in a hushed voice gasped, "My son."

Did I say the wrong thing? What's the matter? Mary cleared her throat. "Where does he live?"

"I'm not sure he's alive."

Mary reached for her hand and then hesitated. "You poor dear, what happened? Sorry. I didn't mean to intrude. You needn't tell me."

Clara withdrew a hankie from her pocket and wiped her eyes. She shook her head. "Actually, I go late to eat because I have a hard time talking about it."

"And here I interrupted you . . . if there's anything I can do to help . . ." Mary rose. She probed her mind for something comforting to say.

"Please don't."

Don't WHAT? Mary shifted her weight. "You want me to stay?"

"Please do," Clara pleaded. Mary took a seat and picked up the menu. "I'm here if you need to talk." *I've lost my appetite. What would it be like to have a missing child?*

The same waiter returned. "Have you ladies decided?"

"A cup of black coffee and some toast for me, please. Do you want something, Clara? After we eat, I'll walk with you up top." Clara stared at her lap. "Do you want coffee?" Clara nodded. "Toast and eggs?" She nodded again. Mary addressed the waiter. "Could you bring us two glasses of orange juice as well?" They ate in silence.

Mary dotted her mouth with her napkin and brushed the crumbs from her lap. "I'll be up top if you want to join me." She patted the woman's shoulder and moved toward the stairs. On the bottom step, Mary turned to see if Clara followed, but she sat motionless.

At every meal thereafter, Mary searched for Clara to no avail. *Should I ask the captain? Is he allowed to give me her room number?* She decided to talk to him at dinner. "Captain, may I speak with you privately for a moment?"

After explaining the situation with Clara, the captain agreed Mary should check on the woman. He gave her the room number with orders to report back. Mary left immediately. She knocked softly on Clara's door. "Clara? It's me, Mary. May I come in?" No reply. She knocked again. "Clara, are you ill?

May I talk with you, please?" The door opened a crack. "Hello, would you like to come out and get some dinner with me?" The woman shook her head.

"How about if I bring you something? You must be hungry." Clara relented. Mary took off before she changed her mind. She found the captain. "She's in her room and I'm taking dinner to her. I'll see if I can eat with her."

"Good. I'll have the waiter follow you. Thanks for checking."

They returned to Clara's cabin. Mary knocked, handed her a tray and asked for permission to join. Clara opened the door. Mary listened intently as she related receiving a letter from her son's employer saying their fishing boat had never returned.

"How horrible! Why, during the war, I worried about my sons every day, not knowing their whereabouts or what they were facing. Maybe I can relate a little." She steered the conversation away from the fearful topic. Two hours later, they sat laughing over an incident from Mary's childhood.

"Thanks so much, Mary. I feel you are a true friend."

They exchanged addresses and promised to keep in touch.

CHAPTER 4

Ralph waited on the dock at Seldovia. He recognized Mary before she spotted him, hurried down to carry her luggage and helped her into his small boat for the journey to Ismailof Island. Mary thought of the young man lost at sea. She grasped the sides of the boat and prayed. Her face paled. "Open your eyes!" Ralph shouted over the noise of the engine. "You're missing the scenery." Mary opened them for a moment but squeezed them shut again when waves slapped the sides of the boat.

Peg heard the motor droning in the distance. She grabbed her daughter and flew down to the dock. "Mom!"

Ralph cut the motor. "We're home."

Mary stood on shaky legs and held her hand to Ralph who steadied her.

"So happy you made it!" Peg gave her a bear hug. "This is our daughter." Peg held her baby forward, causing Little Peggy to cry.

"Oh! My little Peggy! But I don't want to scare her. Let's give her some time."

"Come! See our place!" Peg led the way to their home. "How did your trip go?"

While the women visited, Ralph brought in Mary's bag and offered, "I'll sleep out in the tent and let you gals stay here inside."

The baby yawned and rubbed her eyes. After they placed the baby in her bed, they sat out in the sunshine. Mary told of her delight in the captain, the dancing and making new friends. "But one sad thing, my friend Clara's son has gone missing. His fishing boat didn't return."

"How long has he been missing?" Ralph asked with genuine concern.

"A month or so."

Ralph warned, "I'm afraid she won't find him. Probably in a liquid grave." After thinking for a moment, he added, "So, that's why you kept closing your eyes on the boat!" Mary winced and raised her shoulders.

"I have sad news, too. Our friend, Tante Norton, died right before you arrived," Peg said.

"Oh, no, what happened?"

"She went to Anchorage to have a tooth pulled. Septic poison set in. She died a couple days later. Reminds me of what happened to my brother Gene," Peg sniffled.

Mary reached for her hand. "How's her husband doing?"

"Not sure. Would you mind if we stopped to check on him tomorrow while we're in Homer? His name is Gene, too." Mary hesitated. Peg noticed and promised, "It's not far across the bay. We'll go slow as we'll be dragging the dory to bring home coal."

"Coal?"

"Across the bay, there's a big cliff with seams of natural coal open to the weather. The cold and heat split the coal into various sized chunks which fall onto the beach. The tide comes in and washes it. When the tide goes out, the people living in the bay take barges or scows to gather it for heating and cooking."

"Anyone can have it for free?"

"Yes, the cliffs in the reserve protected by Teddy Roosevelt, so no one's allowed to mine it. If we're still there at night, we'll see a constant red glow over the coal deposit from a perpetual fire deep in the ground.

The next morning, they headed to Homer Spit. Sun skimmed over craggy mountains that bolted straight up from the sea. Waves chased each other. Ralph guided the fishing boat, pulling the dory where Peg, the baby and Mary rode. Halfway there, the tail of a whale breached the surface. Then, a whole pod appeared. One rose and slapped its tail. Mary screamed and grabbed Peg's arm. "They'll tip us over!" she shouted over the motor. Two whales broke the surface. Mary squeezed her eyes shut. Peg bent forward to catch every detail. The last whale jumped, twisted and smacked the water with his back. He splashed the boat and waved his fin as if saying goodbye. Mary shuddered and gripped the sides until her feet hit shore.

Below snowy peaks and dense forest, Homer Spit jutted out into the bay. Fog nestled like a scarf between mountain cleavage. Peg and Mary strolled along tranquil beaches of gravel and sand, filling their buckets with hunks of coal, then dumped them in the dory. Ralph pointed out the coal seams in the clay cliff above Kachemak. Seals sunned themselves. Mary counted eleven on one rock. She picked up a feather left from a bald eagle and waved to a man slipping by in his canoe.

After a picnic lunch, Peg threw leftover biscuits to the fish and tapped the crumbs from the bottom of the pail. "We need to get there before the tide rises if we want to pick blueberries."

Mary surveyed the area. "Blueberries?"

"They're bog berries and a pain to pick 'cause the plants grow close to the ground. Come see." Peg picked her way through tidepools and driftwood, leading her mother to a patch. Mary stopped next to a pool teeming with life. She recognized clams and starfish. Crawling along on all fours, Peg held up a stem loaded with berries. "They fall off, so you'll have to gather them from the ground, too."

After thirty minutes of picking, Mary stood, stretched and noticed the tide had risen noticeably. Ralph moved the baby back into the shade. He came to her and held out his hand for the bucket. "Here, let me dump those for you. I think we'd better leave soon. The tide changes every six hours. Ocean will be thirty feet higher in a few hours."

Mary rubbed the back of her neck. "Thirty feet?"

"Yep. Every six hours. Twice a day, every day. Millions of gallons gushing in and out. Let's catch a bite at the Salty Dawg and head home."

Mary studied the rising ocean and shuddered. "Won't it get dark soon?"

"Naw, sunset this time of year is close ta midnight."

As they entered the Salty Dawg, a man yelled, "Peg!" "Uncle Gene" Norton waved them to his table.

"Gene!" Peg threaded her way through the tables. Ralph handed the baby to Peg and stole a chair from another table. Peg introduced her mother who held out a blueberry-stained hand. "I've heard about you!"

His eyes brightened, "You have?"

"Yes, Peg writes to me about all her friends."

Uncle Gene spoke over her head to Peg. "You folks staying a few days?" His hopeful face tugged her heartstrings.

"No, but we'll stay until an hour before sunset," Peg promised.

Mary pushed the menu aside. *He's lonely. I understand.* She rested her chin on her hand and gave him her full attention. "Tell me about your life here."

Uncle Gene took a deep breath. Two hours later, he commenced another tale and Ralph rose. "Better get back."

Mary hesitated when Uncle Gene's shoulders dropped, and he gave a weak smile.

"Come over and visit us. Mom's here for two months," Peg suggested as she picked up her coat.

Outside, the sunset dipped marsh grass in gold. Ralph handed the sleeping baby to Peg, helped Mary into the boat, and hit the starter. Choking and roaring to life, the engine caused the baby to startle. "Shusssh," Peg patted her back and climbed aboard. The steady engine purred, lulling the baby back to sleep. Mink and river otters foraged along the beaches. A black bear slouched at the edge of the forest.

The next morning, the family sat on the dock, watching the sun skim over the mountains. Peg asked, "Mom, how about a visit to Mount McKinley? Ralph and I have been wanting to see it."

Mary, who dozed along with the baby she rocked, roused. "What? Where?"

"The highest mountain in North America. Do you want to see it?"

"It's impressive," Ralph added. "According to Athabascan legend, the mountain rose when a mighty warrior named Yahoo built a canoe and paddled west to find a wife in Raven Chief's village. Raven Chief hated Yahoo but respected his strong medicine."

"Then what happened?" Mary asked.

Ralph set his mug down with a self-satisfied smile and launched into the rest of the story: "When he found the village, a raven sang to the chief, revealing Yahoo's wishes. The Raven Chief's wife secretly offered her daughter to Yahoo, but warned, 'Take her and go quickly. Your enemy, Raven Chief, is preparing to kill you!'

The young woman agreed to marry Yahoo, so they jumped in the canoe and paddled off. The Raven Chief pursued and caused a huge storm. When Yahoo calmed the water with a magic stone, the Raven Chief threw a spear. Yahoo used his medicine and turned the great wave into a mountain of stone, deflecting the spear. Next, he used all his power to make a bigger mountain. Raven King's second spear shot into the sky as his canoe struck the second mountain, throwing him onto the rocks. The chief transformed into a raven and soared to the top of the mountain.

Exhausted from the fight, Yahoo fell asleep. When he awoke, he saw the two mountains he'd created, a mighty dome and a smaller one to the west. The tallest he named Denali, The Great One."

Mary responded, "Interesting. I'd love to see it. As a child, my neighbor, Mr. Beale, kept a raven as a pet. He nursed the injured bird who stayed after it recovered. The raven shook his tail feathers every time Mr. Beale talked to him. We loved to place shiny objects around the yard and watch the bird swoop down to retrieve them. They say ravens have the intelligence of a three-year-old."

"They're also thought to be a sign of good luck if you see one while hunting. We can go to McKinley on Saturday if you like. I'll bet the foliage is turning. Should be beautiful."

Saturday, Ralph, Peg and Mary dropped Peggy off with the Nutbeams and headed north by train. From the park they rode horses higher to camp. A cornucopia of fall colors spilled over the mountain. Entering a stand of trees, they crunched through a carpet of leaves. The Fireweed Willows had turned from bright pink to cotton. Snow filled the crevices of sharp mountain peaks that pierced the clouds, causing icy tears to fall. Red crept up the base of the mountains, and Mountain Ash waved bright red berries. A sea of Aspen saplings bowed in submission to the wind.

Mary stopped to catch her breath. "What's the rusty color over there?"

"Dwarf Birch," Peg replied. "Animals won't eat it, and it's known for catching your laces and untying your shoes!" She noticed Mary's red face. "Let's rest." A moose thrashed through trees twenty-five yards away.

Ralph put a finger to his lips. "Don't move. It's rutting season. If it comes this way and flattens its ears, we'll run for it!" He motioned toward a nearby tree.

Mary froze. *He thinks I can climb that? If it comes my way, I'm dead!*

Luckily, the moose moved on. Ralph broke the silence, "He's most likely found a female. If she finds enough food, she'll probably give birth to twins next spring."

"What will they eat up here in the winter?" Peg asked.

Delighted by his attentive audience, Ralph stood tall and cleared his throat, "They eat twigs in winter and willows in summer. Moose are too tall to bend down and eat grass." He motioned the women forward. "'Bout lunch time, isn't it?"

After lunch, they placed their backpacks under their heads and warmed their bones in the sun. Their rest halted when a howl split the air. Ralph sat up, listening intently and howled in return.

Mary rolled over and stretched forward on one elbow. She shaded her eyes, expecting to spot wolves. "Why are you trying to call them?"

Ralph reached for his gun. "That's a human howl. When I answer, it's a signal to whoever is out there, that we're not cheechakos. Hopefully, they move on." They studied the area, but nobody appeared.

"Over there!" Peg pointed. The clouds parted and Denali's face shone under a brilliant blue sky. Wisps along the lower mountains drifted along as if admiring the golden red tapestry below. On the crest, two bull caribou locked horns. Below, streams braided themselves into a glacial river, rushing to the ocean.

"You're looking at the most dangerous thing in Alaska," Ralph proclaimed as they took in the landscape.

Mary followed his gaze. A frown creased her brow. "Where?"

"Rivers! They kill more people here than anything else."

On the return trip, Miko alerted them to a pack of wolves in the valley ripping apart a baby moose. Peg grabbed his collar. "Stay!" Miko whined and strained. Ralph squatted beside him and wrapped his arm around his neck. Mary pointed west where a grizzly pounded its way into the scene. Afraid of losing their meal, the frenzied wolves tore into the meat.

As Peg watched the scene, her mother's dinner table admonition came to mind: "You don't need to WOLF down your food!" Now it made sense. As soon as the top predator arrived, the wolves scattered.

Each evening on the way back to their base camp, the little troop sat around the campfire. Black shadows from the fire danced across their faces. They gazed into heaven's vault full of stars long enough to see midnight fling the Northern Lights across the sky. The wind wandered through trembling aspen leaves. Finally, tired from the day's journey, the trio tumbled into their bed rolls and dozed off in awe of the universe.

Ten days later, they returned to pick up Peggy at the Nut-beams. Alice begged them to stay the night. "We want to hear all about your trip!" The savory smell of moose stew bubbling on the stove helped convince them. Little Peggy jumped into her mother's arms and refused to leave them. "Good as gold. We're going to miss her!" Alice reported.

After Ralph told a couple stories, Peg asked, "What's new around here?"

"Sad news about a friend up in Turnagain Arm. He strayed too close to the water and died on the mudflats," Ted shared.

"How?" Mary asked, having no knowledge of the mudflats.

"Mudflats act like quicksand. Once you step in, mud closes around your feet and traps you. He drowned in the rising tide. They found his body when the bore tide swept him into the inlet. Glacial silt is deadly."

"Yep!" Ralph interjected. "Alaska's beautiful but unforgiving. Come on, ladies. Time we head home."

A week later, Mary carried her suitcase to the porch. "Ralph's ready, Mom." Peg's voice caught in her throat. She swallowed a cry.

"Oh, dear," Mary hugged her daughter and patted her back. "We'll see each other in a few months. Who knows? Next time

I may bring Mud with me. After I tell him about this great adventure, I'm sure he won't be able to stay away, especially after I show him my photos."

"That would be wonderful!" Peg's face brightened.

Mary tied a red scarf under her chin. "This has been a highlight of my life, dear. I'll never forget it. I understand now why you love it here."

Ralph picked up Mary's luggage. "Ready?" He took a handkerchief from his back pocket to wipe his brow and the back of his neck. "Better leave if you want to make your boat."

Mary reached for her granddaughter. She held her close and attempted to memorize every feature. "I'll show the family your picture," she promised the little girl. "When you come to Grandma's, your cousins will recognize you." She handed her back to her mother. "Can you wave bye-bye?"

Peggy's chubby little hand opened and closed.

CHAPTER 5

Two months after her mother left, Peg stirred white beans bubbling on the Yukon stove. With her other arm, she balanced her nine-month-old daughter dangling from her hip while last night's dream replayed in her mind:

A black thundercloud shot hail into a sharp wind. It stung her cheeks. She raised her hood and ran to the beach. A red-haired man stepped from the pier. Peg froze. "Charlie?" she gasped. *How did he find me?*

He sprinted up the beach and skidded to a stop ten feet away. "Peg, it *is* you! I've been searching for you ever since you left. Why did you leave?"

Peg grasped the front of her coat with both hands. "You got married, remember?"

He hurried toward her. "It didn't last. I love you." She froze. His head dropped. "I can't go on without you."

Her mouth hung open. "Why did you push me away? Why did you marry Florence?" She stepped back. "It's . . . too late, Charlie." She stammered, "I . . . I . . . I'm married with a little girl."

He reached for her, took her hands and scrutinized her face. "Are you happy?"

She awoke before she could answer. The dream still felt real. She remembered the green and brown plaid shirt Charlie wore, the sheen of sweat on his brow and the moisture making his red hair curl at the nape of his neck. Her heart had raced at the sight of him and still thumped as she awoke.

I know the answer to his question. I'm not fooling anyone, not even myself. I love Alaska and my daughter, but not my marriage. Did Charlie leave Florence? Mother never said anything about it in her last letter. Would she? How can I find out?

The baby's head lulled against her breast. Peg replaced the lid on the pot, put the spoon in the dishpan and settled little Peggy in her crib.

Her jaw clenched as her husband wobbled into the tent. "What are you *celebrating* now?" she accused. He pushed his hat onto the back of his head, glared and wove his way through the laundry strung from the tent poles to the bed in the corner. Soon, soft snoring filled the room. He twitched and clenched the half-empty bottle to his chest. Little Peggy stirred in her crib, brown eyes blinking.

"Shush, Baby," Peg whispered. A low flutter in her swelling stomach reminded her she'd need the crib for another child in a few months. She threw herself into a chair. *What shall I do? This seemed like such a great adventure to elope with Ralph to Alaska. I'm still young, and he's old and set in his ways. Winter in Alaska can cause depression in the heartiest souls, but he used to be positive and clever. Ever since he lost his job and his fishing venture with Sundsby proved unprofitable, he's found solace in drinking. Well, I know what he does at "work."*

Peg heaved herself up and felt the drying laundry. Opening the clothes pins and dropping them in her apron pocket, she gathered clean diapers and deposited them on the table. She sat with a hard plop and stared at her rounding stomach. *I wonder how much money we have left. I could find a job, but with two babies? Who would take care of them? I don't want to leave them with anyone.* Her fingertips pressed her lips. *I could go home, but my pride won't let me. Things have to improve come spring.*

Ralph murmured, mouth moving like a fish, his whiskered Adam's apple bobbing. He shivered. *If he's sick . . . that's all I need! Well, I'm stuck. I'll do anything for my children.* She smiled at the small lump, moved to the crib and patted the baby's bottom. *I'm still amazed how I love her. I realize now what my parents felt about me. At least Dad won't ever find out about my marriage, unless he can see me from heaven. And I wouldn't worry Mother for anything. I need to figure this out.*

Peg collapsed in the rocker, shut her eyes and fell asleep. After an hour, the baby's babbling woke her. Bending over to pick her up, she hit her head on the shelf. "Dang!" Her eyes watered. When the pain subsided, she noticed the books she'd brought back after her last visit home. She ran her fingers over the spines, stopping on *The Holy Bible. Maybe this will help.* She lifted the baby from her crib and set her on the floor. Little Peggy crawled off to pet the sleeping dog. Peg rubbed the tooled-leather cover, then opened the book. It fell to Romans 12:12: "Rejoicing in hope, patient in tribulation, continuing steadfastly in prayer."

Humm, good advice. Maybe I can find hope through prayer. She bowed her head. *Lord, help me know what to do. I want the best for my little ones. Amen.*

Three days later, three days alone with the baby, Peg's worry over Ralph's whereabouts took its toll, creating darkness and apprehension. Her unflagging optimism faded. Still battling nausea from pregnancy, she stopped to sip water. *I don't want to end up dehydrated and in the hospital like last time. What would happen if I had to leave my baby? Maybe my friend, Amka, would tend to her. I wish I could rely on Ralph, but I can't.*

In the late afternoon, she gathered her knitting from a basket which held half-finished booties for the coming baby. Something stirred outside the tent. Moving to the crib, she put her hand on the sleeping baby next to her. The blanket rose and fell rhythmically. She reached for the old 30-30 Winchester and levered a round into the chamber. *Maybe it's just Ralph coming home drunk again.* She crept to the tent door and undid the top tie. Squinting through the twilight, she spotted someone slumped on a pile of snow at the end of the path. "Ralph?" she called. The body groaned. Miko came to life and barked loudly.

After returning to check the baby one more time, she hunched over and pulled on her boots. "Come on, Miko," she commanded, hoping his barking would scare off the intruder. She opened the door and peered out. A man rose to his knees, swayed and fell again. She raised the gun. "Hold it right there!"

"Help me," a low voice moaned.

Peg advanced cautiously and demanded, "Who are you?"

A man tried to speak, his mouth moving with inaudible speech. Finally, he gasped, "Ki . . . d."

Peg sprinted over. "Kid! What happened?"

He slipped into unconsciousness.

She searched the timberline. Nothing. Blood seeped from Kid's pant leg. Multiple lacerations covered his arms and face. His torn calf extended to a bootless foot. Blood and dirt matted his blond hair. She spotted a large lump on the back of his head.

"Ralph, where are you when I need you?" she hissed, hurried to Kid and patted the wounded man's hand. "You made it. Hang on. You're okay, Kid." Her previous medical training surfaced. After checking him for broken bones, she propped the gun on his chest, reached under his arms and dragged him inside the tent, leaving a bloody trail in the snow. Her heart thumped harder. *From fear or exertion?* She went to work. Opening his coat, she cut his shirt and pant legs, examining his injuries. The leg wound needed attention first. It had already created a dark pool of blood on the floor. After pressing a clean diaper to the gash, she stepped out, filled the big pot with snow and set it on the stove. By the time she had cleaned and bandaged all his wounds, the sun shimmied over the mountain tops.

She elevated Kid's legs slightly and covered him with a wool blanket. Next, she shoved a log in the Yukon stove and boiled more water. *What now? He needs to get to a hospital. Where are his dogs? I don't dare leave him. Damn you, Ralph! Where are you?* She felt Kid's head. No fever.

The baby stirred and cried for her breakfast. Peg washed sticky blood from her hands and arms as the cry turned to a howl. "You hang in there, Little Miss. Mama's coming." Chubby fists pounded the air. "You're not starving, Little One." She tossed the blood-stained water out the tent door, picked up the baby, sagged onto the chair and unbuttoned her shirt. Soon, greedy sucking sounds and sighs of pleasure came from under the blanket. Peg gazed into the sweet face of her daughter and fierce love filled her heart.

A soft moan drew her attention back to Kid. She chewed her lip as she burped the baby. "There, Little One, hold tight. I'll be right back."

After placing the baby in her bed, she bent to check her patient. "Kid, can you hear me?" His eyelids fluttered. "What happened?"

No answer.

"Don't worry. You're safe." Blood soaked through the bandage on his leg. She pressed another clean diaper to it. Before she finished wrapping his leg, the baby demanded the rest of her breakfast.

Peg checked the clock. Almost nine. She finished up and lifted the baby to her breast. *Should I try to lift Kid in the sled to take him to Amka's place? No, better not move him yet.*

A faint noise moved closer. She stopped rocking, straining to hear. Ralph's off-tune singing filled the air. He came swaying and slurring the words to a song:

> How happy I am when I crawl into bed
> And a rattlesnake rattles a tune in my head.
> And the gay little centipede, void of all fear,
> Crawls over my pillow and into my ear.
> And the nice little bedbug, so cheerful and bright,
> Keeps me a-scratching full half of the night.
> And the gay little flea with toes sharp as a tack
> Plays "Why don't you catch me?" all over my back.
> How happy am I on my government claim
> Where I've nothing to lose and nothing to gain,
> Nothing to eat and nothing to wear.

Nothin' from nothin' is honest and square.
But here I am stuck, and here I must stay.
My money's all gone, and I can't get away.
There's nothing to make a man hard and profane
Like starving to death on a government claim.[1]

Fumbling with tent ties, he careened in. Peg's anger flared. "Where have you been?"

"Bought drinks for all my friends," he announced proudly.

"Be quiet. You'll wake the baby!" she shushed him and dashed to close the tent door he left flapping in the wind.

He blinked his bloodshot eyes and teetered over to peer at Kid asleep on the floor, "Who's that?"

"Don't step on him! It's Kid." Peg warned.

"What's HE doin' here?" Ralph bellowed. The baby woke up crying, and Kid moaned.

Peg growled and hurried to comfort the baby. "See what you've done!"

Ralph inclined his head toward Kid and demanded again, "Why's HE here?"

"He's hurt."

Ralph finally noticed the bloody bandage. "What happened to him?"

"I don't know."

He planted his hands on his hips and demanded more firmly, "So, why's he HERE?"

"I don't know," Peg snapped while bouncing the baby in her arms. "He collapsed not far from here. I heard him, dragged him in and bandaged his wounds. He hasn't been conscious."

---

1 Starving to Death on a Government Claim by Vance Randolph, https://www.loc.gov/item/ihas.200197141/

"Humph, he shoulda gone to Sundsby's," Ralph complained.

"What is *wrong* with you, other than being drunk *again?* He didn't plan to get hurt and end up here."

"Don't be so sure," Ralph muttered.

Peg lifted her chin. "You crazy fool!"

Ralph flopped on the bed, shoes and all, burped loudly and promptly fell asleep.

"Don't know why I wanted you home. You're worse than no help," Peg lamented.

Holding the baby in one arm, she bent to feel Kid's head and threw the blanket back over him. She sat the rocker next to her patient in case he awoke.

Homesickness cut across her heart. *If only I could ask Dr. Phillips how to best nurse Kid. I miss Mother, her advice and support. I miss my brother, Mud. Should I go home? I'm exhausted and overwhelmed.* She rubbed her temples and squeezed her eyes tightly, blinking back tears.

CHAPTER 6

Wind tossed handfuls of snow. The dense air next to the sea sharpened winter's harsh grip. Peg tensed as she carried buckets of snow to melt on the stove. Awakened by a blast of frigid air through the open door, Ralph rolled over in bed, pinched his eyebrows together and raised his eyelids halfway. He pressed his fingers to his temples and croaked, "So thirsty!"

Peg handed him a tin cup. The water slopped in his shaking hands. Her face twisted in disgust. "Drinking worth it?" He moaned and fell back on his pillow. Turning to check on Kid, she noticed he hadn't moved all night. She removed the blanket, checked his wounds, lifted his head and held a cup to his lips. "Kid, try to drink."

He parted his lips. She tipped the cup, poured a little in his mouth and wiped the drips from his chin. "It's Peg, Kid. Can you open your eyes?" she coaxed as she felt his head for fever.

Ralph watched, his mouth twisting to the side. Peg felt his eyes boring into her back. She glanced up. The anger in his eyes made her flinch.

"What?" she challenged.

"More concerned about your boyfriend than your husband," he accused.

She flung back her reply, "He's NOT my boyfriend! He didn't CHOOSE his suffering."

Ralph's jealousy erupted. "I see . . . he's a better man, is he?"

Peg's back stiffened. "Get yourself together, so you can help me!"

"What?"

"Go get Amka. Tell her to bring her medicine bag. Please . . ."

"Why don't YOU?" he huffed.

Peg sighed deeply, pushed her fist to her forehead and clenched her eyes shut. "I need to nurse Little Peg . . . unless you can!" She picked the baby up and felt her soggy bottom.

Ralph uncoiled from the bed and balanced on the edge. "Make me some coffee and I'll take him to her."

"He's in no shape to be moved and it's too cold," she snapped, leaving out her thought: *Thinking of yourself first again, aren't you?*

"So, why do YOU have to nurse him?" his words dripped with resentment.

She placed the baby on the bed and removed the wet diaper. Little Peg's wobbly grin softened her heart. "Because I found him, and he needs help. Please. When he's well enough to move, you can take him to Amka's. The sooner he heals, the sooner he's gone," she tried to reason with him.

Ralph poured a cup of coffee and dropped on the chair next to the fire to chew on Peg's answer. He gave in. "Where's the snowshoes?"

Peg inclined her head, pointing across the room as she settled the baby on her breast. He wobbled over and picked them up.

"Maybe Sundsby can come with her. Tell them Kid's taken a tumble. If they have anything for pain, bring some."

He mumbled a complaint and grabbed his coat. She heaved a sigh of relief as he huffed out, leaving the tent flap open again. Kid stirred. Peg kept a close watch.

His eyelids weighed twenty pounds. Kid's mind searched his foggy brain for answers. *Why is my head pounding, my leg aching? Where am I?* His foggy brain didn't answer. *I remember falling, my dogs yelping, a blur of snow-laden trees rushing by. That huge black dog . . .* The darkness enveloped him again.

"Kid?" Peg squatted next to him. "Are you awake? Can you hear me?" She touched his arm. He flinched. "It's me, Peg. You've been hurt. What happened?" Peg touched his cheek. "Come back. What's happened to you?"

No response.

She reached for the cup of water on the table and encouraged him to drink. It dribbled from his mouth. "Kid, please try. Take just a little." A wind rattled the trees outside making the tent walls billow. *Oh, this cursed weather! How long 'til we can get him to the doctor?*

CHAPTER 7

Ralph returned with Sundsby in tow. Peg met them at the door. "Where's Amka?" she shouted over the storm.

"Sick," Sundsby explained. "Brought medici . . . " The tempest carried off the rest of his words. He and Ralph kicked the snow from their boots and brushed it from their hats.

Ralph crossed to the stove and wrestled more wood in. Sundsby saw Kid on the floor and asked Peg. "Any better?"

"Not any worse. No fever. He rests easy. I'm trying to keep water in him. Earlier, when I asked what happened, he muttered something I didn't understand."

Sundsby looked up. "What?"

Peg's forehead wrinkled. "Kluktucky?"

"You mean Klutuck?"

"Maybe. What is a Klutuck?"

Sundsby sat on a chair to tug off a boot. "A person."

"Who?"

"A crazed Eskimo, a fur trapper, but doubt he'd come to these parts." Sundsby removed his socks and rubbed his cold toes. "Got a cabin on the Nushagak River. Kills trappers who stray into his territory."

"Think Kid went there?" Peg asked in disbelief.

Sundsby tipped back his chair. "Doubt it. It's more than a hundred miles east of here."

She hesitated. "Maybe. He didn't say."

"Coulda' been. Klutuck killed a couple of natives last year. Rumor has it he bragged it felt no different than killing a moose. Said he'd kill anyone who invaded his area."

Peg shivered. "Creepy!"

"Yeah. Travels with a big black dog, too," Sundsby related.

Ralph shot Sundsby a warning glare. "Probably some superstition."

Sundsby shrugged. "He's wily. Anyway with the mosquitoes and bogs, who'd want to track him? Area's full of Grizzlies, too."

"Sounds like a good place to hide," Peg commented.

Ralph stepped forward. "Kid well enough to move yet?"

"No!" Peg protested. "Besides, Amka's not feeling well."

"Throwing up," Sundsby confirmed.

"He's not hurting you!" Peg hissed as she moved to Kid's bed on the floor.

"He's in the way," Ralph snarled.

Tension crowded the small tent. Sundsby edged to the door. "Better go."

"Can you wait until the storm passes?" Peg suggested.

"Nah, got to check Amka." Sundsby pulled on his coat and plunged his feet into his boots.

CHAPTER 8

At the end of the week, Kid sat up and sipped soup. "You're a great nurse, Peg," he stated, tipping the bowl to get the last drop, "and cook, too!" He wiped a drip from his wispy blond beard onto his sleeve and handed Peg the bowl.

"So happy you're feeling better. Now, tell us what happened to you!" After taking the bowl, Peg handed him a cup of hot coffee. Steam rose in the cold air. "Who would hurt you like this?"

Ralph cleared his throat, "A number of people."

Kid dug out a frown. "Not sure if I can. I was traveling fast when a large black dog darted out of the underbrush, ran next to my sled snarling and attacked my lead dog. Next thing I remember, I woke up in your cabin. Are my dogs hurt?"

"I don't know. You came here alone," Peg reported.

Kid heaved his sore body forward, a ball of anger churning in his chest. My dogs? *My dogs left me? They don't do that!* He sprang up with a shriek. "What the hell? Where are they? They didn't bring me here?"

Peg reached out. "Careful. Sit down. You've been here a week. There's been no sign of them."

Kid bowed his head and placed it between his hands. "I've let them down!" His jaw jutted forth. "If someone stole them . . ." He clenched his fists, unable to finish his sentence. A wave of grief washed over him, cutting him to the core, causing him more pain than any of his physical injuries.

Peg tried to calm him. "Time to rest. They could have returned home."

"If they did, there'd be no one there to care for them!" he worried.

Ralph rose. "Gotta head to Homer today. Take care of some business. I'll stop in at the Salty Dawg and see what I can find out for ya."

"'preciate it." Kid croaked as he lay his spinning head back down.

"How long will you be gone?" Peg's surprise made her voice rise.

"Dunno."

"What BUSINESS?" she pressed.

Ralph ignored her as he shoved clothes into a cloth bag. He threw it over his shoulder, hitched his pants up on his skinny hips and left without a word.

The next morning, fragrant coffee spurred Kid from his bed to the table. He eased himself onto a chair. "Ralph doesn't want me here."

Peg set a steaming plate of sourdough pancakes in front of him. "Don't worry about it."

"I'm feeling better. I'll be gone before he returns," he promised. "What did I do?"

Peg rolled her eyes. "Nothing. He's jealous of you."

Kid flinched. "Why?"

"Who knows? Maybe because you are young and handsome," she teased.

Kid blushed. "I appreciate all you've done for me. Don't want to cause trouble for you. How can I repay?"

"I don't expect payment, but would you mail a letter for me? I'll give you postage." She stepped to the shelf and reached for their tin of money. It felt light. She pried up the lid and froze wide-eyed. *Empty.* "I guess I'll wait on the letter," she stammered, trying unsuccessfully to hide her frustration and anger.

Kid guessed the problem and reached for the letter. "It's okay. I owe you anyway."

Peg's eyes narrowed. She flopped on the edge of the closest chair and rested her chin on her fist. Her voice trembled as she confided, "It's just Ralph isn't working, and he's drinking again."

"He was drinking before this winter when you went home . . . for your dad's funeral," he hesitated, not sure how much to disclose.

"Oh, I know. I'm praying things will improve this spring. He's a good father, loves our daughter and I'm expecting another baby." She arose with resolve. "Well, things have to change."

Kid cleared his throat. "I hope for your sake they do."

Peg bristled a little. "I'm okay. He doesn't hit me or any-thing." She pushed her chair back. "Let's change those bandages. You must heal, so you can find your dogs!"

Two days later, Ralph returned with news. But first, he scanned the cabin. "Where is he?"

"Sundsby's. He didn't feel welcome here," Peg simmered as she finished feeding Little Peg.

Ralph knelt next to them and beamed at his daughter. "Hey, Baby Doll, Daddy missed you!"

The baby sat up and babbled, "Da, Da."

"You hear that?" Ralph crowed.

Maybe we can be a family now. "What did you find out in Homer? She wiped the baby's face and hands.

A smug flat-lipped smile swept over Ralph's face as he folded his arms and declared, "Everything's going to be skookum!"

"What?"

"Skookum, a native term for good. Bought us a new boat!"

She spun around. "Where did you find the money?"

He ignored her question and gave his attention to the baby. "Can you patty cake for Daddy?" He took her hands and tapped them together. "Patty cake, patty cake, baker's man. Bake me a cake as fast as you can."

What? I can't believe it! That's where the money went. And you without a job! Peg swooped in and picked the baby up. "I asked you a question."

"I won it," he admitted. Little Peg patty caked.

"Gambling at The Salty Dawg?"

"Does it matter? We're set up for the fishing season now. We can realize our dreams of starting our fishing business." He swaggered to the stove, picked up the coffee pot and poured himself a cup.

"Do we have any money left?" she asked, although she already knew.

He gulped coffee. "A little, but soon as it thaws some, we'll be in Fat City!" He dropped his heavy travel bag onto the table. "See what I got in Homer!" He drew coffee, sugar, flour and canned vegetables out, lining them up on the table like a magician.

"The money tin is empty," Peg growled.

"Of course, it is. How do you think I paid for all this?" He waved his hand over the groceries.

"And how much did it cost?"

"Didn't give me a receipt," he bristled with resentment, continuing to empty the bag.

Peg softened a little when she noticed two cans of sweet potatoes. She picked one up and turned it in her hand. *Well, at least now I can make a pie.* She handed the baby to Ralph and picked up two more cans. No one spoke as Ralph rocked the baby and Peg slammed the cans onto the shelf.

He doesn't understand, or does he and he just doesn't care?

Then she remembered. "Hey, did you find out anything about Kid's accident? Anyone see his dogs?"

"Nope."

CHAPTER 9

The month of May brought Break-Up. Winter grudgingly declined. Ice groaned and popped, rivers gurgled, and water dripped. Birds twittered and squirrels clamored up trees. Gray turned green. In the cracks of beach boulders, small yellow flowers bloomed on hairy leafy stalks. Light pink Bog Laurel unfurled on shrubs. Grass muscled through patchy snow, stretching to reach the sun. Peg felt starved for color and devoured it.

On the way to the woodpile, she stepped in a puddle and sank ten inches in slushy water. "Rats!" Sloshing back to the tent, she struggled out of her boots, peeled off her wet socks and hung them over the back of a chair to dry. The sooty smell of fire rushed into her face when she opened the stove to add a log. She shoved it shut and glanced at the crib to see if the noise had awakened Little Peg. The toddler still napped, so she decided to write a letter.

Ishmailof Island, Alaska

May 7, 1926

Dear Family,

Winter's finally receding. The joke is Alaska's seasons are almost winter, winter, and still winter, or June, July, August and winter. It's also said Alaska is lighter, darker, wetter, colder and snowier, but greener than anywhere else. And it's turning green! Sourdoughs say when the birch leaves are the size of squirrel ears, there'll be no more frost. I'm keeping a close watch on those leaves as I want to plant a garden. With the long summer days, vegetables grow huge here.

Another piece of sourdough wisdom: Clap your hands together and count the mosquitoes you killed. If there are fifteen or more, watch out. You're in for a heavy mosquito year! It's still too cold to conduct the test.

Ralph bought a new fishing boat and is anxious to use it. Please pray he's successful.

She set her pencil down. *Winter's over and he's got work. He'd better quit drinking, or what will I do? I can't leave my little ones for a job.* She swallowed hard and wiped a tear from her cheek before it dripped onto the letter. *I won't worry Mom.*

Many here are upset over a new law which requires all goods leaving or arriving in Alaska to be on American carriers. They have to dock in Seattle before getting shipped on. This is making Seattle businessmen rich and taking money out of Alaskans's pockets. Because Alaska is not a state, we don't receive the same protection under the law.

I'm going to have another baby this fall! Peggy will be almost two, so she'll have a playmate. I loved having seven siblings and miss them all.

Little Peggy is the joy of my life. She's sweet, smart as a whip, and pretty, too. However, unlike me, she doesn't care for animals. She recoils when a kitten or dog comes close and won't pet them. She did pick up a big fish, but dropped it, or the slimy thing slid from her fingers.

Please write soon and tell me ALL the news from home.

Love,

Peg

A wolf howled. Peg stepped outside and surveyed the mountains draped in shadows. A pale orange-purple light, the Alpenglow, stained the peaks. An eagle high in the pines turned its head a few degrees at a time. In the brush, birds pecked at snow-covered red berries. She scanned the beach and wondered: *Will Ralph be home soon?*

The next morning, she awoke with a start when Ralph touched her shoulder.

"Guess what?"

Peg sat up in bed. "You've been drinking," she answered sarcastically.

His good mood evaporated. "Why ya always gotta be so negative?" He toppled onto the bed.

"Maybe because I've been up most of the night worried about my husband." She scooted out the end of the bed, grabbed her shawl and positioned the rocker close to the stove.

What am I going to do? I've made a mistake. Lord, help me. The baby inside her kicked, prompting her not to give up. She rocked herself to sleep and woke with a crick in her neck. Ralph snored. Cold crawled up her ankles, telling her the fire needed wood. She yawned, rubbed her sore muscles and checked to see if Little Peg still slept. She did.

With a tug, the stove door scraped open, resuscitating coals that crackled and pulsated. Peg watched, hypnotized. *Maybe I can breathe some life back into my marriage. I need to at least try.*

As morning light filled the room, Little Peg awakened and sang out, "Da! Da! Da!" as she held the side of the crib and jumped. Ralph rolled over and chuckled.

"*SOMEONE'S* always happy to see me. Hand her to me, will ya?" He bent forward and gathered the covers up to his stubbled chin.

Peg faltered on stiff legs to the crib and lifted the toddler over the side. "You need dry pants." She moved a plank of wood from atop a bucket full of wet diapers and set it next to Ralph. "Change her while I heat up her bath water, please."

Too big for the dishpan, the baby's bottom almost filled it and her chubby legs hung over. She splashed and giggled, making both parents smile.

"How about an outing, girls?" Ralph suggested.

"Where?" Peg jumped back as Peggy threw water at her. Ralph handed her a towel.

"There's a fox farm not far from here." Miko ambled over and pushed his head onto Ralph's lap. He pet the dog as he explained further. "Remember I told you there's a doctor and dentist who raise blue and silver foxes?"

"Oh, yes, the doctor planned on helping us deliver the baby, but a storm blew in."

"And we did fine without him," Ralph pointed out. "Anyway, I hear there's big money to be made selling furs."

"But we just bought a boat!" Peg protested.

"Yes, and we'll make money to invest in a fox farm with it," Ralph assured her.

Another one of your schemes! But an outing sounds divine. "Let's check it out. I'll take the baby to Amka's to keep her out of the cold. She can play with little Karl if Amka's feeling better. If she's not, count me out."

Ralph put on his coat. "I'll get the sled ready. Come on, Miko. Let's go." The dog jumped up and wagged its tail.

Connected pens divided a large area near the beach. Chicken wire covered the sides and top. A small wooden house stood in each enclosure. Another fence protected the perimeter. As they drew closer, an awful stench grew.

Peg held her nose. "Why do they stink so?"

The Dr. Barclay chuckled, "Scent glands. They use them and their potent urine to mark their territory."

"Such a great deal of fencing!" Peg shouted above the cacophony of barking foxes.

"They're little escape artists," the doctor reported as he threw a big hunk of salmon into the pen. The fox opened his mouth, jumped and seized his meal with sharp teeth. It shook the fish and enjoyed its dinner. In the next pen, a fox jumped three feet in the air and dove headfirst into the snow.

Peg laughed aloud. "What's he doing?"

"There's field mice under an icy blanket," the doctor explained. They watched, amused, as the fox moved his head from side-to-side listening diving again and again. It faced north, dove and jumped up with a mouse in his mouth.

"What's it take to start a farm?" Ralph inquired.

They strolled to the next pen. The doctor drew another salmon from his bucket and tossed it to the fox. "Money and hard work. To start with less capital, you can lease an island for twenty-five dollars a year from the forest supervisor and let the foxes run free. But you'd have to build feeding pens outside their dens with trap doors for harvesting. You harvest pelts in December. A pair of breeders can cost up to three hundred dollars.

Ralph took a pencil and notepad from his shirt pocket. "Then what?"

"You'll spend most of the day procuring food for them: fishing, hunting or trapping animals like snowshoe hare. They'll even eat porcupines." A goat bleated.

"You give them milk?"

"Goat meat."

"What do you earn for each pelt?" Ralph asked as he mentally counted each pen.

"Depends. A blue fox pelt goes for over one hundred dollars and a silver pelt can easily go over two hundred. But you won't see a profit for a few years."

Ralph jotted down a few notes. "If ya don't mind my asking, how much did it take to set up here?"

"Over seven thousand."

Ralph let out a low whistle. "Ever recover your investment?"

"Oh, yes," the doctor answered with a satisfied smile.

When they returned home, Ralph sat up night after night, calculating at the kitchen table. Over the next three months, he interviewed everyone he met about fox farming. His research required many trips into Homer.

"Do fox farmers congregate at the saloon?" Peg asked when he returned home drunk again. She had no patience after five days chasing after an active toddler while being six months pregnant.

"Yup, that's where all men congregate. 'Fore long, we'll have 'nuff ta start."

Peg kept a close watch on the money tin, hidden behind canned goods on the shelf. With the success of their new fishing boat, it grew steadily. She secreted a little each time Ralph left. Some nights he puzzled, "Musta been too drunk to add this right."

When he left the next morning, Peg again moved the rag rug, removed up a loose floorboard and strained over her swollen belly for the wooden box. *I need an escape plan if next winter is anything like the last. I don't want my children growing up around drinking.* She stretched and groped around in the dirt, hoping not to come in contact with a mouse. The box slipped from her hand. She rolled on her side and tried again. Little Peg toddled over to investigate and straddled her prostrate mother. Peg got the giggles. Someone approached. She panicked and struggled to sit up. Just as she pushed the rug back, the door opened. Ralph entered, "Whatcha doin' on the floor?"

"Playing with the baby. What did you forget?" Peg prayed he'd not seen her distress.

"My lunch. Where'd ya put it?"

Peg pointed. "You left it next to the chair."

He bent to pick it up and straightened the wrinkled rug. "You be careful. You're getting too big to crawl around. See ya tonight."

She closed her eyes and exhaled.

CHAPTER 10

"Is he in jail?" Peg gasped.

"Dunno. Life's cheap here, 'specially native life. Not the first time a man's beat his live-in," Ralph replied.

"But she died!" Peg protested.

Ralph shrugged his shoulders. "Hard to prove when the body's found in the wilderness."

Her voice rose, "There are people who can testify he regularly beat her!"

"Maybe, but doesn't prove he killed her." Ralph removed the lid from the pot, bubbling on the wood stove, peered in and frowned. "Stew again?"

"Until you bring back groceries from Homer," she fired back.

"I didn't kill her!" He slammed down the pot's lid and stomped outside.

I remember seeing her in Homer, her head down, trailing after that brute. With her hair hanging over her face, I didn't see any bruises, but Amka's told me she has. If he's not punished, what's to stop another murder?

Sunshine beckoned. Peg unhooked a fabric bag full of wooden blocks from a nail. She remembered how she and Ralph had sanded scraps from the tent floor to create blocks for their daughter. *Such happy times. Ralph surprised me with paints and brushes after a trip to Homer. Painting them bright colors and adding letters and pictures to them had filled lonely nights with Ralph gone.*

"Come on, Sweetie. Let's play outside," Peg invited. She lugged out a chair and Little Peggy toddled after. Leaning back, she pressed her palms on her lower back to relieve the pressure created by her swollen belly. The unborn baby kicked. Peg grew sleepy in the sunshine. Her back hurt. Retrieving a blanket from the tent, she stretched out next to her daughter.

She awoke with a start. "Peggy?" She fumbled into a sitting position, pushed up to her knees and scanned the area. "Peggy?" Her heart skipped a beat. "Peggy!" *How long did I sleep?* "Miko!" she screamed for her dog. No answer. *Where's my baby? I should've watched her better!*

Plodding down the beach, she held her hands under her stomach for support. Images of ferocious wolves, bears and wolverines dragging Peggy away filled her mind. She imagined Peggy floating lifeless in the ocean. A wounded animal sound rose from her throat. Her shoulders curled over her chest, and she fell to her knees. "God, help me!" A thought came to her mind. *Check the sand.* She noticed little footprints leading into the trees.

She's not in the water. Her relief soon vanished. "Peggy!" she cried in panic as she rushed into the forest, ignoring the branches whipping her legs and face. *How long has it been? Should I go for help?* "Peggy!" she screamed until her throat burned. The needles on the forest floor hid any tracks. She stopped, her chest heaving. *Which way now?* Tears dripped from her chin. *I've got to find her before dark!* "Peggy!" she croaked.

Two hours later, she sagged onto a fallen tree, huffing and bowing her head. *Dear God, please help me find my baby!* She listened. The flapping of wings drew her eyes up. An eagle landed atop a tall pine. "Have you seen my baby?" she asked aloud. *What should I do?*

She sobbed uncontrollably. *Get a hold of yourself.* She wiped her face on her sleeve. *Think like a tracker. Are there any broken branches?* Sunlight filtered through the trees, illuminating a spider's web. Peg moved closer. *Someone or something has passed this way.* She moved north, watching for more signs. Shadows blanketed the forest. Peg took note of the sinking sun, so she could find her way home and retraced her steps. *I must have missed something!* Her head throbbed. A wolf howled. *I'd better find help and a light.*

By the time she got to the edge of the forest, one leg felt numb. Shivering and disoriented, she tripped over a fallen log and landed with a thump. The combination of grief and regret crushed her. *How could I have lost my daughter?* She winced, rose to all fours and crawled back to the tent.

Ralph heard something scraping outside. When Peg's sobs reached him, he dashed out the door and rushed to her side. "What's happened? Where's Peggy?" His question wrenched a new cry from Peg.

"Lost," she choked out.

Ralph looked beyond her crumpled figure. "In the woods?"

"I think . . . so," her voice rose with each word. "Her footprints led that way, but I couldn't find her."

Ralph stepped behind her, put his hands under her armpits and hauled her to her feet. "Let's get you inside and I'll find a light."

"Can you ask Amka and Sundsby to help, too?"

Inside, Ralph pawed through a box for another lantern. "Good idea, but you'll have to stay here. You can watch their little boy."

"But I can't just sit here and wait!" she wailed.

Ralph placed his hands on her shoulders. "Listen to me! You want to have this baby early, too? You're in no shape to be traipsing through the woods in the dark."

It's true. I'm beat. "All right," she croaked through ragged sobbing.

"Where's Miko?" Ralph asked as he threw on his coat.

She paused as hope lifted her heart, "Maybe with Peggy, although I didn't see his tracks next to hers."

Ralph hurried off and Peg fell to her knees. "Oh, Lord, help them find my baby."

Shadows from the lantern jerked alongside Ralph as he jogged to Sundsbys. "Help!" he shouted when the neighbor's tent came into sight. "Help!"

Sundsby put down a fishing fly he'd been tying, cocked his head and listened. "Amka, you hear something?" He spun in time to see her dart out the door. Grabbing his gun, Sundsby bounded off the porch after her.

"Peggy's lost!" Ralph cried when his friends got close.

Perilous scenes played through Sundby's head. "How long?"

Ralph bent over, rested his arms on his thighs and caught his breath. "This morning," he huffed, "she wandered into the forest. Peg's searched since 'bout noon."

Amka went back for lanterns while the men discussed options. When she returned with one in each hand, Sundsby directed, "Wake little Karl up. We'll take him to Peg, so you can help us search. I'll get the dogs. If you find her, fire twice." The three sprinted with the child and dogs to Ralph's tent.

Peg gave Sundsby her little girl's blankets, then settled Karl in her bed. Worry made sleep impossible. She dragged herself up, stoked up the stove and waited outside. Lights blinked intermittently among the trees. *Where is my baby? Is she hurt, alive, scared, frozen?* Her stomach rolled. She reached up to knead her tight shoulders. Tears left stinging trails down her face. She wiped them away in anger. *Why did I lie down? How can I ever forgive myself if they don't find her?*

Amka scrutinized the forest floor for any sign as she advanced into the depth of the woods. *Had the baby followed her dog?* She whistled and called, "Here, Miko! Here, boy!"

Ralph tripped over a fallen log. His lantern sputtered out. He squinted into the log. *Would she crawl in this for warmth?* He relit his lantern, leaned over and peered in, seeing nothing but an old squirrel nest. *Is she freezing?* He staggered around fallen limbs as fear pushed him forward.

By three the following morning, Sundsby's hope evaporated. He pushed his coat sleeve back and lifted the lantern to see his watch. *At least four more hours until sunrise. Many grown men haven't survived a night in Alaska's unforgiving wilderness.* He recalled last summer when a miner friend told him of finding bones. The miner hadn't thought anything of it until he happened on a human skull nearby. *There are a thousand ways to die in Alaska. A lost toddler's chances of survival are slim.* The dogs yanked him farther into the inky forest.

Peg paced and ran her fingers through her hair. Dark circles sagged under red-rimmed eyes and her nose ran raw from weeping. Little Karl whimpered in her bed. She lumbered over, lay next to him and patted his back until they both fell asleep.

Sundsby's dog stopped, cocked his head and perked his ear. "What is it, boy?" The man strained to see. "Peggy!" he yelled. The dog tore into the forest, jumping over fallen logs and crashing through brush. Sundsby shoved branches aside and plunged through the undergrowth. "Peggy!" His dog circled a snarling wolf. He jerked the gun from his back, cocked the hammer and squinted down the sight. Snow swirled in a gust of wind, obstructing his view. He crept closer and waited. Something darted forward. He shot and missed loaded and fired again. The body dropped. He inched in. His heart fell. *I've shot my own dog!* The wolf dodged into the trees. Sundsby crouched down and placed his hand on the dog. *Too late.*

A freezing gale battered Amka. She hugged herself and thought of her own child safe and warm. A stiff gust pushed tears into her ears. Holding still to commune with the spirits of nature, she asked the wind to subside. She asked the forest's spirit to guide her to the lost child. Two gunshots reverberated through the air. She spun toward the sound. *Did someone find her?* Lifting her lantern, she raced to the blast. "Sundsby! Ralph!" she called, but the wind swallowed her cry.

Ralph heard the gunfire. Engulfed in relief, he dropped to his knees. *She's found!* He wept, staggered up and headed home. The sun squeezed through the storm, lighting the tops of trees. The thin light kindled hope as he trudged home exhausted.

Too exhausted to wake, Peg didn't feel little Karl crawl from the bed. He whimpered when his feet hit the freezing floor, rubbed his eyes and moved close to the warm stove. "Mama?" he whispered. In the semi-darkness, he returned to the bed and touched Peg's back. "Mama?" Peg stirred. When she lifted her head, he cried, "Mama! Mama!"

Peg rolled to the edge of the bed and held her arms out. "Come here, Karl. It's okay." An owl hooted. He dove into her arms. A shiver snaked down her spine. *Natives say an owl appears when someone dies and accompanies their soul to the after-life.* She remembered Sundsby telling her when Amka jumped after seeing a large snow owl. *It's just a superstition.* She reassured herself. Remembering the reason for Karl's presence, she sat on the bed. The clock ticked loudly in the silence. Six-thirty. *Have they found her? Is she alive?*

"Mama," cried the frightened boy as he slid off the bed and pattered to the door.

"No, Karl! Stay here," Peg called. She threw her legs off the bed. *If he goes outside, I may not be able to catch him.* "Come here, Honey. Are you hungry? Come on. Let's find you some breakfast." She tried to sound cheerful. "Do you want a biscuit?" She found a tin box, stuck her fingernails under the lid and pried it open.

The little boy wept again for his mama.

"Karl, you know me." Peg's stress caused a sharp edge to her voice. *I doubt he's ever slept away from home.* She reached in the crib for the Eskimo doll she'd made Peggy. "Here, Karl, come see." She held the doll forth.

He edged over, running his chubby hand over the doll's fur clothing.

"There, there. I'll fix the fire and we'll make a hot breakfast." *I am hungry. Haven't eaten since yesterday morning.* She put the coffee pot on and scooped a spoonful of lard into the skillet. When it melted, she threw in a slab of moose meat and opened a can of peaches. The coffee pot bubbled. She poured a cup. The warmth brought some comfort. The smell of coffee and meat sizzling on the stove made her stomach growl.

As Ralph approached, the wind drew smoke from the tent's stovepipe. He rubbed his numb hands and lumbered on. "Peg!" he called, hoping to find her. She dashed to the door. Her heart fell when she noticed his empty arms. "You didn't find her?" she wailed.

"Did you hear the gun? He fought to enunciate the words with cold lips. "Two shots. They haven't returned yet?"

Peg slouched in disappointment.

"They'll be along with her." Ralph placed his arm around her shoulder and guided her inside. "Got hot coffee? Something smells good!"

"Do you think she's alive?" Her words begged for hope.

Ralph took a swig from her abandoned coffee cup. "Can you help me get these boots off? I'll eat some food, warm up and go back out there."

Amka trudged in the direction of the shots. *Did I hear something?* She froze and again pleaded with the spirits to guide her. *Was that a cry?* The storm moved on. A rising sun penetrated the forest canopy. She scoured the ground for tracks, but the wind had blown the ground into a blank white canvas. A deer sprang over a snow-covered bush. *Sounds like a cat mewling.*

From behind, a snarling dog jumped at her and knocked her to the ground. She waited for the bite. Nothing. Slowly, she lifted her head. "Miko?" The dog's hackles rose. She removed her hat. "It's me, Miko. Here, boy. Here, Miko!" A cry came from the bottom of a snow mound. "Peggy!"

Amka crouched. Miko disappeared into the mound. She crawled in and called, "Peggy?" The little girl tried to lift her head. "Good boy, Miko!" The dog had stayed with the girl and kept her alive, but her breath came slow and shallow. Amka gently lifted her. She tucked her inside her fur parka and backed out. Hugging Peggy to her body, she trekked back.

Sundsby knelt next to his dog. He brushed a tear from his face and patted its head. *Goodbye, old friend. Too bushed to carry you out, and it's too cold to dig you a grave. Got to go get warm.*

After eating, Ralph's head bobbed. "Lie down for awhile. You can't go on," Peg declared. "You rest here with Karl and I'll go." With his head on his chest, Ralph didn't hear and didn't protest. Peg pocketed a handful of bullets and struck out.

She hesitated at the edge of the forest, trying to decide which way to start when a shadow off to her left caught her eye. Squinting against the sun, she saw movement. *Amka?* "Amka!" Afraid of the news, she hesitated, then broke into a run. "Did you find her?" she yelled.

Amka opened the top of her coat to reveal soft brown hair. Peg fell to her knees. "Oh, thank God! Thank God! Bring her in. Ralph!" she screamed. "Ralph!"

Ralph's eyes closed and head tipped forward in thanks. He took a deep breath and dashed outside. "How is she?"

"She's alive!" Peg sobbed. "Amka's got her!"

The trio rushed inside where Amka unbuttoned her coat to reveal the girl sleeping against her chest. Peg scooped her up and bent her cheek to the little head as tears fell. "Ralph, warm some milk and get warm water in the hot water bottle." She removed the toddler's wet clothing and wrapped her in blankets. When Ralph handed her the water bottle, she placed it atop the blanket and sat in the rocker. "Her breathing seems normal. How did you find her, Amka?"

"Miko," Amka answered. "Miko keep warm."

"I'm going to give that dog a steak!" Ralph declared.

CHAPTER 11

A month later, Peg relaxed in the sunshine. A Chinook blew in mild, moist air and the warmth beckoned. She combed Peggy's snarled hair. The toddler babbled at her friend in the hand mirror, turned to her mother and giggled. It kept her from protesting the untangling. Peg patted her round stomach. "Soon, you'll have a sibling to play with."

When Peg put the mirror back on the shelf, she caught a glance of herself. *I could use some grooming!* Her hair had grown six inches since she left home. Winding the thick tresses into a bun, she noticed a white spot at her right temple. *Am I going gray already?*

When Ralph came home, she pointed it out. "I can't believe I've got gray hair. I'm only twenty-two!"

He moved closer to see for himself. "Yep! Maybe people won't call you my daughter now."

"But I always enjoyed the expression on their faces when you told them I'm your wife," she chuckled.

"Well, I did know of a woman whose hair turned white from a frightening experience. Maybe losing Peggy caused it." He threw his coat over a chair. "By the way, I checked with the doc over at the fox farm today. He's planning on coming over next week and staying until you have the baby."

Peg's eyebrows shot up. "Where will we put him?"

"Said he'd bring a tent. He also reported missing a couple dogs. Wonder if it's the same person who stole Kid's." He picked up his little girl and threw her in the air until she laughed. "You like, my little Eskimo? I'll ask Amka about finding a walrus hide, so we can blanket toss."

I wonder if Kid's recovered, Peg thought, but she knew better than to ask Ralph.

When Kid arrived home, he shivered in the eerie silence. The sight of empty kennels stung. He tucked his fists under his arms. *I swear. Come hell or high water, I WILL find my dogs!*

He limped into his tiny log home and slammed the door. Elk antlers on the wall teetered forward and threatened to fall. Cupboards created from wooden crates rocked. Snowshoes hanging over the bed shuddered. His breath formed clouds in the freezing air. A pitcher on the table held ice. A bundle of furs sat on his bed. He blew on his hands and opened the cold stove. *Might as well clean it out.* Ashes sifted through the air as he shoveled them into a metal bucket.

When he heard a scratching at the door, he dove for his gun. He jumped behind the bed and hit his shoulder on the frame. Rubbing the pain, he held his breath and listened intently. Nothing. He edged to the window and inched up. A white tipped tail disappeared around the corner of the house. He straightened up and peeked out. Only dog tracks in the snow. *Is someone watching the house?*

Easing the door open, he squinted at the frozen landscape and ventured out. Suddenly, something from behind knocked him to the ground. He flipped over, ready to fight for his life. A rough wet tongue licked his face. "Frostbite! Where'd ya come from?"

Drawing himself up to his knees, he put an arm around the animal and scrutinized the area, hoping to spot more of his dogs. Nothing. He rubbed his dog's head and ran his hand down its sides. "Where ya been, boy? You're thin as a rail! Let's get ya some grub."

Finding one dog brought Kid new determination. The next day, he and Frostbite made their way to The Salty Dawg. "Kid, where ya been hiding?" the bartender called out.

"I got attacked," he revealed.

"Do tell! By what?"

Kid glared. "That's the worst part. I don't know. Woke up hurting in Peg's cabin. Dogs and sled gone."

An eavesdropping miner at the bar piped up, "Heard there's dog fights about. Could'a been stole fer fights."

"Doubt it. My malemutes are sled dogs. More likely a musher."

"Ya never know. Oughta check it out." He slinked to a table in the corner to nurse his drink.

The bartender dropped his voice and whispered to Kid, "Pay 'em no mind. He don't know beans from bedbugs."

CHAPTER 12

Ralph left early to check his traps. Fog rolled in from the ocean. Mist filled the air, making fall colors on the mountains melt and run. He turned up his collar, shifted the pack on his back and lowered the brim of his hat.

Peggy stirred in her crib, calling out, "Mama? Mama?" In the dark tent, she couldn't see her mother in the bed next to her.

Peg opened one eye. *If I don't answer, maybe she'll go back to sleep.* Outside, rain hissed. She burrowed deeper under the quilts. Still half asleep, she thought she heard radio static crackling and sat up. *But we don't have a radio.* Rain drummed the roof of the tent.

"Mama!" the little girl called out as she held out her arms.

Wanting to stay in bed, Peg shifted her swollen body over and reached for her daughter. "Why, you're as cold as a little frog!" She pressed into the warmth of the bed and snuggled in. They both drifted back to sleep until thunder rumbled in the distance. Lightning flashed as a camera bulb. *Better stoke the fire.*

A week later, Peg woke to a dull ache. She changed position to ease the discomfort and rubbed her lower back. Her stomach tightened. *It's too early!* She collapsed onto a chair and took a deep breath. A contraction seized her. Little Peggy glanced up from coloring. "Mama?"

"Yes, baby. It's okay." She frowneded as her stomach cramped. *Where is Ralph? If this doesn't subside, I'd better go to Amka's.* She threw clothes for herself and daughter into the rucksack. Another pain gripped. "Come on, Honey. Let's get your coat on. We're going to visit!" Peg bundled herself and the little one, shrugged the rucksack onto her back and tied a rope around the toddler's waist. *If she ran off, I couldn't catch her, and I'm not losing her again!*

She opened the door to a blinding blizzard, wrapped the rope around her mitten and led her daughter down the beach two hundred feet. Warmth seeped down her legs. *Oh! My water broke.* A roaring gale created whiteout conditions, demanding they return to shelter.

Peg crouched and gathered her little one into her arms. *I need to go inside.* She shouldered into the ruthless wind that slapped her face as she pressed home. Stumbling into the tent, she collapsed on the floor. The storm hurled snow in after her. The little girl whimpered. Peg heaved herself up and secured the door, cried out and doubled over in pain. Her daughter felt the tension and began bawling. *I'd better get things ready.* She put a pan of water on the stove.

Meanwhile, the sky hammered down silver nails of rain. The storm, a gray and black beast, howled through the sky. Ralph scanned the landscape for shelter. A jagged firebolt snaked through the trees. Ten seconds later, thunder exploded. He dove into a clump of low shrubs, then peeked out when rain turned to snow. Balancing his snowshoes on top of the bushes to create a roof, he cut branches from a nearby pine to place over them and hunkered underneath to wait out the storm. As snow piled up, he scooped it into a wall to break the wind. Pushing his pack next to the wall to steady it, he prayed the storm wouldn't last long and fell asleep. An hour later, a growling close by brought him to his knees. He fumbled in the dark for his gun.

A dark pointed face nosed its way into the shelter. Ralph whipped back and brought up the barrel of his gun. A dog-sized wolverine lurched forward with powerful jaws snapping. Ralph pushed the gun into its belly and fired.

"Hush. Hush. You're safe," Peg whispered as she gave little Peggy her blanket and placed her into the crib. *When Amka gave birth, she didn't lie down.* Water bubbled on the stove. Peg set it off and washed her hands. She sterilized their sharpest knife and set it along with towels next to a chair. Next, she found some string to tie off the cord. A calm fell over her. When the next contraction came, she panted through it. *Soon, I'll be rewarded with a baby!*

Little Peggy peered over the side of her crib. As if sensing the magnitude of the moment, she didn't make a sound, but watched her mother. Outside, the storm bellowed. Peg paced in between contractions. *Why do storms start my labor?* When the urge to push came, she squatted next to the chair, grabbed the seat for support and arranged blankets beneath herself. With each pain, she pushed. As the baby's head became visible, she reached to support it and gently guided the baby as contractions forced it out. She caught the slippery child, wrapped her in a towel and held her close. *Another beautiful girl!*

Peg counted the baby's fingers and toes. Amid newborn cries, she kissed the top of her head. "I'll name you Lois, Lois Jean."

Ralph turned the animal's body over. He put his heels against the torso and with his legs shoved it to the edge of the shelter, hoping blood wouldn't draw more predators. He dug his knife from his pack.

After dragging the body into the open, he skinned the animal before it turned to ice. Blood pooled on the ground and froze into the dark brown fur. He flung the entrails as far away as possible and retreated to the shelter. The exercise had warmed him, but he knew better than to start out. The conditions were still too dangerous.

A hushed clean landscape greeted him when he crawled from his cave once the wind died down. With his forearm, he pushed the snow from his snowshoe roof, yanked them free and banged them together to remove clinging ice. He tied them on and worked to stay on top of the knee-deep powder as he slogged his way home. Rivulets of sweat ran down his back, but he felt the need to move quickly. *How long have I been gone?* Under the dark sky, he couldn't tell time. Snowshoes swooshed as flakes gathered on his shoulders and head.

Two hours later, Ralph saw smoke curling in the distance. He allowed himself a few moments to rest, but his anxiety intensified. He toiled on. Miko saw his approach and bounded through the snow to meet him. "Hey, boy! How's everything?" Ralph pulled the pack from his back. Miko promptly nosed it, smelling the dead wolverine. "No! Leave it be." He batted the dog away and lugged it to the door.

As he entered, Peg stirred in bed. "Well, slug a bug . . ." he started, then noticed bloody towels and froze. "What happened here?"

Peg uncovered the little one beneath her arm. He blinked dumbfounded. "You had the baby?"

CHAPTER 13

Homer's local deputy, Herb Dempsy, swaggered into The Salty Dawg and scrutinized the barroom. He removed a sweat-stained hat to reveal thick salt and pepper hair and steely eyes under scraggly eyebrows. A polished silver star shone from his leather vest. Twin revolvers swung in holsters at his hips. Muddy boot tracks trailed behind him all the way to the bar. He whispered to the bartender, "Seen Kid?"

"While ago."

"Where?" Dempsy puffed.

The bartender motioned toward the door. "Might try the post office. Sometimes spells the postmaster while he checks his traps."

"Heard tell of people missing their dogs lately?" the deputy asked as he sat next to a man with a sunburned face. He poured himself a glass of whisky and downed it.

"Yep." The bartender held out his hand for payment.

Dempsey dug into his pocket and threw a silver dollar on the bar. "Who?"

The bartender slid the coin across the bar into his hand. "Ben lost a couple while staying at a roadhouse 'long his route."

"Ben who?" Dempsey used his sleeve to wipe whiskey from his mustache.

"Man with the government contract to deliver mail 'round here."

Dempsey plucked a stubby pencil and dirty little book from his back pocket. "How long ago?" He licked the pencil.

"Last week sometime." The bartender moved to serve another customer.

"Hey, not finished with you," Dempsey protested. The bartender held up a finger as he poured a drink for a bearded man who'd sat at the bar. "What else he say?" the deputy prodded.

The bartender moved back and cleared his throat. "Threw a canvas mail pouch with a lock up on the bar."

The deputy lowered his voice. "Learn anything about the contents?"

"Nah."

"Find out his destination?"

"Nah."

The deputy turned and muttered to himself, "Yursa dad-blamed mindless wouldn't see a bear 'til it slapped yer face."

The sunburned man chuckled, "Don't let 'em fool ya. Bartender takes in all that goes on 'round here."

The deputy tramped out and let the door slam. He surveyed the street and headed to the post office. Upon arrival, he kicked mud from his boots on the wooden walkway and pushed against the door. Kid worked behind the counter sorting mail. He set a letter down, moved his hand to his hip and eased out his gun. Holding it below the counter, he cocked it and waited. The deputy pushed the water-swollen door open with his shoulder. "Hey, Kid. What's up?"

"Hey."

"You turned mailman?" The deputy smirked.

Kid placed his gun back in the holster. "'Fraid so. At least until I find my dogs."

"Can ya tell me what you had in the mail when you got attacked?" Dempsey threw his hat on the counter.

Kid frowned. "Dunno for sure. Bag was already loaded on my sled, so I took off. He stared into the distance. "Load felt heavier than usual now that I think about it."

After launching a stream of brown tobacco into the spittoon, Dempsey sat on a rickety chair. "I'm wondering if that's why you got ambushed."

"You think someone wanted the mailbag?" Kid wondered.

"It's possible. There a way to track the mail?"

"Not unless it got registered." Kid located a thick book from under the counter. He swiped a cobweb from the calendar hanging on the wall behind him. "Let's see. Couple of weeks ago on a Friday the 13th."

"Makes sense," Dempsey snorted. "Sure an unlucky day for you." He moved to the counter. "This book'll tell ya what came in that day?"

Kid thumbed through dusty pages. "Maybe, just depends if it got written down." He squinted at scrawled notes in the ledger as he ran his finger down the page. "Nothing on the 13th."

"Check out the day before," Dempsey suggested. Kid let out a low whistle. Dempsey moved to the back side of the counter and stretched to see. "What?"

Kid pushed the book to him and pointed. "There on the 12th. The Seattle Merchants Association sent a locked canvas bag to Einar Nilsen on Ismailof Island. I must'a been transporting it."

"Ya see anyone? Who is this Einar guy?"

"Don't know the man. Right before I got attacked, I noticed a big black dog coming at my lead dog in a blur of speed. Next thing I remember, I woke up at Peg's place."

"Ever find your dogs and sled?"

"Frostbite came home half-starved a week ago. Nothing else."

Dempsey scratched his head. "Could'a been a wild dog."

"Yeah, but why couldn't the rest of my dogs handle one wild one?" Kid puzzled.

"Good question."

CHAPTER 14

February 8, 1927

Newport, Washington

Dear Peg,

I keep thinking of you with two children in that bitter cold. Wish you'd come home during winter and just summer there. What are your plans when Peggy's old enough for school?

Gilbert Mercantile had a big year-end sale. I found cute dresses for your girls but knew the shipping would be more than the cost of the dresses. Plus, I didn't know what size to buy or when I'll see you next, so passed them up. Tell Peggy I hope she had a wonderful birthday. I can't believe she's five years old. How's my little Jean?

Saw Mrs. ~~Waterman~~ Simms in Kelly Drug Store yesterday. Her boy starts school this year!

Remember how surprised we felt when she had a baby at her age? Cute little towhead. My dear friend, Eliza, passed away last week. She's had indigestion for some time. Doc Phillips never found the cause.

There's been a shocking murder near Usk. A man employed by Joe Black went missing. Some men wanting to buy the old Ferguson land discovered a Masonic charm in the roadway. Guess it belonged to the missing man. A search party returned and found the man shot in the back. Marshal's got a couple of men in custody.

We're happy the Interstate Bridge across the PendOreille River is almost complete. The sawmill is hiring. Ralph could get a job there if you bring Peggy home for school.

Love,

Mom

P.S. The enclosed money is for Peggy's birthday and some extra for you. Buy something you've been wanting for yourself.

Peg folded the letter and put it back in its envelope. *I won't tell Ralph there's money in here.*

"What's new?" Ralph tapped ash from his cigarette.

"There's been a murder near Usk and Mom misses us." She stashed the letter in her knitting basket.

He rose. "What happened?"

Peg related the details. "I guess there's danger, no matter where you live."

"I heard there's been another Spenard divorce in Anchorage."

She tensed. *Can he tell I'm thinking of leaving him?* She reached for her knitting. "A what?"

He took a long drag from his cigarette and coughed. Peggy toddled over and held her arms up. He heaved her to his knee. "Some woman blew a hole through husband soon as he walked through the door."

"What did you call it?"

"Spenard divorce. Named for a red-light district of Anchorage. Boom towns always attract sleazy business . . . lotta violence." He stubbed out his cigarette.

Peg put down her needles and sympathized, "I'll bet the poor woman had been abused. Probably at the end of her rope. Is she in jail?"

"I imagine."

Peg tutted. "Poor thing. Better off there." *Remember, things could be worse.* "So many women, especially natives, aren't treated right here." She sat up straight. "But women can fight back. Do you believe the rumor that President Harding's wife murdered him for a string of affairs and illegitimate children?"

Ralph shook his head. "Nope, more prone to believe the suicide rumors since his cronies got involved in all those scandals. But I sure would like to find out who absconded with the golden spike." Peggy slid from Ralph's lap and made her way toward her mother.

Peg dropped her knitting, picked up the child and planted a kiss on top of her head. "Golden spike?"

"Yep, over at Nenana. President Harding drove a golden spike to commemorate the completion of the Alaskan railroad. Now no one knows where it is."

"That doesn't surprise me."

A pot of water on the stove boiled. "Could you lift that off?" Peg set Peggy down and got the washboard.

Ralph poured part of the steaming pot into a tub half full of cool water. "Test it and see if you want it warmer."

Peg ran her hand through the tub and set the washboard against it. "A little more, please."

He tipped the pot. "While the girls nap and you do laundry, I'll head to Sundsby's and see if we can catch some fish."

Peg's eyebrows scrunched and eyes squinted. *How 'bout you do the laundry and I'll fish?* She grabbed homemade lye soap and took out her frustration scrubbing and slapping the clothes. After wringing out the first shirt, she sat on her heels . . . *Oh well, he can't nurse the baby.*

She mulled over the letter from her mother as she scrubbed and tried to find a good reason to stay in Alaska.

CHAPTER 15

Florence handed her daughter Belle a lunchbox and straightened a bow atop the mass of red curls. "Don't dally. School starts in fifteen minutes." She watched from the porch until Belle turned the corner. Then, Florence went in and gathered the breakfast dishes. The coffee pot steamed. Hot coffee bubbled in the glass dome of the lid. Florence poured herself a cup and shuffled through a pile of unpaid bills on the countertop. The bottle in the high cupboard beckoned. *It's too early.*

She sorted the laundry and rolled her washing machine close to the kitchen sink to fill the tub. After putting in a pile of whites, she added soap and bluing, turned on the agitator and filled the nearby sink with cool water. The bottle called again. She gritted her teeth. The churning clothes matched her thoughts. Round and round, they tumbled. *How will I pay those bills? What will become of us?* She fed a pair of Charlie's pants through the wringer and guided them into the rinse water. A dog barked. She saw her husband through the window. Charlie opened the gate and moseyed up the walk.

She dried her hands and met him at the door. "Why aren't you at work?"

He shuddered and raised his hands.

"Well?" she pressed in the intimidating tone she used whenever Charlie's behavior didn't measure up to her expectations.

He ignored her comments, went to the bedroom and shut the door. She followed. "I asked you a question!"

Charlie flopped onto the bed and closed his eyes.

She stood with hands on hips. "Well?"

Charlie rolled over, turning his back to her.

Florence stuck out her jaw. "Do I have to do everything around here?" She rubbed her temples and slammed the bedroom door. *Maybe Doc can give me something for these headaches.* In the kitchen, she pulled the stool from the broom closet and climbed to reach the bottle in the high cupboard.

Later that afternoon, Belle skipped up the stairs and flung open the door. "Mama?" She stepped over a pile of clothes next to the washing machine. "I'm home. Where are you?" Walking to her parents' bedroom, she opened the door and peeked in, finding her father asleep on the bed. She found the living room empty. *Maybe Mama's in the bathroom.* The door stood ajar. No one there. "Mama?" Down the hall, she went into her bedroom and found it empty, too.

Throwing her lunchbox and sweater on her bed, she returned to the kitchen and opened the ice box. She poured a glass of milk, climbed on the stool, took the lid off the cookie jar and took two peanut butter cookies. After eating her snack, she swept crumbs from the table to the floor and put her glass in the sink, still full of breakfast dishes. She searched through the house again for her mother but saw only her sleeping father. *I love my daddy.* Back in her room, she found her jump rope on the closet shelf and bounced outside.

Skulking in the shadows, an older man watched Belle. He waited for a few minutes, then followed at a distance. Belle looked over her shoulder when the neighbor's dog barked. A man with rumpled clothes and greasy hair popped into view. He waved at Belle who froze as he approached.

The stranger gave a sly wink as he sidled up to her. "Hello, little girl. What's your name?"

Belle shrunk back from the smell of body odor and alcohol. "Who are you?"

"I'm your grandpa."

CHAPTER 16

Kid returned from lunch at The Salty Dawg. As he slogged through slushy mud from the last storm, his dogs spotted him and barked a chorus. The postmaster pushed open the swollen door with his shoulder. "You're back. Already loaded the mail in the sled for you."

"Gee, thanks!" Kid checked the load and tightened a rope. "See ya later! Don't take any wooden nickels." He waved and jumped on the sled's footboards. "Mush!" The dogs heaved themselves forward. Kid grasped the handle and raised his eyes to the mountains. The tops had progressed from termination dust to thick white blankets. Black clouds skidded over. "Mush!" He glanced up anxiously and adjusted his goggles over his eyes. *Hope I beat the storm.*

Menacing gusts of wind thrust snow up from the ground. Dogs with lolling tongues and frosted muzzles hurtled over barren land and through open woods. Weak sunlight leaked from leafless trees. Suddenly, a squall roared, and Kid couldn't see the brush bow of the sled. The lead dog gave a high-pitched bark that turned to yelping, then a whimper. The sled flipped. Its stanchions cracked. A man pounded from behind Kid and smacked the back of his head with a thick stick.

"Let's get!" the stranger shouted to his partner at the head of the sled. The attacker lugged his unconscious victim to the edge of a ravine and threw him over. He returned and righted the sled. "Mush!"

When Kid awoke two hours later, he moaned and worked to force himself to his knees. He reached to the pain in his head and brought back a bloody mitten. *Where am I? What happened? My dogs!* He tried to stand. Another sharp pain shot through his calf. He crumpled to the ground. Astonished to see a wall of rock to his right, he asked himself, *Did I fall from there?* It felt like a drummer played inside his head.

Later, he awoke shivering and in pain. *Can't stay here or I'll freeze. Need to find my dogs. Where am I?* He called. No answer. Moving forward in an army crawl, he surveyed the rock wall above, recognized it and remembered: *I took the mail to the island. That wall's not far from Peg's place, if I can get there.* He gritted his teeth and began the agonizing journey. A commonly quoted saying came to his mind: *"Your first mistake in Alaska is often your last."*

<h1 style="text-align:center">CHAPTER 17</h1>

October 17, 1927

Newport, Washington

Dear Peg,

I keep having dreams that you need me, do you? You know your family is always here for you.

We're ready for winter. The boys have split and stacked until the woodshed is bulging. We've smoked a couple hogs and I've almost finished up the canning. Yesterday, I sat on the stool in the root cellar feeling gratified by all my work. Sun beamed through the open door and hit the bottles turning them into gems. Cherries, peaches, pears, beans and beets glittered like Aladdin's cave of rubies, diamonds, emeralds and garnets. We've picked bushels of apples, squash and potatoes and the sandpit is full of carrots. Wish I could send some your way! The granary is full and haystacks tower over cut fields.

Nature's awash in fall colors. I think this is my favorite time of year. It brings such a feeling of accomplishment and security along with warm days and cool nights. Maybe I enjoy them more knowing what's around the corner. I imagine winter's already blasted Alaska.

Newport purchased Boundary Island. There's talk of turning it into a cemetery or recreation area. I think a place for families to camp and fish would be popular.

Rose came down twice this summer and stayed for the weekend. We didn't see much of her. Of course, she and Henry spent every minute together. Such a lovely girl. Henry would be foolish to let her escape!

Well, there's a bushel of windfall apples in the kitchen waiting to be turned into apple butter. Write soon. I miss you all and can't wait to meet little Jean!

Love,

Mom

Peg read the letter three times, closed her eyes and tucked sweet memories in her heart: lugging bushels full of apples, the wire handles cutting her hands . . . the derrick swinging loads of fresh hay to the top of the stack . . . working with Mud to store piles of striped and marbled winter squash . . . the cellar with giant pumpkins hulking in the corner and having to duck between braided onions and garlic hanging from the ceiling . . . the kitchen, full of steam and sweetness . . . apple butter bubbling on the stove.

I want my girls to experience my idyllic childhood. Should I go home? Haunted by the thoughts of winter stuck in the tent with two small children and a hung-over husband, she squeezed her hands into fists and rocked back and forth. Worries returned and set up camp in her head.

She found a pencil and sharpened it with her pocketknife.

Ishamailof Island, Alaska

November 10, 1927

Dear Mom,

I loved reading about autumn at home. It brought back such fond memories. You guessed right about winter here. Today a snowstorm pummeled us.

Miko sprang to his feet and barked. Peg put the letter aside and crossed to the door. A dog sled appeared in the distance. *Who's that?*

"Whoa!" echoed through frigid stillness. The sled sprayed snow over Miko as he bounded close. "Whoa!"

Peg stepped back in, checked the baby in the crib and grabbed her gun, *just in case.* "Stay here, Peggy." She dashed to the porch and cocked the gun.

The driver removed his goggles. *Kid? Not his sled . . . or his dogs.*

"Peg!" Kid beat his hat against his leg to remove the snow. He staked the dogs. "How's my nurse?"

"As I live and breathe!" She lowered the gun. "Question is, how are you? I've been wondering. Come in and warm up!" She held the tent open. Peggy ducked behind her mother who reached down to pick up the little girl. "Don't be afraid, Honey. It's Mama's friend, Kid." Peggy buried her head in her mother's shoulder. Peg backed into the room. "Whose outfit you using? Where's yours?"

Standing soldier straight, he replied in formal tone: "Neither rain, nor sleet, nor dark of night shall stay these couriers from the swift completion of their appointed rounds."

Peg's hearty laugh belted forth. "Can't believe you've memorized that!"

"Why not? Had to memorize poems a lot in school." He kicked snow from his boots and shucked off his coat.

Peg moved inside and shoved a chair from the table toward Kid. "So good to see you healthy . . . Have a seat. I'll pour you a hot drink."

Kid scooted the chair closer to the stove and held his hands to the warmth. "Peg," he choked up, "thanks for what you did. I'd be dead if not for you."

"You're the one who dragged yourself here." Peg's voice quavered a little. "Ever remember what happened?"

Kid shook his head. "No, my dogs stay with me if I fall. Every time I've been thrown from the sled, they've always stopped and waited. Makes me think I got ambushed for something in that mail."

"How would someone know what you carried?" Peg thought aloud.

"No idea, but Dempsey's checking into it." Kid gulped the last of his coffee. "Just wish he'd find my dogs."

93

CHAPTER 18

Questions crowding her mind held her body hostage. By two in the morning, Peg gave up and crawled from bed. *May as well finish my letter.*

> I'm not surprised about Rose and Henry.
> I think they're a good match. Next time you see her,
> ask her to send me a line.
>
> Pretty exciting news about Boundry Island.
> I sure have grown to love our little Ismailof Island.
> It's hourglass shaped, sits at the entrance to
> Halibut Cove and only a little over one mile long.
> I've explored it many times. During summer, I live
> in a world of blue and green. Most people here
> are involved with the herring fishery or work in
> salteries. Steamers come to the cove on a regular
> basis to load kegs of salted fish.
>
> I've been canning and drying fish for winter.
> Last summer, I planted a big garden and canned
> everything we didn't eat. Thanks, Mom, for
> teaching me how! I also planted flowers beside our
> walkway and around the birch tree in our yard.
> Our tree wore a skirt of flowers!
>
> Winter has its own beauty. Then my world is

blue and white. Jack Frost sugarcoats every needle and limb on the trees. Even the weeds are pretty. He also coats people! Ralph came home with a frost-covered beard yesterday and tried to convince Peggy he was Santa Claus. She held firm and kept saying, "No. Daddy. No. Daddy!"

Peg set the pencil down and propped her chin on her fists. Her thoughts continued to tangle. *Ralph does love his girls. Do I want to leave him? What's best for my daughters? Will he change for them?* Hope ignited a fragile flame in her heart.

We're thinking about coming home this spring after Breakup. I want the girls to love my family.

And I need to clear my head. Decide if I want to continue living here . . . with Ralph.

He stirred and reached across the bed for Peg. When he found her side empty, he sat up. "Whaddya doing? Come back to bed."

"Couldn't sleep. I'm writing to Mother. Almost finished."

"It's cold out there. Finish up." He gathered the covers to his chin and studied her. *She's not happy anymore. And I know it's my fault, but I'm going to change.* He sat up, reached for a cigarette, lit it, took a drag and commenced his campaign, "Peg, can we talk?"

She braced herself. *Here it comes again.* "Now?" she whispered. "The girls are still sleeping."

"That's why it's a good time," he exhaled, creating a scarf of tobacco smoke around his neck.

Peg's back stiffened. *I've heard this too many times.* "More promises?"

"Son of a gun, Girl. You know I'm trying! Business hasn't gone well as I'd planned."

It's always some excuse. She spun around. "I don't think you CAN quit, Ralph. Life is full of disappointments. There'll always be SOME reason to drink. *And I'm tired of having my hopes dashed, of wondering when you'll fall off the wagon again and not being able to count on you. I don't want my girls to grow up around this.*

Her assault forced him to roll into a fetal position and bury himself in the covers. *I feel gutted as a fish,* Ralph thought.

She moved to the rocker, drew a quilt over her shoulders and huddled closer to the stove.

As winter stretched on, worry wrung Peg's heart. Her girls became the only bright spots in her long dreary days. While they napped, she took her Bible from the shelf. Lately, she'd found solace there and reread the verses she'd written in her journal from past days.

Let not your hearts be troubled.
Believe in God. Believe also in me. John 14:1

Be gracious unto me, O Lord, for I am languishing; heal me, O Lord, for my bones are troubled. My soul also is greatly troubled. But you, O Lord how long? Turn, Lord, deliver my life. Save me for the sake of your steadfast love. Psalm 6:2-4
Say to those who have an anxious heart, Be strong; fear not! Behold, your God will come with vengeance, with the recompense of God. He will come and save you.
Isaiah 35:4

Will He come to save ME? Her doubt faded as her mother's voice came into her mind: *"The Lord helps those who help themselves."*

CHAPTER 19

MAY 1927

Spring arrived and Mother Nature awoke. Stretching from her long winter nap, she sent cracks racing down frozen rivers. When Peg's spirits rose with the lengthening days, Mother Nature rolled over and resumed her slumber. Slushy mud puddles refroze, driving arguing squirrels back into their nests.

Peg turned the calendar to May. The thaw crawled into the mountains. Colors melted from the sky onto the landscape. Northern Lights, exhausted from their long winter dance, retired. Nature throbbed with life, creating a restlessness in Peg. *Time for a change, Peg. Time for a change.*

After Ralph left for the day, she folded the rug over, removed the floorboard and dug out her stash. Months of saving a few dollars here and there had added up. The roll of bills fit tightly inside the box. *This needs to be more accessible. I'll sew it into the lining of my travel bag. How much will I need to go home? Hopefully, the baby won't need a ticket.* While her girls slept, she unpicked the seam inside her bag and stuffed the money in. It created a telltale lump. *That will never do!* Disappointed, she scanned the tent and spotted their coats hanging. *I'll sew money into them!* The job took most of the morning.

When Jean stirred, Peg picked her up and hummed. *Now I have some security. What's my next step? Should I enlist Kid's help? No, I don't want him involved. Ralph already loathes him. I don't want to worry about his safety. I could disappear with the girls.* As she nursed the baby, they both fell asleep in the rocking chair.

"Peg! You came back!" Charlie jogged toward her with outstretched arms and a broad smile. He was his old self: young, confident, happy. The sun setting behind him burnished his red curly hair. His bright blue eyes shone with excitement.

Her heart jolted. But he's married and so am I. Where am I? Her head darted from side to side. Oh, . . . the train depot. *I don't remember coming home. I've missed him.* She dropped her suitcase at her feet. "Good to see you, Charlie."

She remembered her children. She dashed alongside the tracks. Nowhere in sight. All of a sudden, Charlie materialized at her elbow. She swung around. "Have you seen my girls?" *Where could they be?* Her mind froze. In a tightening chest, panic wrenched her heart, and she began to hyperventilate.

A bewildered look crossed Charlie's face. He stepped close, circled Peg in his arms and whispered in her ear, "Don't you remember? You left them in Alaska."

"I did?"

Peg jerked awake. The baby, asleep on her lap, startled and threw her little arms above her head. Peg gasped, stared into the baby's face and sagged in relief against the chair. She pressed her palm to her heart and lifted the sweet bundle to her shoulder. *Oh, it was just a dream. But I'll* NEVER *leave my girls!* She pushed her toes against the floor and set the rocker in motion again until Jean settled down. *What does the dream mean? Should I go home? I know Charlie's not waiting for me. Or is he? Why can't I just forget him?* A tear fell on the baby's soft hair. Peg sniffled and gently kissed it away. *Ralph's not all bad. I can't say I don't care about him.* Outside, a hawk's screeching shook her from her musings. *Well, enough pity party! It's time to put this place in order.* Rising carefully, she placed Jean in her crib and checked Peggy who stirred and turned over but didn't wake.

First, she attacked the dirt and wood chips beneath the Yukon stove squatting in the corner. She finished quickly, pleased her homemade broom worked so well. The pot of water on top of the stove simmered. After pouring some into the dishpan, she set in last night's dishes to soak. The rest of the hot water went into the bucket. But no matter how hard she scrubbed the floor, an orchestra of worries and questions played on.

How can I tell him I'm leaving. Should I? I could go home for a visit and not return. No, that's the coward's way. But what if he tries to stop me or tries to keep the girls here? She wrung out the mop rag. *I know he loves his girls. Will the girls miss their dad and want to return? Have I tried everything to make this marriage work?* After scrubbing the floor, she got clean water and tackled the table and dishes. While Peg was lost in her thoughts, Peggy rose from her nap hungry. She peeled and sliced an apple for her. By the time Ralph returned, she'd made up her mind.

Ralph knew as soon as he saw her face. He steeled himself. "What's the matter?"

She took a deep breath. "I want to go home. Peggy's old enough to go to school and there's not one close."

He winced. "Is that the whole reason?" *Or an excuse?*

I may as well tell the truth. He already knows it. She dropped her head. "No, I'm not happy here anymore."

He cocked his head. "You mean you're not coming back?" His eyes widened and he felt his stomach sinking. He grabbed the back of a chair to steady himself. *Please say you're not leaving me!* "But it's spring. Things will change." *I know my drinking makes her worry.* "I'll change," he pleaded.

Peg glared. "I don't believe you. You take one drink, and the drink takes you. I'm so tired of excuses and I don't believe them anymore."

His fear roared forth in anger. "You can't take my kids! How will you care for them?" He scooped the baby from the crib and held her tightly.

Peg's chest tightened. "Think about what's best for them," she implored with a tremulous smile.

He took a step back. "You're being selfish. How will the girls feel when I'm not there to be their dad. How will you provide for them? I won't allow a divorce. Is it best for them or best for you?"

She drew herself to her full height. "Both."

His shoulders fell and chin trembled. He handed her the baby, backed to the tent door and fumbled with the ties.

CHAPTER 20

August 4, 1936

Ismailof Island, Alaska

Dear Mom,

I'm leaving Ralph, bringing the girls and moving home. All year I've prayed we could work things out, that things would change. They haven't. Four months ago, I told Ralph, but nothing's changed. He's still drinking too much. I've tried. Really I have, but I have to think about what's best for my daughters. May I stay with you a while until I find a job and a place of my own? You can expect us sometime in the middle of August.

Love,

Peg

She felt relief and trepidation as she folded the letter into an envelope. *Never thought I'd be a "grass widow!" People shun divorcees.* Turning over the envelope, she wrote her old address. Anticipation sprouted in her heart. Thinking of home and her loved ones brought hope. Next, she wrote to her husband.

Dear Ralph,

We'll be gone when you read this. I can't stay here any longer. It's not just your drinking. I feel abandoned, neglected and emotionally deserted. I'm almost a single parent. At least if I go home, I'll have my family's help.

I can't stay with you because we're not true partners. You make decisions without me, decisions I don't agree with. Your decisions have created an unstable life for me and the girls.

I realize you love our daughters and you're welcome to come visit them, but you can't keep them here. They're too young to be left alone while you work.

Thanks for bringing me to Alaska and giving me two wonderful girls. I wish you the best.

Peg

She licked both envelopes and left Ralph's letter on the bed. Next, she opened the seam in her coat where she'd sewn part of her stash and stashed her mother's letter inside next to her money. "Get your coat, Peggy. We're leaving."

Peggy paused from stacking blocks and peered up through her bangs. "Where, Mama?"

I need to cut her hair again. "We're going to explore Homer Spit." Peg wrapped the baby up. "Then, we're going to see Grandma."

Peggy's brow wrinkled. "Don't want to see spit."

Peg's shoulders relaxed as her belly laugh rang out. "It's where the ocean spit up gravel."

"OK, let's go." Peg placed the blocks back in the cloth bag.

On the way to the ferry, Peg passed Amka's house. *Should I tell her I'm leaving? I don't want Ralph to find out until we're gone, just in case. I trust her, but don't trust she'll understand me leaving.* As they came near, Peg recognized a fishing boat in the distance. *Hum, Amka's out. Oh well, that decides for me.* She stopped and waved.

The ferry sloshed to a stop at the Homer dock. Peg's stomach churned. The ship to the outside didn't leave for three hours, and she needed to keep the kids happy. She placed Jean on her hip, turned and reached for Peggy's hand. "Come on, Sweetheart. It's time to leave."

"Hey, Peg!" Kid called as he sprinted down the dock.

Peg whipped around. "How did you know to expect me?"

"Didn't. I just met the ferry to collect mail." He reached out his hand to lift her onto the dock. She handed him Jean, then grabbed Peggy under her arms and boosted her up. "Coming to the post office?"

Peg sprang onto the dock. "No, that is if you can mail a letter for me. I want to take the girls out to explore Homer Spit."

"Sure thing."

As Peg fumbled in her coat lining for the letter, a wad of bills fell out. Kid picked them up. "Be careful," he warned in a hushed tone and checked to see if anyone had noticed the money.

A rough deckhand watched them. He swung around when Kid met his eyes.

Peg noticed. As she gave Kid money for the letter, chills tip-toed up her spine. Sensing Kid's subtle warning, she whispered, "Do you think it will be safe for me to take the girls to the Spit alone?"

Kid took her suitcase and escorted them up the dock. "Usually there's people fishing, picking berries or beach combing. I think you'll be fine."

"Oh, I should have brought a pail to pick blueberries!" Peg lamented.

Kid tossed her a smile. "Hang on. I'll see if I can rustle one up. Got to be something around here close."

She shifted Jean on her hip and herded Peggy up the bank to a hewn log bench overlooking the ocean. The wind lifted its arms. An eagle rode the current and swooped down to snatch a fish for lunch. *I'll miss this place.* Down at the harbor, moored boats rocked gently while the sun fought its way through clouds.

A few minutes later, Kid returned with a bail bucket "You think of everything!" Peg crowed with delight. "How can I ever repay you?"

"Already have. Never forget that you saved my life." He held his hand out. "Leave your bags here in the office 'til the ship comes. That way you won't have to haul them around."

Next, he held out a leash for Jean. "This way you won't have such a time keeping two kids out of the water." When Peg buckled it around her waist, Jean howled in earnest. "Shus . . . sh, shus . . . sh, shus . . . sh." Peg tried to soothe her.

"Mama, she doesn't like it!" her big sister protested.

Peg patted her head. "She'll forget about it once we start walking." Jean tugged at the leash. "Well, we're off! Thanks again, Kid. Where should I leave these things when we're finished?"

"You'll have to take the bucket home, unless you eat all the blueberries," he teased.

He doesn't realize we're not going home. Should I tell him? Harbor seals barked, "Arp! Arp!" Grunts, moans, growls and an occasional roar filled the air as they jockeyed for the best place on the beach.

On impulse, she gave Kid a hug. He blushed. "No trouble." The trio meandered down to the beach. Water licked the beach, eroding the sand. Peggy combed the shore for treasures as majestic eagles gilded overhead. When she startled an otter sunning on a rock, it cried, "Haah!" She squealed. It gamboled into the water, chirping and humming to warn those in the ocean of the threat. The playful otters dove to safety and the little girl ran to her mother, screaming.

Peg hurried over with open arms. "It's all right." She hugged her daughter. "See that little flat rock over there? Bring it to Mama and I'll show you something." The girl's fear dissipated as she hopped over to collect the rock. Peg chose a few more stones, skipping them across the inlet. She demonstrated the throw. "Now, you try."

Peggy drew her arm over her head, releasing the rock with a plop that created circles on the surface and sank. She turned to her mother in disappointment. A baby moose with a humped back and rounded nose stopped to study them. Ralph's warning popped into her mind: *Unlike bears, if you meet a moose, do NOT stand your ground. RUN!* Peg scanned the area searching for the mother but didn't spot her.

"See those bushes?" Peg pointed in the distance. "Let's pick some blueberries. Here, you hold the pail." Peggy's eyes lit as she trotted back with her hand held out for the bucket. Peg kept a watchful eye as they plucked the big berries, but her mind traveled home.

CHAPTER 21

Florence stumbled up the crumbling cement step and pushed open a sagging screen door. Charlie sat on a metal chair at the kitchen table. "Where have you been?" he asked with reproach.

"Why do you care?" Florence snarled.

Charlie stood. "Where's Belle?"

Florence threw a flinty glare as she drew back. *She's not here?* "Maybe if you'd get off your duff, you'd know what's going on."

"I thought she was with you." Charlie dashed to the window.

Florence threw her purse on the table. "Well, obviously not. Did you hear her come home from school?"

"No, but her lunchbox and sweater are on her bed." He moved to the bedroom to check again. Florence followed. She picked up the lunch box and flipped up the latch. "Didn't touch her sandwich."

"Have any idea where she's gone?" Charlie worked his way through the small house, checking every room. When he returned to the kitchen, he stepped over a pile of dirty clothes. "You didn't finish the laundry."

"And what have *YOU* done today?"

He held his temper. "Let's not quarrel. Where do you think Belle could be?"

"Maybe she's . . ." she paused when she saw Belle, skipping up the street through the window, "there."

Charlie peered over her shoulder. "Thank heavens!" He scooted around Florence and opened the door. "Hi, Baby! Where have you been?"

Belle hopped up the steps. "Hi, Daddy!" she chimed as she jumped into his arms. Florence scowled from the doorway. *Why does she love him more when I'm the one who does the most for her?* She returned to the kitchen and threw towels into the washer. *It's because he spoils her. I always have to be the one to discipline her and make her do chores.*

Charlie sat on the front step and placed Belle on his lap. "What did you do today?"

Belle tilted her head on his chest and fingered the buttons on his shirt. "I played jacks with Clara." She sat up with a start and pushed her face close to his. "Hey, could we play dominoes?"

He pushed a curl from her eyes. "After dinner. What else did you do?"

"Talked to Grandpa."

Charlie stiffened. She jumped from his lap and grabbed his hand. "I'll find the box."

He drew her back. "Just a minute. Where did you see Grandpa?" She pointed down the street and ran into the house.

Charlie followed. "Florence, did you see my dad in town today?"

She dunked a handful of clothes into the sink. "No."

Charlie moved closer. "Belle said she talked to Grandpa."

Florence swiped stray hair from her eyes. "Well, my dad's still in prison."

"Who could it have been?" Charlie worried. "Belle, come here, please."

She appeared in the hall, clutching a wooden box of dominoes. "Can we play before dinner?" she asked, hoping that he'd changed his mind.

He glanced at Florence scrubbing socks on the washboard. "Sure, I think we have time."

"Oh, goody! I love you, Daddy!"

Florence pinched her lips and slapped the socks on the board. *There he goes again, giving her whatever she wants! He's going to ruin her."*

Charlie turned the dominoes over one by one, face down on the table. "Chicken foot?"

"That's my favorite!"

He placed his hands on the tiles and mixed them on the tabletop. "Why didn't you eat your sandwich today?"

She moved onto her knees replying, "Not hungry." She drew tiles to her side of the table and set them up in front of her.

"Why not?" Florence interrupted.

Belle placed a domino at the end of the chain. "Grandpa gave me candy before school and I ate it."

Charlie's panicked eyes shot a question over Belle's head. Florence's eyes widened as her hand flew to her mouth. Charlie sent her a warning with a quick shake of his head. "Grandpa from the farm?"

"No," she replied, "Nother grandpa. Chicken foot!" she exclaimed triumphantly.

Charlie threw down a fist of dominoes. "He short or tall? Thin or heavy? Describe him!"

Belle drew back and blinked. "Just old."

Charlie grabbed Belle's hands. "That could be anyone! You've got to tell Daddy EXACTLY what he looked like!"

"I don't remember," Belle whimpered, recognizing the serious tone in her dad's voice.

Florence stepped to Belle's side and put her arm protectively around her daughter's shoulder. "Calm down. She doesn't have a photogenic memory!"

CHAPTER 22

Peggy grinned up at her mother, with a round face and teeth stained from blueberries, her little purple hands clutched the bucket. "Come here," Peg beckoned. "Let's wash up." They stepped close to the water. Peg bent over to scrub the little face and hands, then took the girl's shoes off. "You can wade a little while."

After untying the leash holding Jean, Peg lifted her with a kiss. She searched for a place to feed her toddler and found a rock in the sun. Peggy giggled as she scampered across the wet sand, leaving little footprints chasing after her.

The scene tugged at Peg's heart and her resolve faltered. *I'll miss the ocean. I hate to leave you, Alaska.* Sun caressed Peg's back and shoulders as if reassuring her. She called Peggy. "Time to go!" She used the edge of the blanket to clean the sand from Peggy's feet, then worked to push the little damp foot back into a sock.

"No shoes!" Peggy protested.

"OK, but walk on the sand. Watch out for sharp shells. You can go barefoot until we reach the dock."

Peggy stopped at a tide pool and picked up a broken abalone shell. The mother of pearl luster enchanted her. She dropped it into the bucket. Peg checked her watch. "Come along. We need to catch the ferry." Clouds crouching along the tops of the mountains caused her to worry over a storm.

She took a few minutes to drink in the scene. *I'm going to miss the briny smell of sea and the cry of gulls.* As they neared the dock, a gull skimmed above the oily water and landed on one of the pilings. Down the beach, a man in a canoe slipped into shore. In the distance, immense mountains still wore beards of snow.

Peg collected her luggage and led Peggy along to the boat dock. A well-dressed man with prowling eyes made Peg's skin tingle and created a longing for Ralph's protection and a wish she had a gun. The man took note of her two little girls and commented to his younger companion with a sneer, "Many leave the States to get lost in Alaska, but only the hardy stay."

A sunbaked dock worker overheard and turned his hoary head to Peg. "Don't let Mr. Hunt bother you, lady. He's just a no-account swindler. Now, me, I'm the real McCoy. Been here since Gold Rush days!" he bragged. "It's purt near time. Let me hep ya." He reached for Peg's travel bag.

"I've got it. Thank you." *I can't trust anyone.* "Come along, Peggy," she coaxed the girl forward.

Peggy held back, hesitant to continue, "Where are we going? Where's Daddy?"

"Follow along, Sweetheart. We're going to see Grandma! She's got a pond to fish in and a lake where we'll swim. There's lots of cousins to play with and Grandma will help you make a dress for your dolly."

Peggy's eyes lit in anticipation. "Is Daddy coming, too?"

"Not this trip." *Am I doing the right thing? Will he come after us? Is this the best for my girls?* Peg shifted Jean to her other arm and offered her hand. "If we hurry, we can sit by the window and maybe we'll see a whale."

"Will Daddy come later?"

Peg swallowed and rubbed the back of her neck. *Don't fight me, please.* "He can if he wants to."

Convinced, Peggy hopped alongside. After they found a seat, Peg tucked her bag under her feet, so she'd detect any movement. She handed a picture book to her daughters. Reclining, she closed her eyes. *I made it.* The swaying ship rocked her to sleep.

CHAPTER 23

After Charlie tucked Belle into bed, he returned to the kitchen where Florence sat at the table, embroidering a quilt block. "Don't let Belle go anywhere alone," he ordered.

She cut the thread on the back of her sewing. "You think she's in danger? Here, in little Newport?"

"Until we know who 'Grandpa' is, someone needs to be with her."

She returned to her stitching. "You're paranoid."

Slamming his fist on the table, Charlie snapped, "I mean it. Don't you let her go *anywhere* alone!"

Florence flinched, drew her lips tight and lifted her chin. "That's ridiculous! How am I supposed to do my housework?" She threw her hands up.

"Never mind! I'll take care of her!" Charlie's face turned purple. He clenched his fists and swung around.

Florence shot up. "YOU have to go to work!"

"Not anymore," Charlie muttered.

"I'm tired of living in this old shack I grew up in. You promised we'd move!" Florence raised her voice. "I married you to escape this place!" *When my brother comes back, this house will be his. Since Charlie can't hold a job, I guess I'll have to find one.* She threw her sewing on the floor and flounced outside, letting the door slam.

Charlie propped himself against the wall and took several deep breaths. *Calm down. Relax. Do it for Belle.* He steadied himself against the door frame for a minute and tiptoed in to check on his sleeping daughter.

Her sweet peaceful sleep wrung his heart. *I'll protect you. Daddy won't let anyone hurt you or worse.* He shuddered. When he touched her hand, Belle sighed and burrowed deeper beneath the covers.

Florence *collapsed* on the bottom step with her head in her hands. *I thought life with Charlie would solve my problems, but nothing's changed. I still have no money, no friends, no future, and now a child to worry about. I wish I could fade into Bolivian!*

Gravel in the driveway crunched. She tensed as Marshal Ben Fox opened the door to his patrol car. After raking his hair back with his fingers, Ben donned a charcoal gray fedora and strode toward the porch.

"Evening, Florence." He hesitated and gave an apologetic smile. "Charlie home?" A porch light across the street came on. A face peered from the window.

"What's wrong?" Florence squeaked, fearful of his news.

Stepping closer, he lowered his voice. "May I come in? I need to talk with you."

Not trusting her voice, she motioned toward the door. Charlie appeared behind the screen door and cracked it open. The marshal assisted Florence to her feet. "Hello, Charlie. May I speak with you and your wife for a minute?" Recognizing the intensity in Ben's voice, Charlie stepped back. After entering, the marshal eased the front door shut.

"Have a seat?" Charlie pointed to the kitchen chairs. Florence, her hand at her throat, dropped on the nearest one.

Charlie moved next to her and placed his trembling hand on her shoulder. "What's up?"

Ben removed his hat and cleared his throat. "Well . . . I got a notice from Warden McCauley at The Walls." Florence clutched the table edge in apprehension. "Harris escaped last night from the prison infirmary. Wanted you to know in case he shows up."

"I think he has," Charlie announced.

Ben shot up. "When?"

"Belle told us that on the way to school today, a man gave her candy. When we asked who, she said, 'Grandpa.'"

Ben's eyes narrowed. "Does she know him?"

Charlie's hands trembled. "No, but he told her to call him Grandpa."

"Could it have been your dad, Charlie?"

"We asked her, and she said no."

"Has Belle mentioned seeing him any other time?"

"No, but I'll ask her tomorrow. She's asleep."

Ben picked up his hat. "I hate being the bearer of bad news, but I thought you should know, just in case. Thanks for your time. Sorry to upset you, Florence. I'll let myself out."

As soon as the door shut, Charlie opened the high kitchen cupboards. "What are you searching for?" Florence asked.

"Bullets for my gun."

Florence rose in a panic. "I'll find them. You go check Belle's window." *I can't let Charlie see my stash.*

CHAPTER 24

Peg shepherded the girls up on deck. A school of fish threaded through the water below. "Come here, Peggy!" she called. The little girl ran to the side, giggling. "Can we feed them?"

She grabbed the back of her dress as Peggy peered over the side. "No, don't fall in!" When Peggy lost interest and scampered back to the deck chair, Peg's eyes swept to the imperious mountains splitting the sky. Whispers of fog nuzzled their peaks. In the distance an oil well's pump jack bowed its goodbye. A trail of white water followed the ship as it propelled its way to the outside. *See you, Alaska. I hope to come again sometime.*

By the time they arrived in Washington, Peg's gloomy mood lifted. Filled with anticipation to see her family, she whistled as she packed their bags.

"How much longer? When will we see Grandma?" Peggy pestered.

Peg shut the suitcase and lifted it off the bed. "We'll ride on a train named Dinky for a while before we arrive in Newport."

"Is the train little? Is that where Grandma lives? How long will it take?" Peggy fired one question after another.

Peg laughed. "Now you sound like me!"

As the Dinky puffed down the tracks, Peg's mind wandered. *I hope Mother got the letter about me coming home. What will Mud think? I need to find a job soon. Wonder if Doc Phillips can give me some hours. I can probably help in the store 'til then. Maybe I can work there until Peggy starts school, but who will watch Jean?* The train whistled as it approached a turn. Ponderosa pines streaked by the window in a green blur. Rocking to the rhythm of the train, Peggy snored softly against her shoulder. Peg kissed Jean's soft hair. *Mom will love having these girls of mine close. I wish Dad were here to play with them.*

"Wah-wooooooooooo woo, woo, woo," Dinky sang out, informing Mr. Scott of three passengers for lunch. Peg gathered her things. "Here, Peggy, take your dolly. We're here!" The train shuddered to a stop. She lifted Jean to her hip and bent to grab her suitcase.

Peggy danced in place. "Is Grandma here?"

"No, Grandma didn't know for sure which day we'd arrive. Come on," she coaxed Peggy forward and squeezed down the aisle.

Stepping down from the train, she set down her luggage and drank in the familiar view. *Everything stayed the same.* Just ahead, Peggy tripped over her untied shoe. "Wait. Let Mama help you before you fall." She knelt to tie Peggy's shoe.

"Can I help?" a male voice asked.

Peg rose in surprise. "Henry! What are you doing here?"

He chuckled, "These beauties must be your girls." He swept off his hat.

"You're pretty," the little girl whispered to him.

Henry's laugh bounced about as he tied her shoe.

"Hum," Peg commented with a wry smile, "some things never change. Still wooing the ladies?"

"Why not?" He responded. "But not for too long," he added, a wink in his voice.

Peg set down her luggage. "Henry, have you got a sweetheart?"

"That's why I'm here," he boasted.

Peg gasped. *Surely not for me!* "What do you mean?" Her heart skipped. *I'm not interested in another man!*

"Can you keep a secret?" He raised one eyebrow.

Peg hesitated, "Yes . . . "

"Promise?"

"I promise."

He produced a small package from his pocket. "I came to the train to pick this up." His eyebrows raised as he threw out another mysterious wink.

"What is it? Who is it for?"

"A ring," he teased with a whisper.

Peg snorted. "You're kidding?"

"Nope."

"Did you and Rose . . . is it for Rose?"

His lips pressed together as the corners of his mouth twitched up. He put his finger to his mouth. "Shh, it's a secret."

"Oh, Henry! That's exciting!" Peg clapped.

"Keep it down," he warned as heads turned their way.

Peg remembered Peggy who'd wandered off. "Peggy!" She dashed toward the office.

Henry picked up her forgotten suitcase and followed.

The conductor turned at Peg's approach. "Have you seen a little . . . girl?" She stopped when she spotted Peggy sitting on the bench, swinging her legs.

The conductor turned his head and blew his nose. "She's okay. Wanted to ask me questions about the train." He brushed ashes from his shoulders and stepped into the office.

"You stay by Mama," Peg admonished. *I should have watched her better. You'd think I'd have learned my lesson!*

Henry laughed. "Curious like her mom, huh?"

"Yes, but she usually won't talk to strangers. I don't know what got into her." She noticed her suitcase in his hand. "Oh, thanks. I'm tired and got thrown off balance when I couldn't see Peggy."

"No problem. I heard the train announce three for lunch. Is that you?

"One of them. We'd better eat while I decide how to get home."

He scanned the area. "No one is coming to meet you?"

"I couldn't tell them an exact date, so no. I'm not sure they got my letter. Afraid I didn't plan well," she admitted sheepishly.

"How about I buy lunch? Do you want me to give you a ride?"

Relieved, she replied, "Oh, yes, that would be great!"

Mr. Brown in his pressed pants, vest and crisp bow tie held the door open. "Miss Tarbet, I mean Sparks," he corrected.

Peg returned a wistful smile. *I love how things are the same, but I've never seen him flustered.* "Still have meatloaf?" she inquired.

"We do. Want your usual?"

Her heart lifted. "I would, please, but would you bring two extra plates, and no pie this time."

Henry helped Peggy onto the chair, then sat across from Peg. "I'll bet you're tired."

"You know it, but Henry, hearts all over will break when they hear your news," Peg kidded.

He threw his head back with a hearty laugh. "Tell me all about your adventures in Alaska."

Mr. Brown brought her order. She cut the meatloaf into bite sized pieces for her daughters and spooned potatoes on their plates. "You go first. My mouth will soon be full!" She took a big bite of meatloaf. *Mmm, memories in a mouthful.*

"Sad thing about Charlie and Florence, huh?"

Peg's head popped up. Her heart sank. She dropped her knife. "What happened?"

CHAPTER 25

Florence flipped the bacon and stirred the eggs as Charlie entered the kitchen. "Smells good! I'm famished."

He sounds better today. "Where you headed?"

"Guess I forgot to tell you in all the excitement with the marshal last night. Dad needs some help on the farm. He'll pay me." Charlie took a bite of bacon.

Florence wiped her hands on her apron. "Great! What time should I have dinner ready?"

"Don't know. You and Belle eat without me. I'll bet Mom will feed me along with the hands." He gulped some coffee. "Florence . . ."

She set the spatula on the stove. "Yes?"

He reached out and clutched her shoulders. "Remember, don't let Belle out of your sight. Promise me? Or I could take her."

Florence rubbed her temples. "Maybe you should. I didn't sleep at all last night."

"Fine. Get her ready. Mom will be happy to see her."

As soon as they left, Florence pushed a chair to the high cupboard over the sink. She felt for the bottle, nothing. Rising on tiptoes, she stretched higher and inched her hand farther back.

"Whatcha lookin fer?" a man's familiar voice floated in from the doorway and interrupted the silence.

Startled, Florence's heart stopped. She teetered, tipped the chair over and landed with a wail as her ankle twisted beneath her. She drew the chair to her as a shield. "What are you doing here?"

"Got thirsty. Thanks for keeping a bottle fer yer 'ol dad," he smirked as he entered the kitchen.

"Get OUT! Leave right now!" She winced in pain. "I'll call the law! Don't you think I won't."

His eyes narrowed as he cracked his knuckles. "Doesn't seem like you're moving too well, does it? Now, where's that pretty granddaughter of mine?"

"You leave HER alone!" Florence screamed. She began to shake uncontrollably as flashbacks of her own abuse slashed through her mind.

"She in her room?" He took off down the hall.

Florence limped in pain toward the door. "Help! Help!"

Harris scrambled back to the kitchen, seized Florence and covered her mouth. "Shut up. If you know what's good for ya, ya hear?" he threatened. She bit his hand. He yanked her head back. "Why, ya little sow! Still don't respect your elders, do ya?"

Florence opened her mouth to scream as a fist slammed into the side of her head, knocking her unconscious. She fell to the floor with a thud.

Harris took the opportunity to search for cash. He rummaged through cupboards, rooted through closets and under beds. Nothing. *Damn! Better skedaddle! He* peeked out the door. Seeing the empty street, he scurried out the back door.

When Florence regained consciousness, her head spun. In sheer panic, she crawled to a nearby chair and tried to stand. A sharp pain in her ankle brought it all back. Shaking and sobbing, she dropped to the floor again. Determined not to let her father get to Belle, she continued crawling on her hands and knees out the front door. "Help! Help!" she croaked.

Across the street, Margaret took the clothespin from her mouth and pushed it onto the corner of the pillowcase. *What was that?* She froze and turned her head, straining to hear. *Is someone calling?* She reached for another sheet.

"Help!"

Margaret let the wet laundry fall to the ground and ran to the front yard to see Florence incapacitated on the porch. "Florence!" She dashed across the street to her side. "Lord, have mercy! What happened?" she cried, noticing Florence's swollen face and black eye.

"Call the marshal," Florence whimpered.

Margaret rushed home. With shaking hands, she tore the phone mouthpiece from its hook. "Number please?" the operator asked.

"This is Margaret Shaw," she gasped. "Tell Marshal Fox to come, fast!"

"What's the matter, Margaret?" the operator asked calmly.

"It's Florence. She's hurt!" She dropped the phone. It dangled by its cord as she sprinted back.

"Margaret? Margaret, are you still there? Margaret?" the operator's voice echoed through the empty kitchen.

Florence lay in a fetal position on the porch. Margaret reached for her. Florence roused and pushed her away. "Don't. I hurt my ankle!"

"What happened to you?" Margaret asked in genuine concern.

"He's back." Florence wiped tears from her bruised face. "My dad broke out of prison. He beat me up. Now he's after Belle," she sobbed. "Oh, help me save my baby girl!"

Margaret gulped, "Did he take her?" She stared down the vacant street.

CHAPTER 26

"What happened to Charlie?" Peg grabbed Henry's arm and repeated her question.

Henry's mouth dropped, "You mean you haven't heard?" He shrugged. "But I guess mail's slow to Alaska, huh?"

"What happened?" Peg demanded.

He lowered his voice. "Well, I guess it happened to Florence."

"What?" Peg hissed, impatient with Henry's telling.

Henry scanned the room, then whispered. "She's in jail."

Little Peggy put down her glass. "Jail?"

Henry mouthed, "Later?"

Mr. Brown appeared and refilled the water glasses. Peg glanced down at her daughter. "Yes, but now I have no appetite."

"Forgive me," Henry begged, "I didn't realize you hadn't heard." Peg swallowed hard. She closed her eyes, gritted her teeth and stared outside where russet leaves spun in the breeze and twirled to the ground. Henry jiggled his leg, considering what to do next. *I should have waited to tell her!* He stared at his feet.

Peg gazed out the window for several minutes. *Why's Florence in jail? Did she hurt Charlie? Did he need me, and I wasn't there?* She tapped Peggy's shoulder. "Honey, finish your meal.

Henry's giving us a ride to Grandma's." She jammed her hands into her armpits and paced. *I can't eat! How is Charlie?* Jean sensed the tension and whimpered. Peg collected her traveling bag. "I'll load the luggage while Peggy finishes."

"No, I'll do it. Meet you at the car." Relieved to have something to do, Henry jumped up to pay the bill.

Peg hustled her daughters out the door and motioned toward a towering ash tree. "Why don't you go and play in the leaves with your sister for a few minutes while I talk with my friend?"

"Where's my dolly?" Peggy asked, worried she'd left it on the train.

"Right here," her mother announced as she produced an Inuit doll with a carved soapstone head and fur clothes from her bag. Its legs dangled revealing a missing moccasin. Peggy rubbed the soft fur against Jean's cheek, making her giggle. After settling her girls under the golden ash tree, Peg jogged back to Henry. "Tell me what happened!"

He whispered, "Florence killed her father."

"What? I thought he was in prison!" Fear gripped her brain and cold crept into her heart. She spun around to make sure her girls still played under the tree.

Henry read her mind and took her hands. "Don't worry. They're safe. Old Harris escaped from the prison hospital. He came here to steal money from Florence and Charlie. Thank goodness Belle and Charlie weren't home. When Florence told him to leave, he knocked her out. Luckily an old lady across the street heard her cries when she came to, ran for help and called the marshal."

"But he's gone now?" *Maybe I shouldn't have come home!*

"Yes, it's gonna be okay, Peg. He's gone for good.

Peg's stomach fell. "How did she kill him?"

"She didn't, at least not then."

"What do you mean?" Peg mouthed. The girls giggled. As leaves floated down, Jean's chubby hand reached up for them. A cool wind nipped their faces.

A car chugged past and honked at Henry. He waved it on. "She killed him a couple of days later. I guess there's an old cabin on Boundary Island. Florence realized he might be hiding there. She found him passed out and shot him."

Peg sagged in relief. Across the street, a worker swept leaves from the front porch of the hardware store. "But that's first-degree murder!"

Henry continued, "Yes. it is, but I guess her dad sexually abused Florence from the time her mom left. Kind of makes sense now."

"Why didn't she tell Uncle Ben? Where's Charlie? Is their daughter safe?"

"I think so. Heard Florence feared for her daughter's safety. That's why she went after her ol' man. No way was she going to allow her dad to touch Belle. Some say she's justified for killing him. Charlie and his little girl are back living with Charlie's parents."

A waterfall of emotions poured over Peg. Tears ran down her cheeks." *Poor Charlie! I doubt he can take much more trauma.*

Henry brushed them away. "Hey, are you okay? It's over. Everyone's safe."

"Sorry. It's so sad. Now Charlie's little girl must grow up without her mother." She went to collect her children. *Who'd have thought that Charlie'd marry a murderer and I'd marry an ol' drunk?*

CHAPTER 27

The jailer frisked Charlie before leading the way down the hall. He stopped at the second cell, lifted a chain full of keys from his belt and inserted a large key into an oversized lock. "You have thirty minutes." The door creaked open on rusty hinges.

Charlie tumbled in and blinked to adjust to the dark. The door clanged shut.

Florence lifted her head from the pillow and pushed hair from her eyes. She pursed her mouth, swallowed a sob, turned from Charlie's dejected face and stared out the barred window.

"How did you know where to find him?" Charlie blurted the question that had been bouncing through his brain ever since the marshal shared the details of Florence's dad's murder.

"I lived with him for nineteen years. Not that hard to dissolve that mystery." Her back stiffened. "Him coming for Belle was the last stick that broke the camel's back! I'm not about to let him abuse her like he did me!"

"Maybe the judge will take that into consideration," Charlie suggested as he perched on the edge of the bed and placed his hand over hers. "Belle is doing fine. You don't have to worry about her. How are you?"

"How do you think?" she demanded. "I'm in jail! I'm charged with murder! I can't see my little girl!" Her words dripped with bitterness. She yanked her hand back and hid her face.

Charlie put his arm over her shoulder. "I'll get a lawyer and . . ."

She pushed him aside, bolted up and interrupted, "Right! How will you pay a lawyer? You can't even pay our bills."

Charlie hung his head. "I'll find a way."

Florence sneered. "Sure, you will. I've heard that before." Her words dripped with resentment. "You can't help me. Nobody can. Just like nobody helped me all those years when he abused me. People claimed my accusations were just a pigment of my imagination!" She flopped back. The metal bed springs screeched. "Go!" She ducked her head and fought back tears.

A tear trickled from Charlie's chin. "I have twenty more minutes."

"Aw, go chase yourself," Florence retorted.

CHAPTER 28

Henry opened the door of his dark blue 1928 Ford Phaeton and helped Peggy into the back. He stowed the luggage in the rear-mounted trunk.

Peg walked around the car and whistled. "Wow! Henry, when did you buy this beauty? Won't Rose love being chauffeured around in this!"

Henry grinned proudly. "Saved every extra penny for two years." He put up the black soft top and attached it to the windshield. "With this breeze, I don't want your girls to feel chilly."

Peg slid into the passenger seat with Jean on her lap. "I've never ridden in such a fancy car! What a nice welcome home!"

Henry hopped in, turned over the engine, moved the stick shift and checked out the back window. "How long ya staying?"

"I guess news doesn't make it home any faster than it does to Alaska." She paused. *How much should I tell him? Oh well, everyone will know soon enough.* "I'm home to stay."

"Wow! When will Ralph arrive?"

Peg peeked over her shoulder at her daughter who had already fallen asleep. "He won't."

"Oh, did he stay back to sell out?" A dog ran in front of the car and Henry hit the brake.

Peg flung forward. "No, I've left him," she confessed. Jean stirred. Peg switched the child to her other shoulder and patted her back to sleep.

He squirmed. *Wow! I blew that.* He cleared his throat. "Oh, sorry, Peg."

"Don't worry. You didn't know. I'm afraid that Mom didn't receive my letter letting her know we're coming."

"Now it's your turn not to worry. I'm sure she'll be delighted to have you home." Henry squeezed her hand.

"I hope so."

They rode in silence until the Tarbet homestead appeared. "Oh, I do love this place," Peg sighed. *But there are things I'll miss about Alaska, too.*

Mary wrestled the sheet blowing in the wind to pin it to the clothesline. When Henry honked the horn, she paused. He stopped the car, ran around, opened Peg's door and helped her out. In the back seat, Peggy woke up and peered out the window. "We to Grandma's?"

"They're here!" Mary announced with delight.

Peggy spotted her. "Grandma!" She ran across the lawn to her open arms.

"There. I told you that you needn't worry," Henry stated. "I'll let you settle in and catch up on all the news later."

"I'd love that! Let me know as soon as Rose comes down, too. When is the wedding date?" Peg asked.

Henry laughed. "Remember, I haven't asked her yet!"

"Oh, that's right. I won't say a word until she accepts."

"Hopefully, she will."

Peg hugged him. "I'm sure of it! Thanks again for the ride and lunch, too."

Mary approached holding Peggy's hand. "Who's that in your arms, Peg?" she teased.

Peg woke Jean who began to fuss.

Mary enfolded her. "It's okay. I'm your grandma. Nice to meet you," she cooed at the toddler. "She's beautiful, Peg."

"Did you get my letter, Mom?" Peg wondered aloud.

"I did. Already talked with Dr. Phillips in confidence, and he's anxious for you to return to your old job."

"Thanks. My prayers have been answered. People here are so kind."

"You worked hard for him. We've all made mistakes.

Peg hung her head. "I made a poor choice, didn't I?"

"Maybe. But you got two wonderful girls out of it."

Peg's face brightened. "You're right!

Mary put her arm around Peg's waist. "Come on in. I have a raspberry rhubarb pie. Your room's ready. I freshened up the guest room next to it for the girls. It's so good to have you home!

Peg's eyes filled with tears.

CHAPTER 29

Charlie pulled a handkerchief from the front pocket of his overalls and wiped his brow. He took a moment to absorb the vibrant fall leaves and take a gulp of water from his old military canteen. The morning chill had burned off. Geese in classic V shape honked overhead. It reminded him of planes using that same formation to reduce wind resistance. *Nature teaches many things.*

Suddenly, he hit the ground and covered his head with his hands. He crawled on his stomach into the uncut wheat, praying the enemy hadn't already spotted him and waited for the whistling sound of dropping bombs. "Chickadee-dee-dee," a bird called to alert the flock of the abundance of wheat. He broke out in a nervous sweat. When no bombs landed, he eased onto his hands and knees and crawled through the wheat to the farmhouse. His vision blurred. He grabbed the door casing and lunged into the house.

He fell into the armchair and tipped his head against the back. His racing heart finally slowed. When his mother came in with a basket full of apples, she heard him talking and wondered who had dropped by. Anna set the apples on the table and stuck her head around the door. "Charlie?" He jumped up wild-eyed. "Charlie, who was here?"

"Leprechaun, where is he? Is he shot?" He crossed to the front door.

Anna's heart forced her to hustle in and take his hand. "Charlie, your friend isn't here. Come in now."

"Wh . . . ere di . . . d he go?" he stammered.

"Why don't you lie down for a while?" She led him to his bed, took off his shoes and sat next to him until he fell asleep.

When Charlie's father came in for supper, Anna met him in the yard to warn him, "Charlie had another episode today."

James sat on the porch, removed his work boots and followed her inside. "What happened this time?" He pumped the handle next to the sink until a stream of water filled it, then scrubbed his hands and face. "Have a towel?"

Anna tossed him a clean cloth. "I found him sitting in the parlor talking to himself. He's still worried about his friend, Leprechaun."

"That guy from the war who got killed?"

She lowered her voice. "Yes, he got shot the day the war ended. Remember how upset Charlie sounded in his letter?"

He grunted as he dried his off. "I'm starving. Supper ready?"

"Hang on. Here comes Belle." She opened the screen door and called, "Supper's ready." Belle skipped to the porch. "How are your kittens today?"

Belle beamed. "Boots is the biggest. His eyes are open, but Lucy scratched me!" She held up her arm for inspection.

"Sorry, but that's what cats do," her grandmother sympathized. "Go on. Clean it with soap and wash your hands, too." She returned to the wood stove, filled bowls with mashed potatoes and string beans, then forked fried chicken onto the platter. From the ice box, she served sliced peaches and poured glasses of milk.

Belle tugged at the water pump handle.

Her grandpa waited at the table. "Talked with guys at the store today. They read an article in the paper to me about a Dr. Hurst who's been treating shell shock victims in England."

His wife put her finger to her lips. "Belle, go wake your father. Tell him it's time to eat." As soon as Belle left, she questioned him, "What's he doing for them?"

James took a swig of milk. "Hypnosis, massage, diet."

"Does it work?"

"They said so."

Belle appeared leading her father by his finger. "Come on, Daddy. It's your favorite, fried chicken and peaches. I'll say the prayer."

"Go ahead," Grandpa agreed.

Belle bowed her head. "Dear God, thanks for my kitten, Grandma and Grandpa. Please bless this food and bless my daddy to get better. And can you help Mom get out of jail? Amen."

CHAPTER 30

When Peg walked into Dr. Phillips's office and heard the bell above the door jingle, time froze. The unmistakable antiseptic smell, the black and white checkerboard floor, and two patients sitting on white enamel chairs, all combined to make Peg feel like she'd never left.

Mrs. Waterman's, now Simms's, chair creaked as she swiveled. "As I live and breathe! Peg's back."

Peg's face flushed as the men in the waiting room stared. "Didn't Doc tell you?"

"He did, but he didn't know when." Mrs. Simms marched into the foyer. To Peg's astonishment, she enfolded her into her ample body. "Welcome home."

Peg coughed and stepped back. "Thanks. When should I start?"

"What are you doing today?" asked Mrs. Simms over her shoulder as she returned to her chair.

Peg followed her behind the counter. "I can work today."

Mrs. Simms continued, "Well, things 'round here are pretty caught up. Can you work for me?"

Peg's confused look made the nurse's eyes twinkle.

"Tomorrow is my son's birthday party. I need a cake. Do you bake?"

"I can." *With my mother's help.* "How old is he?"

"Seven. After work, I've got two bushels of tomatoes to put up and green beans to pick. Time that's finished, I'll be bushed!"

"What kind of cake does he want?"

"Chocolate. And I need a big one. He's invited six boys."

She's certainly changed. It's hard to imagine her hosting a little boy's party.

"Well?" Mrs. Simms prompted.

"Mom has a big pan I'll use. She makes three cakes when our family gathers and I used to help her."

"Good. If Mary's taught you, I know it'll be tasty. What about games?"

"What about them?"

"This is the first party where I've invited kids. Since Arthur Junior goes to school now, he's decided he wants friends to come. What kind of games do kids play at parties?"

"Duck, duck, goose, tug of war, baseball, marbles, drop the handkerchief, kick the can, ring toss, capture the flag . . ."

"Goodness! Could I pay you to be in charge of games, too?"

Peg hesitated, "Well, I'd have to see if Mom would watch the girls for me."

"If you'll do it, you can bring your girls. I'll tend the little one."

Peg's eyes widened. *I can't believe it! Who are you?* "Deal! I'll bring the cake when we come. What time?"

"Come at two. Party's a half-hour later. Report back here Monday at 8:30." She drew a breath. "By the way, did you do any nursing in Alaska?"

"Yes, I helped at a hospital a little and nursed a friend who got attacked."

"What happened to him?"

"That's the problem. He's not sure. I found him nearly dead near my home. I think someone must have hit him over the head, stole his dogs and the mail."

She gave Peg her full attention. "He's the mail carrier?"

"Yes, and I've often wondered what that mailbag held."

"He didn't know?"

"Nope." *I wonder if they've found anything out. I'll write to Kid this afternoon.*

CHAPTER 31

"Mom!" Peggy ran out the door when she spotted Peg walking down the drive. Mary followed with Jean toddling behind.

"Did they behave for you?" Peg asked as she reached for Jean.

"Of course."

"I imagine so. When they have everything they want, they ARE good!" Peg teased. She hunched over to Peggy's level. "How would you like to go to a birthday party tomorrow?"

"Yes!" Peggy squealed. "Whose birthday?"

"Arthur Junior. He's turning seven, your age. You'll be in the same class when school starts."

Peggy frowned. "I don't want to go to a boy's party."

"We'll have fun. I'm going to help with games. And guess what? We're going to make the cake!"

"How'd that happen?" Mary asked, somewhat surprised.

Peg laughed. "I know. Mrs. Waterman, I mean Simms, hugged me. She said she's too busy to make the cake. She even offered to pay me if I'd make it and help with games."

"Having a child softens a person," Mary observed.

"But get this," Peg added, "she told me to bring the girls and she'd tend Jean!"

"Oh, I can watch her for you," Mary protested.

"Thanks, Mom, but you'll have plenty of chances for that."

"Chances for what?" boomed Gene as he swung open the back door.

Peggy noticed her cousin behind him, "Betty!" she squealed. The two girls embraced and ran upstairs.

"I love her having cousins close," Peg declared as she hugged her oldest brother.

"Good to have you and your girls here." He took the lid off a pot on the stove. "Mmm, what do I smell?"

"Chili." Mary took the lid from him. "I'm always in the mood for it when the weather turns. "I'm making cornbread and apple pie. Think your wife will join us for dinner?"

"If she's back. She went to her cousin's funeral. Poor family. The same cousin's daughter has been diagnosed with polio."

Peg grabbed his arm. "Gene, that's serious. Betty hasn't been around the girl, has she? It's contagious and can lead to paralysis."

Gene opened the pie safe and took a piece of raspberry pie. "That's what comes from working in a doctor's office. You worry too much. Want some pie?" He sat at the big round table. "Mom, got a copy of the newspaper here?"

"In the parlor. Peg, will you find it?"

Peg returned with the local paper. "I'm not kidding, Gene. Polio isn't something to mess with." She brought over the newspaper and set it on the table.

He unfolded the paper. "Whadda ya know, Diamond Match bought two big tracts in our county." He took a bite of pie. "Wow, three hundred million feet. Mills will be built to cut fifty thousand feet a day. Maybe I'll quit driving trucks and pick up a job there, so I can be home more."

"That's a good idea," Mary agreed. "I'd love having you closer."

Gene polished off the pie and turned the page. "You know that fire at Kelly's Store? Says here the fire department had to break in the iron doors at the rear of the building. It burned two holes in the floor of the storage room. All the sugar and flour stock got ruined by water. The window in the top floor and plate glass window in front cracked."

Mary stopped stirring the cornbread batter. "Oh, that's too bad! What caused it?"

He read a little further. "No known cause. There was no fire in the stove yet, but it's covered by insurance. Hey, Peg," he called, "Fid's Opera House's showing Pathe current event movies on Saturdays, during the afternoon matinee. Want to go?"

"What does it cost?"

"Two bits."

Peg kept sweeping a trail of crumbs from the pie safe to the table. "Too rich for my blood."

He closed the newspaper. "My welcome home treat."

"I have two kids to take care of." She dumped the dustpan out the back door.

"Jean can get in for free and Peggy can come play with Betty."

Peg grinned. "You're on!"

CHAPTER 32

F all blew into winter. But after Alaska, the cold didn't bother Peg. Thoughts skittered through her head like leaves in the wind as she walked to work. *I wonder how Ralph is doing. Did Kid get my letter? I miss Miko, Amka and Sundsby, too. But I love working again with Doc.*

That afternoon brought a surprise. Gene and his wife came into the office. Peg squirmed. *I wonder how Marie feels about me leaving Ralph. It's weird that I'm her mother-in-law now and only three years older and her sister-in-law!* She pasted on a smile. "What's up?"

"Gene fell on his elbow a few days ago," she reported.

Peg opened the door to the back. "Come on, ya big oaf. Let's see. Why ya dancing on your elbow?" Gene sat on the examining table and winced as he pulled up his sleeve.

"Take your shirt off," Peg stated as she shook down the mercury in the thermometer.

Gene slowly slipped it off, exposing a red swollen elbow and lower arm. "My! How did you do that?"

"Jumped out of the truck. My foot hit a patch of ice and down I went."

"That's a lot of weight on one elbow!" she teased and checked the thermometer. "Hum, you have a fever. Let's take your blood pressure."

Gene lifted his unhurt arm. "It's infected."

"Yes, it is."

He grit his teeth as she gently lifted the arm to examine it.

Marie's voice wavered as she explained why they hadn't come in earlier. "I've been worried. He felt so dizzy this morning that he finally agreed to come to the doctor."

"Thanks. He can be bull-headed," Peg teased, trying to ease her worry. Her own fear escalated when she noticed a red streak leading to his armpit. "Lie back, Gene. I'll get Doc."

She darted to his office. "Doc, come quick!"

He jumped up. "What is it?"

"Gene hurt his arm. His temperature is one hundred and three and blood pressure is low."

He rose and picked up his stethoscope.

Peg stopped him and whispered, "Also, there's a red line up to his armpit."

Doc pushed open the door. "Hey, Gene. I hear you've been falling out of trucks."

Gene shivered. Doc examined the wound. "Marie, this is septicemia. We need to take your husband to the hospital immediately."

Marie's hand flew to her throat. "It's what?"

"Blood poisoning. We should have given him antibiotics earlier. He needs to be in the hospital where he'll be monitored closely. I'll call the ambulance and you can meet him there."

Peg swallowed. "Could I nurse him?"

Doc walked to the door. "No, you're not an RN, and he'll be in intensive care. This is a serious infection. Why don't you go home and let your mother know? I'll tell Mrs. Simms you're leaving early."

"Want a ride, Peg?" Marie offered.

"No, it's out of your way. You go to the hospital. I'll be fine." Peg threw her coat on and dashed off.

"Mom!" Peg screamed as soon as she opened the door. Out of breath, she collapsed on a kitchen chair.

Hearing the panic in Peg's voice, Mary scurried in. "What's the matter?"

Seeing her mother, Peg lost control. "Gene's very sick," she choked out between sobs.

Mary hurried to Peg's side. "With what?"

"Blo . . . od poisoning," she whimpered.

Mary grabbed her hat and coat. "We'd better stop by Gene's and pick up Betty. School's almost out."

"It's closer to get both girls at the school," Peg stated. "I'll start the car."

Peg dropped Mary at the hospital and sped to the school. She arrived just as the school doors opened, spilling boisterous children onto the sidewalk. Peggy and Betty emerged hand in hand. Peg scooped up Jean and met them. "Hi, girls. Betty, you are coming over to play with Peggy for a while."

"Yes!" Both girls shouted in unison.

After two days in the hospital, Gene went into a coma. The following evening, he died. After the shocking news, Peg couldn't eat or sleep. A headache hammered at her temples. She sat in the overstuffed chair in the parlor and stared out the window. *He was only forty-one years old. He should have come to the doctor sooner! Poor little Betty. It breaks my heart that she will grow up without her dad. I miss him so much already.*

Peggy crept in and sat at her feet. "Mom, I don't have to have a party tomorrow."

"A party?"

"Yes, tomorrow's my birthday, but you don't have to make a party for me."

Peg flinched, "Oh, Honey, I totally forgot. Of course, you need a party! Eight years old is a big deal. What do you want to do?

"I'd just like Betty to come over. Maybe we could make a cake like we did for Arthur Junior."

"We can, and we'll make a fancy tea party, too. We'll use Grandma's best china. Want to dress up fancy?"

Peggy clapped her hands. "Yes!"

Mary covered the table with the lace tablecloth that had taken her a year to crochet. With no fresh flowers available in February, she made flower shaped cookies with pink frosting and angel food cake topped with whipped cream and strawberry jam. Peg spent the morning making ladyfingers, spritz cookies and fancy little tea sandwiches. When the girls came in from school, Peggy caught her breath, "It's beautiful!"

Peg helped them remove their coats and mittens. "Go wash and change into your party dresses. Then we'll start." The two girls giggled off.

"I needed something to distract me," Peg admitted. "Funny how I enjoyed making all this when I didn't want anything girly as a child."

Mary hugged Peg. "It's gratifying to see the children happy."

"Poor little Betty," Peg mused.

"Children are resilient. She'll make out okay," Mary predicted.

Peggy awoke with a fever and stomachache. "Mama," she cried out. "I don't feel so good." Peg came upstairs and felt her forehead. "You're a little warm." She went to the bathroom for the thermometer. When she returned, Peggy vomited. She grabbed the wastebasket next to the bed and held it for her. "Oh, Honey, maybe you ate too many sweets last night."

The commotion woke Betty sleeping in the same bed. Peg wiped her daughter's face. "Lie back. I'll make you some tea. Come on, Betty. Peggy's not well. We'll need to take you home."

When Peg returned with the tea, her daughter grabbed her throat. "My neck hurts." She set the tea on the nightstand and felt her forehead. Still warm. "Drink this."

"What's in it?"

Peg helped her sit up. "Tea and honey."

Peggy took a sip. She grabbed the back of her neck and winced in pain.

"I'm going to take you to Doc. Find your shoes and coat."

"In my nightgown?"

"No one will see under your coat. Put your arm in here."

Peg went down to the kitchen. "Mom, can you go with me to work this morning? Peggy's got a fever and she says that her throat hurts. I want to make sure it isn't strep. Could you bring her home after?"

Mary dried her hands. "Sure." She took her coat from the hanger and grabbed her purse.

Dr. Phillips entered the room. "Hello, Miss Peggy. Not feeling well today? Let's see. Open your mouth and say, 'Aw'." He swabbed her throat. "Peg, please collect a urine and stool specimen."

Peg raised her eyebrows.

"Just covering all the bases," he reassured her. Turning to Peggy, he instructed, "You go home with Grandma, rest in bed and drink fluids."

As soon as they left, Peg peppered him with questions.

Doc held his hand up. "Let's wait until the test results are ready, please."

"Do you think I could have time off to take care of her? Mother's getting older and I don't want to wear her out."

He stepped to the sink. "Can you stay until lunch?"

"Of course," Peg said with a nod. *Maybe I'm spooked because of Gene.* On the way home, she passed Fid's Opera House. The marquee read: Now playing: New Pathe film: Motor Racing. It stung. *Gene would have loved to see that one!*

CHAPTER 33

Charlie trudged up the stairs from the morning milking, kicked mud from his feet, opened the screen door with his toe and set two foaming milk pails on the kitchen cupboard. He retreated to the back porch and sat on the chair to remove his boots. Sun crept over the hill, setting the fall leaves ablaze and washing the clouds in shades of saffron and salamander. *It's good to be home. Maybe I can heal here. I have to be strong for Belle.* Pregnant boughs on the apple trees hung low, ready for delivery. Frost had bitten the garden's vines back, exposing a kaleidoscope of gourds, squash and pumpkins. Charlie felt a stir of hope. A rooster crowed, birds twittered and the hens scratched for breakfast. *I do appreciate nature more.*

The screen door slammed as Charlie entered the kitchen. Anna worked at the sink straining the milk. Ham and eggs sizzled in cast iron skillets and oatmeal bubbled in a pot. "Good morning, Son. Take some of this fresh cream for your cereal. I cut some peaches, too."

"I will," he agreed, "after I wake Belle." He padded down the hall and paused at the bedside. Hesitant to wake her, he drank her peace and innocence to his parched soul. *She's my hope, my reason to live.*

Under the patchwork quilt, Belle stirred. She opened one eye and reached up, "Daddy."

"Morning, Beautiful. Hungry? Grandma's got a big breakfast ready." Charlie scooped her into his arms and whispered to the mass of fuzzy red curls. "Run to the outhouse and I'll pour you some warm water for washing up." He set her on her feet and plucked her coat from a hook on the door. "You'll want this. It's frosty out there."

Belle peered out from her hair. "Daddy?"

"Yes."

"Did Mom kill my grandpa?"

Charlie froze. *I've dreaded this.* "Who told you that?

"Kids at school."

"She did it to protect you. She worried that he would hurt you."

Her lip quivered. "Am I in trouble?"

"No! Of course not!" Charlie growled.

Tears filled her eyes. "I miss Mom. When's she coming home?"

Charlie's stomach churned. "I don't know, Honey. Daddy's working on it."

Charlie's father came in and hung up his hat. "After breakfast, I'm off to Tarbet's store. Got your list ready, Anna? I'll take Belle, and she can catch the school wagon there."

Charlie spread a thick layer of cream over his oatmeal. *How would I survive without my parents?* He forced a happy face. "Thanks, Dad. I'll service the tractor and split more firewood." As soon as they left, he put his head in his hands, then lowered it onto the kitchen table.

His mother cleared the dishes, then patted Charlie's back. "It will all work out, Son. You know we're here for you."

He raised his head to his hands and whispered, "I shouldn't have married her, Mom," he whispered. "I was so messed up from the war. I just felt that Florence needed me."

"She still does. Belle needs you. We all do." She sat next to him. "Your father heard back from the lawyer in Spokane yesterday. He'll take the case. Surely, Florence's past will have some bearing on the verdict."

"Florence told me to leave last time I visited. I don't know if I should even try to see her again," Charlie confided.

The wind sighed and billowed the kitchen curtains. It banged the screen door and rustled the leaves. Anna rose to shut the doors. "Don't give up, Charlie. Belle needs her mother." She noticed clouds gathering. "Do you think she'd talk to me?"

CHAPTER 34

Homer, Alaska

The Kid climbed steps of a covered porch tacked onto the box-shaped building of the Inlet Trading Post owned by George Bishop. He pushed the door in and took a list from his coat pocket. Bishop handed some change back to a bear of a man wrapped in a fur coat. Though the man adjusted his hood to cover his face as he turned to leave, Kid got a quick glimpse of the Native's face as he crammed huge, calloused hands into his mittens and prepared to battle the cold.

"Morning, Kid. What can I get you?" Bishop closed the till.

Kid handed the list over. "Who was that guy?"

Bishop shrugged. "Haven't seen him before. Didn't seem too friendly. Ignored me when I tried to visit.

Deja vu made Kid shiver. "I'll pick up my things later." He hurried outside and caught sight of the stranger as he disappeared into the Salty Dawg Saloon. Kid followed. The barrel-chested man waited at the bar. Kid took a stool next to him. "Howdy." He turned bloodshot eyes Kid's way. "Haven't seen you in these parts." The stranger downed his drink with two gulps. He slung a coin onto the bar and left mumbling.

Kid spoke to the bartender. "Unfriendly type. Ever seen him before?"

"Yep. Last time I told him no dogs were allowed inside, and he left without buying."

Kid tensed. "What kind of dog?"

"Big black wolf-lookun thing."

"A wolf?" Kid shot up. "Seen Marshal today?"

The bartender wiped up a spill. "Nope."

Kid bolted out, but the man had disappeared. He jogged down the street to the marshal's office and threw open the door.

The marshal reached for his sidearm. His hand fell. "Hey, Kid."

"Come quick!" Kid huffed. "I think I saw the man who attacked me!"

The marshal jumped to his feet and threw Kid a rifle. "Let's go! Don't shoot. Hold him 'til I get there." They charged into the street. Marshal signaled for Kid to go up the street while he headed down. Kid cocked the rifle. He walked warily, searching every possible hiding place. When he got to the edge of town, the snow showed no footprints, so he turned back.

An hour later, he passed the marshal's office and saw him sitting at his desk. Kid walked in. "No luck?"

"No, you see anything?"

Kid blinked rapidly. "How could he just disappear?"

"Seems natives can do that."

Kid's eyes narrowed. "I said nothing about him being Native."

The marshal reached to take his rifle back. "Guess I assumed that for some reason."

Kid walked to the desk. "Did you ask at the bar about a man with a wolf dog?"

He frowned. "Don't think natives would have a wolf. They're more afraid of wolves than bears. Won't even say the word wolf aloud. Believe they have magical powers and can hear what you say." He hung the rifle back on the rack behind him. "But they do like their dogs to breed with wolves for intelligence and endurance."

Kid sat across from him. "Ever hear of Klutuck?"

The marshal blinked. "Of course, but he's not in these parts. What made you think of him?"

"Thought I heard someone say his name during the attack."

The lawman pushed back his chair and steepled his fingers. "Interesting. Could be they were talking about him."

I said nothing about more than one person. "Klutuck have a partner?" Kid probed.

"Don't think so? Why do you ask?"

"You said THEY talked about Kluktuk."

Marshal pushed a pile of papers back. "I did? Well, I'm thinking out loud."

Kid pressed, "Any ideas?"

"Well, mighta taken your dogs for fights. And they're nice dogs, that would be easy to sell or maybe they needed a team for trapping. During the Gold Rush, dog knapping happened a lot, but not much mining around here. Could have been a planned attack or a crime of opportunity."

"Will you ask around about the man in the bar?"

"Sure thing."

Kid made for the door.

"Wait," the marshal called, "this is probably unrelated, but Joe found a dog frozen in a block of ice while checking his trapline."

Kid stomped back in. "What kind of dog?"

"Dunno."

CHAPTER 35

The State of Washington vs. Florence Wilson

The bailiff banged the gavel. "All rise. The Fifth Circuit Court of Washington is now in session. The Honorable Judge Howard Smith presiding."

The clerk stood. "People of the state of Washington against Florence Wilson, docket number 00348."

The judge cleared his throat and picked up the papers on his desk. "Is the defense ready?"

A graying lawyer in a three-piece suit rose next to Florence. "Yes, Your Honor." He nudged Florence under the table with his foot. She lifted her head. Her vacant stare unnerved Charlie who tried to get her attention with a wistful smile.

Turning to the other side of the room, the judge asked, "Prosecution ready?" Florence lowered her head again.

Across the aisle, the prosecutor answered, "Yes, Your Honor."

The judge addressed the clerk, "Swear in the jury."

"Ladies and gentlemen of the jury, please rise. Raise your right hand. Do you solemnly swear to justly try this case and enter a verdict based only on the evidence presented?"

The jury chorused, "I do."

The clerk finished, "You may be seated."

After the jury quieted, the judge continued asking, "Does the prosecution have an opening statement?"

"Yes, Your Honor," the prosecutor, a gangly man in horn rim glasses, moved to face the jury. "Ladies and gentlemen of the jury, the state intends to prove Florence Wilson guilty of premeditated murder, murder in the first degree. We will prove that Mrs. Wilson went to Boundary Island with the intent to kill her father. Instead of contacting the marshal, she took the law into her own hands. She traveled to Boundary Island, where she found her father incapacitated, shot and killed him." The crowd shifted and whispered.

Charlie's mother grabbed his hand.

"Order!" the judge banged his gavel. "Does the defense wish to make an opening statement?"

Florence's lawyer pushed back his chair. "We do, Your Honor. The Defense will show extenuating circumstances that made Florence Wilson fear for her own life and for her daughter's safety. We will show that Mrs. Wilson suffered years of neglect and abuse from her father. Mr. Harris recently contacted his granddaughter, Belle Wilson. He attacked Mrs. Wilson and attempted to rob her. Mrs. Wilson's only objective was to prevent her father from sexually abusing her daughter the way he had previously abused Florence for years after his wife abandoned him, due to Mr. Harris's drinking and associating with local moonshiners.

"Prosecutor, call your first witness."

"I call Marshal Ben Fox."

The marshal took off his hat and entered the stand.

After the clerk swore him in, the prosecutor proceeded, "Marshal Fox, how did you discover that Mr. Harris had been killed?"

The marshal peered over his glasses. "Margaret Shaw called and told me to meet her at Florence's house immediately. Margaret is Florence's neighbor. When I asked what had happened, she said that someone had been shot."

"And what did you do?"

"I asked Mrs. Shaw, 'Who?' She said, 'Hurry!' and hung up, so I rushed to Florence Wilson's home."

"Upon arrival, what did you find?"

"Florence, I mean Mrs. Wilson, sat in a kitchen chair holding a gun on her lap. When I asked for the gun, she put it on the kitchen table."

"Then what?"

"I used my handkerchief to pick it up and asked if she'd shot someone."

"And how did she respond?"

"She didn't respond. She just there sat weeping. I asked Mrs. Shaw why she thought someone had been shot. She said, 'Florence told me.' When I asked Mrs. Wilson again if she had shot someone, she nodded. I thanked Mrs. Shaw for her help and took Florence Wilson down to the station for further questioning."

"What happened after you arrived at the station?"

"I took her into the interrogation room and asked again if she'd shot someone. She admitted to shooting her father and told me about the cabin on Boundary Island. That's where I found the body."

"Did Mrs. Wilson say she killed him in self-defense."

"No."

"Did she?"

"I found no signs of struggle. I found Mr. Harris lying on metal springs from an old bed. He reeked of alcohol."

"Did you find any further evidence relating to the case?"

The marshal sat up straight. "We found footprints outside the window across from the bed and shells that matched the gun I took from Mrs. Wilson.

"In your professional opinion, did she kill him in self-defense?"

"I doubt it."

"Thank you. Your witness." The prosecutor sat down.

The defense attorney approached the stand. "Marshal Fox, had you visited the Wilson home the day before the alleged murder?"

"Yes."

"And why did you go there?"

"Mrs. Wilson's neighbor, Mrs. Shaw, called me to say Florence needed help."

"And what did you find upon your arrival?"

"Mrs. Shaw sat with Mrs. Wilson who lay in her front yard. Mrs. Wilson had a swollen ankle and a cut and bruised face. When I asked how she got hurt, she told me that Mr. Harris broke into her home. She told him to leave, but he refused and continued to rummage through the kitchen cupboards in search of money. When he found no money, he attacked her, causing her to twist an ankle. She fought hard to remain conscious while we waited for the ambulance to arrive, and I put out an APB out on Harris."

"Was that the first domestic violence call you had in connection with Mr. Harris?"

"No, Mrs. Shaw had called me a few times before when she heard screaming from the Harris home."

"How many times?"

"I don't know without checking my records."

"Make a guess. One? Five? Ten?"

"I'd say between five and ten."

"Did you investigate?"

"I did."

"And what did you find?"

"Harris had been drinking and verbally abusing his daughter. Every time I asked Florence if she needed help, she refused. One time I took Florence to the station and had a nurse examine her. She found nothing amiss physically."

"Isn't it true that Mr. Harris escaped from prison while serving time for shooting you, Marshal?"

"Yes, he and a fellow bootlegger didn't want us to discover their operation in the woods above John Tarbet's place."

The defense attorney gave the jury his full attention. "Mr. Harris is a dangerous criminal. Before going to prison, the marshal had been to the Harris house ten times . . ."

The prosecutor interrupted, "Objection, Your Honor, the marshal said between five and ten."

"Sustained."

The defense attorney continued, "Between five and ten times to investigate domestic violence. Three weeks ago, Harris, a convicted felon, returned to Newport and assaulted his daughter, Florence Wilson, during a robbery. No wonder she felt threatened. No more questions, Your Honor."

Charlie quivered. His mother whispered in his ear, "Do you need to leave?" He flexed his fingers repeatedly and shook his head.

CHAPTER 36

Peg stopped by the marshal's office on the way home from work. All day she'd thought about the murder and new questions rose in her mind every hour. She stepped in the door and over to his desk. "Ben, what's going to happen to Florence?"

"Hello, Peg." He pushed aside his paperwork. "She hasn't been sentenced yet."

"Well, when will that happen? What do you think will happen to her? Will she go to prison?"

He lifted his shoulders. "A sad situation. Her lawyer is pleading temporary insanity. If the court accepts that, she'll probably be placed in a mental facility for evaluation and treatment."

"I heard the authorities found Harris's body. He'd passed out drunk on the bed and that's why she can't plead self-defense." Peg sat in the chair across from him.

"Yes, she should have come to me. I could have handled it. Hard to prove self-defense when the man wasn't even conscious."

"Will they consider the fact that she has a little girl? How long will she be away from her family? How is Charlie holding up?"

Ben avoided her questions and simply raised his hands. "I don't know."

"Don't know what?"

"Any of it. Just have to wait and see." He moved to the file cabinet and brought forth a paper.

Peg hesitated before asking her next question: "Did you see Charlie at the trial?"

"Yes." The phone rang and he answered, "Marshal Fox. Yes. Yes, I see. We'll check into it."

Peg fidgeted until the call ended. "How is he holding up? Did you talk with him?"

Ben's brow wrinkled, "Who?"

"Charlie. I'm worried about him, but don't want to invite gossip by visiting his house."

The door opened and the deputy entered. Ben whispered to Peg, "Good idea. Stay away." He addressed the deputy, "Could you check in on Mrs. Dawson? Got a report that the neighbors haven't seen her sitting on her porch for the last three days."

Peg rose to leave. "I hope everything's okay." She walked out with the deputy. All the way home, she debated. *Who could I ask about Charlie? I know Doc won't give me any info about him. Should I ask Mom to make a visit to his house? Maybe I should leave it alone. I know he's married . . . but he's still my friend.*

When she opened the back door, Peggy jumped off the kitchen chair. "Mommy!"

Peg squatted and opened her arms. "Hi, doll, how was school today?"

She gave a toothy grin. "I loved it!"

"What happened today?" Peg straightened up and removed her jacket.

"I made a new friend," the little girl beamed.

"That's wonderful. Boy or girl?"

"Girl."

"What's her name?"

"Belle Wilson."

CHAPTER 37

Charlie stretched out on his bed, attempting to rest. Darkness and night terrors lurked, ever ready to begin another assault. Afraid to sleep, he wandered zombie-like through the house all night. In the morning, he forced cheerfulness to see Belle off to school. As soon as she left, his mother set a plate of eggs and toast on the table. "Come and eat."

"Not hungry."

She took hold of his elbow. "Come on. Try to eat something. Think of Belle. She needs you to be healthy."

"I don't think I'll ever be healthy again. I can't sleep or eat. Sorry to be such a burden, Mom. I should have died with Leprechaun." He hung his head, disgusted with himself and his inability to come to grips with his emotional defeat.

"We're grateful you made it back. I'll bet the stress from this trial has set you off again. Things will improve. Don't give up." She sat next to him and put her arm around his shoulders.

Tears dripped from his chin. "That's the problem. Things are worse. Florence will be away for years. I'm such a dope. I got so fired up to go to war and it ruined my life. I don't think I want to live if this is what my life is."

Anna took his face in her hands. "Charlie, you need help. There's a doctor that's making progress with shell shock victims.

Let's go see him. Belle needs you. We all love and need you. Will you go?"

"What about Belle?"

"She has your dad and me. Kids are resilient. The main thing is to get you better, so you can be there for her. I'll make the doctor's appointment."

He stifled a sob. "OK."

"Eat and see if you can rest." Anna left to find her husband.

James bent over the engine of a rust-eaten farm truck. Its weathered wooden rack shimmied as he slammed the hood. Straw and dirt sifted from the bed. He climbed into the cab over stuffing poking from the cracks in the leather seat and cranked the engine. It lurched forward with a clunking sound. Hens scattered. Anna ran to the truck and waved at him. He stuck his head out the open window and stomped on the brake. "What's up?"

"Turn that noise off, so we can talk, please," she shouted over the engine.

"Can't it wait? Just got 'er going," he complained.

"No!"

As he turned off the key, the engine sputtered to its death. A rooster crowed.

Anna gripped the half-down window. "I'm so worried about Charlie."

"That's nothing new. What's so all-fired important?"

Anna's bottom lip quivered. James creaked open the door and jumped out. "Let's sit." He dropped the tailgate of the truck and climbed onto it. Anna joined him and reached for his hand.

"He told me he doesn't want to live. Let's not have the same tragedy as the Smiths.

James's brow pinched.

Remember how his family found him swinging from the barn rafters? We need to find a doctor for him," she begged. "He's agreed to see one."

"Which one?"

Anna dabbed her eyes. "Doc Phillips recommended one in Spokane. I can't remember his name."

"What will that run?" He ran his hand through thinning hair.

"Does it matter?" she snapped. "We're talking about his life!"

"OK, you arrange it. I'll drive him. You'll have to stay and tend to Belle."

Anna bobbed her head and scurried back to the house.

Charlie sat on the porch, plucking at the collar of his shirt. As soon as his mother arrived, he stated, "I've changed my mind."

Anna's shoulders fell. "No, Charlie, your dad agrees. I'm making an appointment."

He gritted his teeth. "No, it'll cost too much."

"You'll have help from the Veterans Bureau." She put her hands on her hips. "I'll take a job if I need to. You've got to think of Belle," she reasoned. "I'll make the appointment tomorrow when I go to the store." She marched up the wooden stairs, making them creak and into the house before he could respond.

A stripe of sun snaked over the barn and hit Charlie. He raised his head and watched the rope swing in the old alder tree sway as his two border collies brushed past it. They ran to his knees with tongues lolling, scattering leaves in their wake. "Good ol' Max and Mollie." He rubbed their heads and patted their sides. "Let's find you some food." *You're some of the truest friends I have.*

CHAPTER 38

"Come into my office for a minute, Peg," Dr. Phillips beckoned. When he shut the door, Peg tensed. He cleared his throat. "The tests are back for your daughter. I'm sorry to say she has polio."

"Oh, no!" Peg took two steps back and fell back into a chair. Visions of braces, paralyzed children and iron lungs darted through her mind. "I need time off," she muttered. "What can we do?"

"Nothing will cure polio. She needs bed rest, good food and physical therapy to prevent muscle loss. I'll make arrangements with Mrs. Simms for you to have time off. I wish I could do more." He gave an apologetic smile. "You'll need to be careful. The virus lives in an infected person's throat and intestines. It spreads through coughing, sneezing or touching an infected surface. She can shed the virus in her stool for up to six weeks."

After two weeks of bed rest and six weeks of quarantine, Peggy asked again, "When can I go back to school?"

Peg finished hanging clean clothes in the closet. "In a couple weeks. We need to make sure you're strong enough."

"Well, can I play with my sister?"

Am I being too cautious? "This afternoon when she gets home from school, I'll make a tea party for you," Peg promised. *She still tires so easily. If something happened to her . . .*

Peggy clapped her hands. "Can I help you make it? Can I wear a party dress? Can we use the little cups and saucers?"

Peg sat on the bedside. "If you rest until Jean comes home, you can. We'll all make it together."

"I'm tired of reading and coloring. Will you tell me a story like Daddy used to?"

Peg flinched. *I didn't realize she still misses Ralph. Wonder how he's doing. I miss his stories, too. And I miss Amka, Sundsby, Kid and especially Miko.* "How about playing with the cat?"

"No, I don't like animals."

Peg chuckled. "You don't take after me, do you?"

"Take after you?" Peggy puzzled, not understanding the meaning of the phrase.

"I love animals, sports and the outdoors. You prefer sewing, reading and cooking."

"But you like to cook," Peggy pouted.

"Yes, we both do. What do you want to make for your tea party?"

"Popcorn!"

"Popcorn it is. What about some little frosted cakes?"

"Can we make the frosting pink?"

Peg patted her head. "We can. Now, lie back and rest." She went to the kitchen where Mary washed lunch dishes. "Mom, did I do the right thing?"

Mary turned and motioned for Peg to sit. "What exactly are you asking?"

Emotionally exhausted, Peg poured herself onto the chair. "Did I do the right thing by leaving Ralph?"

"Honey, only you can answer that question. If the girls weren't in a good environment or were being mistreated, you should have left. What's made you question it now?"

"Peggy just told me she misses her dad's stories."

"He hasn't contacted them yet, has he?"

"No, Peggy and Jean have sent him letters, but we've received nothing from him. He did let it slip once during a drunken tirade that I'm his third wife."

"Do YOU miss him?" A wind gust slammed the kitchen door shut.

Peg jumped. "Not really."

Mary placed her hand on top of Peg's. "I guess you have your answer."

CHAPTER 39

Even as snow softened the face of the imperious Alaskan mountain, a storm lashed at Kid, reminding him of nature's force and the need to be ever watchful. Wind roared through the trees. One cracked under the weight of snow-laden branches.

As he made his way to the center of town, he thought back to his trip to Anchorage. The muddy streets, stirred by horses and cars, created puddles that reeked from animal and human waste along with huge piles of trash. He'd learned to jump back or duck into doorways to avoid getting splashed by the foul-smelling slop. *At least the mud will freeze.*

He mulled over his last conversation with the marshal. *He knew too much about my accident. Don't think I'll confide in him. But if I can't trust the law, who can help me find my dogs?* His jaw protruded as his hands formed fists. *Oh, Lord, help me when I find that person who stole my dogs!* He kicked the door to The Salty Dawg open and the wind flung it back.

"Hey," the bartender barked, "don't tear it off its hinges!"

"Sorry," Kid wrestled it shut. A combination of alcohol, stale coffee and fish assaulted his nose. At the back of the room, Ralph Sparks drooped over a table. The Kid got a drink and sat across from him. Ralph raised his head. "Kiiid," he fought to remain conscious as he leaned over the table, "ever find yur dogs?"

"No, but when I do . . ." He chose not to finish his sentence. He removed his stocking hat, unwound the scarf from his neck and took a gulp of beer. "How's Peg and kids?"

Ralph lit a cigarette. He inhaled and blew. Tobacco smoke curled over his head as he stared into space. "Gone."

"Gone?" The Kid choked on his drink. "What happened?"

Ralph tapped his ashes into the ashtray. "Left me. Took the girls and went home."

Kid's shoulders relaxed. *They're alive then.* "For the winter?"

"Forever." Ralph picked up his wadded scarf from the table and wiped his nose.

Kid's brow furrowed. "Not coming back?"

Ralph's head hung for a minute. He glanced at Kid and his eyes widened. "Just had a thought. You take Miko. I know you're missing your dogs. And I also know I'm not doing him justice. Hate to see him tied up all day. And when I leave him inside, he destroys things."

Kid's grin spread. "Would it be okay for me to pick him up today?"

Ralph dipped his head. "Sure, he's chained next to the tent."

"Great! Got to get the mail out. I'll stop en route." He jumped up. "And sorry to hear about Peg and the girls." He left with a spring in his step. "Thanks again," he called back and ran off to the post office.

When Frostbite noticed Kid, he leapt but the chain held him back. "Hey, Boy, almost ready. We're getting you a new friend today. You'll love Miko!" He pet the dog, pushed snow from the porch and door of the post office and shouldered it open. Next to the counter sat the mailbag. He hoisted it to his shoulder. A feeling of deja vu overwhelmed him. He hefted the bag onto the counter, undid the buckles and dumped the contents on the rough wood counter. A flurry of letters fell out. The bag still felt heavy. He ran his hand through the interior. Nothing. He organized the mail and found a letter for a person he didn't recognize. *Maybe one of the neighbors will know where to find him.* He buckled the bag up and threw it on the sled. "Hike!" Frostbite sprang forward.

As he approached the site of his attack, he stopped at the edge of the drop-off. Shutting his eyes, he tried to remember anything new. Frostbite whined and pawed at the ground. Kid's eyes squinted. "What do you know, Boy?" He scanned the area, nothing but snow. "Wish you could tell me."

When Kid approached Ralph's tent, Miko jumped forward. His ears narrowed and neck ruff raised. "Hey, Miko," Kid approached cautiously, "you remember me, don't you?" He took off his hat and scarf and held out his hand. Miko relaxed and let Kid pet him. "You're my dog now. What do you think about that? You and Frostbite are gonna be pals." He placed Miko in the harness. Frostbite didn't protest. Kid turned the sled around. *I'll see if Sundsby and Amka know where Albert Johnson lives.*

Amka and Karl worked at the woodpile. Eight-year-old Karl stood almost as tall as his native mother. Kid drove the sled into the yard. Karl ran over to greet the dogs. "Hey, Karl!" Kid stepped from the sled. Amka took her armload of wood to the tent. Kid followed. "Hi, Amka. No mail for you, but I do need some help. Have you heard of Albert Johnson?" She raised her shoulders. "Sundsby home?" *Does she understand what I want?* "When will he be back?"

"Night. Trapping," she responded. "Eat?"

"Need to return before sundown, but thanks!" Kid hopped on the sled. "Bye!"

"Wait!" She held up her hand. "Miko?"

"Ralph gave him to me since Peg and the girls left." He tapped his chest. "Ralph gave to me."

He saw she understood. "Hike!" Kid disappeared in a swirl, leaving tracks in the fresh snow.

Upon returning to Homer, he took the letter for Albert Johnson back to the post office. Again, the door stuck. He heaved it open. "Hey, Eric, when you gonna fix that door?"

He pushed back from his cluttered desk. "Hey, Kid! How's it going?" Kid handed him the letter. Eric turned it over. "Do you know who this is?

"Nope, that's why I returned it."

"Hang on." Eric rummaged through a pile of newspapers. "I think he's that guy the Mounties been chasing. Read this!" He pushed the newspaper to Kid who removed his mittens and carried it to the wooden bench against the wall.

MAD TRAPPER OF RAT RIVER FOUND AND KILLED

After evading the Royal Canadian Mounted Police for over one-month, fugitive Albert Johnson (believed to be a pseudonym) was killed in a shootout.

Last month, The Royal Canadian Mounted Police traveled to Albert Johnson's cabin in the Yukon, to investigate claims that Johnson sabotaged native traps. After being greeted by the barrel of Johnson's gun and told to get out, they returned with two more men and a search warrant.

This time Johnson shot through the door and hit one of the constables. The Mounties took the wounded man to Aklavik and gathered a posse of nine men and forty-two dogs along with twenty pounds of dynamite. Upon returning they thawed the dynamite in their coats and threw it onto the roof of Anderson's cabin. The explosion caved in the roof, but Anderson continued to fire from a dugout below the floor and held off the posse for fifteen hours.

When the thermometer fell to minus forty degrees, the posse returned to Aklavik. Cold weather prevented further investigation for two weeks. Upon their return, they found the cabin empty and tracked Johnson to a nearby thicket. In the following gunfight, Johnson shot Constable Edgar Millen through the heart killing him, and the posse retreated. Next, RCMP hired natives to track the murderer in the back country and blocked two passes over the Richardson Mountains. However, Johnson escaped by climbing over a 7,000 foot peak and disappeared again.

Recently, the RCMP hired veteran aviator Wop May to search for Anderson from a new Bellanca ski plane. He discovered Johnson's tracks on the far side of the Richardson Mountains. On Valentine's Day, he realilzed how Johnson had eluded the law. May spotted footprints from the center of the frozen Eagle River to the bank. By walking in caribou tracks down the river, Anderson had hidden his footprints from his pursuers. May followed tracks to Anderson's camp. He radioed his discovery to the RCMP who later that day found Anderson standing in the middle of the river. Gunfire broke out as Anderson ran for the bank. After Anderson shot one officer, his evil laugh echoed down the river. When the Mounties returned fire, Anderson died in a hail of bullets. Aviator May landed the plane and saved the wounded constable by transporting him to medical help.

The RCMP recovered gold and over $2,000 cash from Anderson's body. At this time, Anderson's true identity or if he was guilty of sabotaging native lines is still undetermined.[2]

Kid let out a long whistle and lowered the paper. "Where's Aklavik?"

"Northern Canada. Long ways from here. Guess I'd better hand this letter over to the marshal."

Kid scratched his head asking, "Then why would a letter for him come here?"

"You got me."

"Let's read it!" Kid suggested.

Eric slipped it beneath the counter. "It's a federal offense to open someone else's mail."

---

2 https://en.wikipedia.org/wiki/Albert_Johnson_(criminal)

CHAPTER 40

Peggy bent over her desk, gripped her pencil and formed the cursive letters carefully. Miss Bennett walked between the desks and stopped at Peggy's. "My, that's nice handwriting." Peggy glanced up with a shy smile. The teacher moved to the front of the room. "OK, students, clean off your desks. Time for lunch." Papers rustled and children's voices rose. "Quiet. Save talking for recess. Line up when you're ready."

In the lunchroom, Belle spied her classmate and ran over to sit beside her. "Hi, Peggy!"

Peggy scooted down the bench. Belle swung one leg over the seat. "Want to play jacks when you're finished?"

"Yes." Peggy pushed her tray back and started to rise.

"But you didn't eat much or drink your milk," Belle observed.

Peggy wrinkled her nose. "I don't like milk."

Holding hands, the girls ran outside to the sidewalk. "You can go first." Belle handed the jacks and ball to Peggy.

Peggy threw the jacks and tossed the ball up. "Onesies." She grabbed a jack. After working her way up to tensies, she handed the game to Belle."

"Wow! You're good!"

"My dad taught me," Peggy confided.

"Your dad?"

"Yup."

"I thought you didn't have a dad," Belle puzzled.

"Everyone has a dad!" Peggy scoffed.

Belle tossed the ball up. "Where is he?"

"Alaska."

"What's he doing there?" Belle scooped up three jacks.

"Fishing."

Belle threw the jacks. "My dad's in the hospital in Spokane."

"With polio?" Peg guessed.

Belle hesitated. "No, he's sick from the war. I'm staying with my grandparents."

A cat-eye marble from a nearby game rolled into the jacks. "Where's your mom?" Peggy wondered and rolled the marble back to the boys.

Belle told her the truth, "In jail."

Peggy blushed. Luckily, Miss Bennett rang the bell as Peggy wondered how to respond. "Oh, recess is over."

Belle gathered up their game. "Think your mom would let you come over to play after school?"

"I'll ask, but since this is my first day back, she might not."

Belle stopped. "We don't have a phone at the farm, so ask if you can tomorrow." They ran to form a line in front of the teacher.

After school, Peggy burst through the door, "Grandma?" No answer. Peggy put her lunch pail in the sink and noticed a note and cookies on the table.

Peggy,

I had to help at the store. Come over after you eat.

Grandma

After Peggy ate a cookie, she rested her head on folded arms on the table.

Mary checked her watch again. "Raymond, will you watch the till?" she asked the teen who helped after school. "I need to check on my granddaughter."

Raymond peeked out of the storage room. "Sure."

Mary untied her apron, hung it in the back room and put on her sweater and scarf. *I hope we didn't send her back to school too soon.* She hustled home and threw open the back door. Peggy snored softly at the table. *Should I send her to bed?* When she touched Peggy's forehead to test for fever, the girl's eyes opened. "Hi, Honey. School good today?" *No fever. Good.*

Peggy sat up. "Grandma, can I play with Belle after school tomorrow?"

"Let's wait to talk with your mom about it when she gets home." *I don't know if that's a good idea.*

"Grandma," Peggy hesitated.

"Yes, dear."

"How come Belle's mom's in jail?"

CHAPTER 41

"Good morning, Charlie. Breakfast in twenty minutes. Time to rise and shine," the pretty little brunette announced as she stepped to the window and raised the blinds. "How did you sleep?"

Charlie threw his arm over his eyes. "Too early."

"You can rest after therapy this afternoon. Get dressed. It's a beautiful day for your morning walk. I'll run you a hot bath. Come on." She squeezed his toes. Sunshine streamed into the room that had been furnished by the Red Cross with new furniture and cheerful bedspreads.

He rolled to his side and threw his legs over. *Hard to tell a sweet nurse like Doris no.* She left for the next room. Charlie lumbered to the sink and took stock of the man staring back. His curly red hair had been shaved to the skin. A red-blonde stubble covered his chin. Bright blue eyes and freckles contrasted with his ashen skin. He rubbed the stubble on his head and chin and turned on the water. Pipes sputtered and hissed. *Exactly how I feel.* Tired of waiting for the water to warm, he splashed his face and shivered. After spreading up his covers, he removed his pajamas, folded them neatly and reached for his pants. Padding down the hall in bare feet, he got in line for the toilet behind a young man with a nervous tremor who stammered, "Morn . . . in'."

Charlie nodded. *So many lives ruined. Has anyone here ever recovered? Wish I could eat breakfast in my room. Seeing all these broken men . . .*

Doris worked her way down the other side of the hall. When she got back to Charlie, she stopped. "Oh, I forgot to tell you, Charlie, your mother plans to visit this afternoon."

A slow smile crept across Charlie's face. *Maybe she's taking me home.*

Anna Wilson herded the cranky farm truck down the highway to Spokane. She prayed the sprinkles of rain wouldn't turn to snow. When the drizzle stopped, fall colors shimmered in the rising sun. Red dogwood stood out among Ponderosa Pine and Douglas Fir trees. Golden coins from Aspen trees floated and collected on the forest floor. A recent freeze had turned sumac seeds a dark rust. Pumpkins nestled down into fields of brown vines. She passed a deserted apple stand, hiding behind a sand cherry bush where purple fruit rested atop bright fuchsia leaves. *This is my favorite time of year. If only Charlie's well enough to help with the harvest . . . Good thing I thought to see the doctor before I visit Charlie. Don't want to give false hope.*

Dr. Brinkley examined his schedule: Anna Wilson at ten this morning. *I wish I had better news for her. Charlie's not progressing.* He reread the report on Dr. Arthur Hurst's treatments for shell shock. *Occupational therapy and intensive mental therapy are working wonders there in England.* The sun crested over the mountain. *Dr. Arthur helps patients humanely and helps them keep their dignity.* He grabbed his notepad, found Charlie's files and scribbled down ideas.

Two hours later, his secretary poked her head in the door. "Mrs. Wilson is here."

He stopped writing. "Send her in."

Anna inched in, clutching a drawstring purse to her breast.

The doctor rose to shake her hand. "Mrs. Wilson, come in. Have a seat, please."

"How's my boy doing?" She perched on the edge of the wooden chair.

Dr. Brinkley folded his hands on his desk. "He's fine. You're planning on seeing him before you leave?"

"Yes, when will he be well enough to come home?"

"Hard to say. It's different for every patient. When Charlie and his doctors feel he is ready, but these things take time. May I ask you some questions?"

"Of course," Anna stated, ready to do anything to assist in her son's recovery.

"Has Charlie threatened suicide?"

"Not in so many words, but he's told me he wished he'd die. He's lost hope of life ever getting better for him."

The doctor jotted down notes. "Depression is common in shell shock cases. What did Charlie enjoy doing before he went to war?"

Anna twisted the strings of her purse. "We don't spend much time enjoying things. With living on a farm, there's always work to do." She stared into space, then added, "But he did like to hunt and fish."

"Well, we don't allow guns here, but possibly, we could arrange a fishing trip. How has he spent his time since he returned home?"

"He helps around the farm when he's feeling up to it and plays with his daughter."

"How's his wife coping?

"She's in jail."

Dr. Brinkley blinked in disbelief. "In jail? For what?"

"Murdering her father."

CHAPTER 42

White roses and greenery tied with pink ribbon festooned every church pew. When the organ played "Here Comes the Bride," guests in their Sunday-best rose as one, turned to the aisle and strained to see. Rose's beautiful blond sixteen-year-old sister stepped down the aisle followed by Peggy throwing rose petals from a white basket. The flower girl's usual shyness faded as she concentrated on her important role. She loved her new pink dress and white Mary Jane shoes. Grandma Tarbet had fastened a pink bow to the toe of each shoe that Peggy admired as she threw petals. She felt as pretty as Shirley Temple.

Squirming in a ruffled pink taffeta dress, Peg adjusted the flowers in her pinned-up hair. *I feel like a trussed-up pig.* She felt a trickle of perspiration down her back. *It's too warm here. Can't wait to rip this getup off! But the chapel's beautiful, appropriate for the place to be filled with roses for Rose's wedding. Glad **I** don't have a flower name.*

The bridesmaids and flower girl stopped in front of Reverend Cunningham, then turned to watch the bride. Rose's white silk train swept down the aisle, gathering up rose petals beneath it. The guests rose. A silver-haired woman in a straw hat whispered to her husband, "She's stunning!" No one noticed Rose's attractive face blushing beneath her veil.

Henry subconsciously hooked a finger in his shirt neck to try to loosen it. He wiped a clammy hand on his pant leg. His dark hair plastered back contrasted with his pale skin. Peg tried not to smile at her childhood friend's nervousness. *Oh, even cool, handsome Henry is jittery today. But many men would trade places with him!*

Nostalgia engulfed Peg. The memory of her own wedding flashed through her mind. She could not help but compare the elegance of Rose's dress to the simple navy-blue suit she wore to stand before the Alaskan Justice of the Peace. *I wonder what Rose is thinking. Does she have that same surreal feeling as I did? They make such a handsome couple.*

The ceremony mesmerized little Peggy. When Henry lifted the veil to kiss Rose, she covered her eyes and the audience giggled. A tear stole into Peg's eye. She brushed it aside. *They are so happy!*

Rose's large father blew his nose. The audience stood. Rose wove her arm through Henry's. Outside the church, they ducked their heads as rice rained about them, and they ran to the waiting car decorated with a wreath of greenery tied to the hood. Henry opened the door for Rose and helped her gather in her long train and veil. As he went to the driver's side, Rose bent forward and yelled gleefully, "Catch!" and launched the bouquet straight to Peg. She took a step back as the flowers landed in her hands. Her face turned red and thrust them to her daughter. Peggy beamed and pushed her face into the petals. The newlyweds waved goodbye amid the sound of church bells ringing. A string of tin cans rattled behind their car.

Peggy tugged her mother's hand. "Can I keep them?" She clutched the bouquet to her chest.

"Yes." *I don't want to get married. Besides, I need to divorce first.* "Come on. We need to finish making the refreshments. She directed Peggy out a side door before anyone could comment on the wedding bouquet.

After Peg made the birthday cake for Mrs. Simms's son, she recommended Peg's baking to many of Dr. Phillips's patients. Word spread quickly that Peg owned a catering business. With the extra income, she'd moved into town and rented the "Double House." It provided her with one side to live in and the other to rent. Plus, she could walk to work at Dr. Phillips's office as she didn't own a car. Every night for the past week, Peg stirred up batches of cookies after work: spritz, pinwheel, raisin-filled and sugar. She needed to add pink frosting to the sugar cookies. *I'm sorry Rose's mother has passed away, but it's given me the opportunity to help with the wedding.*

Henry's family had decorated the church and would provide a meal the next day at the church hall before the reception. Peg had sewn lace aprons with pink ribbon ties for Peggy and Jean to wear while clearing the refreshment tables. All week, Peggy pestered her mom with questions. "Do I get to keep my flower girl dress? Where do I gather rose petals to throw? How many more days 'til the wedding?"

Peg kicked off her shoes as soon as she entered her apartment. She backed up to her daughter. "Peggy, unzip me, please."

Peggy gently worked the zipper while asking, "Can I keep my dress on for a while?" She twirled and grinned as the skirt billowed around her legs.

"Not if you want to help me frost the cookies." Peg peeled off her dress while standing in the middle of the kitchen.

"Mom! Someone might see you in your underwear!" Peggy protested.

Peg threw her dress over a chair. "Then they'd better not look. It's too darn hot for clothes!" She bent over the sink to wash her hands. "Go change. Please help Jean change, too."

Peggy took her sister by the hand and led her to their shared bedroom. "Come on, Sister. Let's change, so we can frost cookies!" Jean hopped alongside, excited by Peggy's enthusiasm.

Peg scooped a lump of butter into the mixing bowl. *Such good girls I'm blessed with. What would I do without them? Maybe I made a mistake by running off to Alaska, but then I wouldn't have my girls! I'd do it a thousand times over to have them.* She stopped mixing frosting when she noticed Rose's wedding bouquet on the table and washed her hands. After cutting the stems, she arranged them in a vase. Peggy returned and squealed, "You ruined my flowers!"

"Honey, if I don't put them in water, they'll die."

She threw herself to the floor and whimpered, "But now I can't play wedding!"

"Of course, you can," Peg countered. "You can carry these when you're ready, and when they die, we'll pick some from the garden. Bring me your slip and I'll show you something."

Peggy's bottom lip quivered, but she produced the requested slip. Her mother set the white half-slip on the little girl's head. "There, you see, a bridal veil!"

When Jean came back, Peggy cried, "Sister, I'm a bride!"

CHAPTER 43

Kid wanted details. "Marshal, I'm shocked. How'd ya figger it out?"

"Remember that locked bag in your delivery the day you got attacked? Found out someone sent it to Einar Nilsen," he reported with a self-satisfied smile.

"And nobody on my route knew him," Kid added.

"Well, turns out that's our postmaster Eric's real name. He was out checking his trapline as the mail got unloaded and didn't intercept the package. You took it on your route. He had to get it back before anyone discovered it held his share of the money for stolen dogs. After that, he and Slim decided to use other criminals' names. Slim sent letters addressed to known criminals to throw us off track. When Eric saw a letter addressed to a famous criminal, he knew to meet Slim to plan their next move."

Kid's forehead wrinkled. "But Eric showed me that article about Albert Johnson in the paper when I couldn't deliver a letter to him."

The marshal smirked. "Fooled you, didn't he? But did he let you open it?"

"No, he said it's a federal offense to open someone's mail."

"Didn't want you to see inside because it incriminated him. You were too curious. I got a warrant to search the mail. When a letter came to Fredy Hardy, I thought it strange."

Kid confessed sheepishly. "Sorry, Marshal. I suspected you. It's because you knew details about my attack . . . but I've never heard of Fred Hardy."

"No surprise. Murdered a couple of prospectors back on Unimak Island 'bout thirty years ago. He gained notoriety as the first man hanged in Alaska for murder." The marshal continued, "Many criminals come to Alaska because it's the Last Frontier, an easy place to get lost. I happened to be in the post office when the letter for Hardy came and remembered that name from my youth. Big news. 'Course, there's always folks with the same name, but when you mentioned hearing the name of Klutuk during the attack, I thought it unusual that I kept running into old criminal names."

"So what did you do next?"

"Had the mail delivered here first. After I intercepted a letter for Ed Krause, I knew I was onto something." The marshal edged forward on his chair, eager to finish the story.

Kid scratched his beard. "I've heard of him but can't remember why he's famous."

Marshal cleared his throat. "He and his gang started stealing foxes from farmers along the Inside Passage. A man disappeared and Krause and his gang took over the guy's farm. Residents suspected murder. Ya know, so many people come and go in Alaska that sometimes it takes months to notice a missing person. But after more disappearances, they hired an investigator. Next, Krause posed as a deputy marshal and kidnapped his ex-girlfriend's husband. Fortunately, a witness saw Krause leave on his boat with his prisoner. When the man's wife put out the word of his disappearance, Krause was the main suspect. He fled and slipped by authorities when he got off the boat in Seattle where a former Alaskan recognized him and notified police who arrested Krause. They shipped him back to Juneau to face kidnapping and murder charges."

Kid got up and stretched. "Wow!"

"Hold up," the marshal continued. "It gets better. A member of Krause's gang helped him escape jail. He threw a beer bottle through the cell's barred window. Got himself arrested and smuggled in a hacksaw. Krause cut through the cell's bars and took off to the docks. When word got out of his escape, a man named Franzen headed home to protect his family on Admiralty Island. Good thing, too. Franzen had his wife sweep the porch as he waited for the criminal. He showed up and ordered Franzen's wife to make him food. When Krause threatened her, the husband shot him dead and got the one-thousand-dollar reward."

"So how'd ya tie this all to Eric?" Kid wondered.

"Went to Kenai last week. I always visit with my old friend who's a marshal there. He told me they're having trouble with illegal dog fighting. Made me wonder if that's why you got attacked and had your dogs stolen."

Kid shot up. "Has he recovered any stolen dogs?"

"Just dead ones."

Kid's lips curled. "The thought of my dogs killed in fights . . ."

"Sorry we couldn't retrieve your dogs. Often, stolen dogs are sold to prospectors. If that's what happened, they're long gone. The fellows who bought them have no idea they have stolen property."

Kid leaned back into the chair. "So how *did* you figger out Eric in it?"

Marshal blew his nose. "Detective work. When I interviewed Eric about your attack, he had an alibi, visiting his friend, Slim in Kenai. When the Kenai marshal told me he suspected Slim of running dog fight rings, I remembered Eric's story. I tracked down Slim in Kenai. He had a huge black dog with him."

Kid's voice rose, "So THOSE TWO attacked me!"

"No proof yet, but it certainly seems like it. That's why Einar Nilsen, alias Eric, is sitting in my jail."

Kid's nostrils flared. He cracked his knuckles. "Let me talk to him!"

The marshal moved his hand to the gun at his hip. "I've already done the interview."

Kid hit his fist against the top of the desk. "But he knows where my dogs are!"

The marshal held up his hand. "Stop right where you are. Already asked him and he doesn't. Something comes up about your dogs, you'll be the first I'll tell."

Kid marched out and slammed the door.

CHAPTER 44

Charlie avoided Dr. Brinkley's eyes. "I *know* what you must think of me."

"What makes you think so?" the doctor inquired.

"'Cause there's nothing physically wrong with me. Been through enough tests to realize that," he confessed with disappointment.

"I understand that soldiers who suffer from shell shock have also suffered from being judged as weak men. But it's not true."

"How come most guys don't have it?" Charlie questioned.

"Many suffer. However, not everyone displays the same symptoms. Amnesia, paralysis, inability to talk or walk are easier to see. Some doctors think that the intense artillery noise caused brain lesions."

He continued, "I find the military's cruel treatment of soldiers deplorable, the shaming, solitary confinement, even submitting some to court martial!" He pressed his lips tightly and exhaled. "However, I'm impressed with Dr. Hurst's success in England treating shell shock victims. He combines rest, massage and hypnosis with occupational therapy. His results appear promising."

Charlie's face brightened. "You mean there's hope?"

"There's always hope, Charlie. Your mother told me that you enjoy fishing. I'm assigning you to help with the lawns and garden here, and I've arranged a fishing trip with a few men next Tuesday."

Charlie's eyes lit. "I'd like that."

On Tuesday, Nurse Doris entered Charlie's room to find a neatly made bed and Charlie absent. "Humm, that's unusual." She checked the window, still locked, then searched the line of men waiting to use the toilet. "Anyone seen Charlie this morning?" She tried not to sound worried. Men grunted and shook their heads. Her heart plummeted. *He seemed to be doing better. We can't have another suicide.* She scurried to the cafeteria and scanned the tables. No Charlie. *Where could he be this early? Is he AWOL?* She found a male worker, clutched his arm and whispered, "Have you seen Charlie?" He pointed to a bench by the front door. Charlie sat, eyes closed, with his head resting against the wall of the building. Sunlight lit his face and set the red stubble sprouting on his head afire.

Doris let out a breath. "He's doing better," she said out loud. A burly man overheard and interjected, "Me, too. Dr. Brinkley's helping all of us." Doris returned to work with a spring in her step.

Charlie studied the river for the best place to fish. A cloudburst materialized. It dimpled and muddied the water. He ducked under the cover of a nearby tree until the rain passed and sun splashed across the river's surface. A meadowlark trilled a flute-like song that seemed to say," This is a beautiful place to live. This is a beautiful place to live." Charlie's spirits stirred. *It's almost October. Soon, I won't hear this.* Hearing the song of another bird, he smiled. *I haven't felt this happy in a long time.*

He moved to a large rock and got comfortable. A large lazy trout rested on his fat belly in the shallow water beneath the overhang as the slow river murmured by. Tired from a full day of yard work, Charlie dozed off in the twilight. A tug at his line pried him from his reverie. When his rod bent, he leapt forward, ready to do battle. After he landed a twenty-inch trout on the bank, he cried, "Well, big feller, you'll make a tasty dinner!"

A man downstream heard the commotion and trotted over. "Charlie, that's a monster! Can you teach me how to fish?"

Charlie sang out, "Yes!"

The bartender tapped Ralph's shoulder. "Time to go home, Buddy." Ralph snorted and snored on. "Ralph, I gotta close. Get up!" he growled. Ralph raised his head and tried to gain his bearings.

"Closing time. Don't care where you go, but you can't stay here," the bartender barked as he bundled himself inside a coat, hat and scarf. "Shake a leg, Sparks! I'm leaving," he thundered.

Ever since Peg and his girls left, Ralph practically lived at the bar. The bartender and everyone else knew why. Tonight because of the foul weather, the usually dispassionate man felt a spark of compassion. A freezing wind railed against the town, causing the few wooden buildings to shudder. "Terrible night out there, Ralph. Where ya staying?" Ralph didn't answer. "Jail again, huh? Come on. I'll walk ya there."

Enveloped in a cloud of sour alcohol, Ralph staggered to the door. The bartender led the way as Ralph shambled along, their heads bent against the storm. When he opened the door to the jail, the marshal flipped around. Papers on the desk flew everywhere. "Shut the door!" he ordered as he rolled his chair back and picked up the scattered papers. "His cell's waiting."

A wood burning stove in the vestibule outside the jail cells provided the prisoners with heat. When the marshal escorted

Ralph to an empty cell, Eric awoke and complained, "Marshal, it's cold in here!"

The marshal locked Ralph in, then opened the door of the stove. "Hang on. Got to split more wood."

Eric himself propped up on his elbow and strained to see the new prisoner through the dark. He recognized Ralph. "Why don't ya put him to work? For an older man, he's a human beaver."

"Not tonight, he's not! But that's a good idea. Tomorrow, he can work off his stay."

"What about me?" Eric asked, hoping to con the marshal.

"You're staying right where you are 'til you see the judge."

After the marshal fed the fire, he shut the door to keep the heat in. Eric, wide awake, had an idea. "Psst, hey, Ralph!" he whispered. No answer. "Ralph!" he called again. Ralph stirred. "Ralph! It's me, Eric."

"Keep it down!" the marshal roared.

Eric gave up when Ralph showed no response, but his mind whirred. By morning, he'd formulated a plan. As soon as Ralph sat up, Eric put it into action. "Morning, Ralph. How'd ya sleep?"

Ralph flinched at the loud voice and rubbed his forehead.

"Hangovers are hell, huh?" Eric empathized. "Could use a drink myself. Days drag on forever here, and I don't sleep well." He sized up Ralph's mood. "You come here often?" Ralph ignored his question. *Now's not a good time. I'll wait 'til after breakfast.*

The cornmeal mush and coffee didn't improve Ralph's mood. The coffee shook in his hands and sloshed onto his pants. He set the cup on the floor and flopped back on the stained mattress.

Eric tested the waters. "Hey, Buddy, have you ever thought of selling your boat?"

Ralph's head bobbed up.

Eric stared through the bars. *Gotta play it cool.* "Just wondering. Tired of post office work. Thought I'd try my hand at fishing. If yur tired a fishing, I could buy ya out, so's ya could move on."

Ralph rubbed his eyes. "Might be. What's yur plan?"

"Well, I spend the winters trapping, fall prospecting. Thinkin' I'd like ta start fishing in the summers. I can pay ya in gold."

"Runs 'bout thirty-five dollars an ounce," Ralph calculated, then asked, "Got a partner?"

"Yup, friend in Kenai, a 'Yarrayulli' who knows everything there is 'bout fishing."

Ralph tipped his head. "A what?"

"Scandinavian. That's what the Natives call 'em as they're always saying, 'Yaa, Yaa.' Say, you ain't one of those remittance men, are you?"

"A what?"

"Remittance man. Their families pay the black sheep to disappear, so's to avoid embarrassing the family."

"Well, I might be a black sheep, but no one's paying me to stay away."

"Could ya use cash then?"

"Yep."

"Have ta pay in gold nuggets."

"It spends."

After negotiating the price, Eric smirked. *I'll get outta here and go north. Ralph's boat is my ticket.*

Before lunch, the marshal came to check the fire. He dug an oversized key from his pocket and unlocked Ralph's cell. "Time to move on. Ain't feeding ya lunch." Ralph gave Eric a thumbs-up when the marshal turned his back.

As Ralph stumbled down the street, he went over Eric's instructions. *Soon as you're out, move your boat into the Homer harbor. Contact Slim, my partner in Kenai, and he'll get you paid.* He returned to Ismailof Island, threw his few belongings into a knapsack and stopped at Sundsby's to say goodbye. At his rap on the tent post, a gun barrel protruded out the door. "Amka! It's me! Ralph!" She drew back the tent flap. Karl sat helping the baby build a tower from the blocks Ralph had made for Peggy. The sight stung. *I miss my girls.* He swallowed and forced a smile. "Sundsby out?"

Amka didn't understand. She touched the knapsack on his back and peered up, a question on her face. "Sold my boat. I'm moving on. Came to tell you goodbye."

"Where?" Amka asked.

"Well, Kenai first. Maybe try my luck in Sitka. Friend from the cannery's up there. You're welcome to anything I left back at my place." He touched Amka's shoulder. "Tell Sundsby bye for me and thanks for being our friends," he corrected himself, "I mean, *my* friend." He bent to tell the children goodbye, adjusted the load on his back and trudged through the snow to his boat.

After a week in Kenai, Ralph still hadn't been able to contact Slim. Noone had information on his whereabouts. He worried and berated himself. *That's what I get for making a deal while coming off a bender. Got to leave that bottle alone. Probably gettin' what I deserve. Wonder if my boat's still in the harbor. Money's almost gone. Guess I'll have to take that cannery job I despise. Or should I return to check on my boat? Maybe if I have a little drink, I'll feel better.* He headed to the local saloon.

"There he is!" a man shouted as soon as Ralph entered. He stepped back and swung his head side to side. When the marshal drew a gun on him, his eyes opened wide and jaw dropped. "Me?"

"You Ralph Sparks?" the marshal demanded.

Everyone in the bar turned his way. Ralph's heart jumped. "Yes, why?"

"You trying to find Slim?" The marshal drew closer.

"Yes, I am. What's going on?" Having a gun drawn on him made him stammer as he tried to explain. "H . . . e owes me money."

"For what?"

Ralph's ire rose. "How's that any of your business?"

"'Cause I'm the law 'round here."

"I haven't broken any law!" Ralph protested as he backed up.

The lawman yelled at a huge, bearded man in a sealskin coat. "Cuff 'em, Dan!"

Ralph swallowed and held up his hands. "Now hold on!" He heard the gun cock and lowered his hands, allowing Dan to throw on handcuffs and lead him outside. "Where ya takun me?"

"Questioning." He pointed the way with his gun. Their boots scuffed down the wooden sidewalk with Big Dan leading the way. Curious faces peered out from storefront windows. Ralph ducked his head and followed meekly. When the sidewalk ended, they plowed through mud, sucking at their heels among the patches of snow. Overhead, eagles danced in the wind. Smoke rose from the chimney of an old log cabin used as the jail. Ralph stopped to admire massive moose antlers hanging above the entrance. A winter supply of wood towered in an adjacent lean-to. Behind the cabin, two deer bounded over a fallen log.

When Dan stopped to open the door, Ralph noticed a jagged scar along the side of his cheek that disappeared into his tangled black beard. He stepped in when the marshal nudged his back and blinked from the smoky interior. On creosote covered walls hung three different sized cast iron frying pans. Steam from an enormous tea kettle floated above a Yukon stove near an oak barrel wearing metal belts. A Grizzly skin covered in dust stretched on the back wall. Laundry hung in one corner near the stove for faster drying. Blazo box shelves held canned goods. On a wooden nightstand sat two bottles of Chamberlain's liniment for sore muscles, making Ralph wonder if the marshal appeared younger than his age. Twin beds hugged two walls, one with leg irons at the foot of the bed and handcuffs at the head. Apparently, the marshal lived in the same room with his prisoner.

He shoved Ralph onto a chair. "How do you know Slim?"

"Don't."

"You said he owed you money?" the marshal pressed.

Ralph let his head fall back in relief. "Yep, but never caught up with him to collect."

"Why does he owe you money?

"How's that your business?"

"He's running dog fighting rings 'round here. That's how it's my business" the marshal disclosed.

"I'd never get into that! Slim and his partner bought my boat," Ralph protested.

"Who's his partner?"

"Eric Nilsen. Told me to collect the money from Slim," Ralph confided.

"You mean Einar Nilsen?"

Ralph's forehead wrinkled. "Don't know any Einar. Eric's who bought my boat."

The marshal continued, "How ya know Eric?"

"He runs the post office in Homer."

The marshal played his winning card. "Isn't it true you spent a night in jail with him?"

Ralph's pulse quickened as he stiffened. "So? Didn't break any laws."

"Unless you helped him escape," he accused.

"He was in jail when I left Homer and I have witnesses," Ralph declared. Then he stopped abruptly. "How'd he escape?"

"Lifted the floorboards and dug himself out," Dan revealed.

Ralph swore, "Damn fool probably stole my boat!"

The marshal's expression confirmed his fear.

"Guess I'm the fool," Ralph grumbled, coming to the realization that he had been hoodwinked out of his boat.

CHAPTER 46

Peg's girls loved spending the night with their grandmother. Aunt Freda and Uncle Ben Fox stayed after dinner for pie and cards. "Peggy, you want to play?" Freda invited as she shuffled the deck. "Your grandma needs a partner."

Peggy jumped at the chance. "Sure." *When adults visit, they often forget I'm young and discuss things that they never would have otherwise.*

After dealing, Freda described the marathon dance contest she and Ben had attended the previous weekend. "I think they rigged it and wish we hadn't wasted twenty-five cents per ticket to watch."

"Why so?" Mary wanted details.

Ben chuckled and added, "Well, we did have ringside seats to the drama."

"What?" Mary questioned further.

Ben studied his hand and discarded. He picked up a card. "Well, dancers got fifteen-minute breaks every hour, but by the end, they walked around with one's head on the other's shoulder, holding each other up. The minute a contestant's knee hit the floor, they got disqualified. One woman sobbed uncontrollably when she fell to the floor." Peggy quietly slid Ben's discard from the pile and worked it into her hand.

"I felt sorry for those amateurs when they fell. I'm sure they needed that five-hundred-dollar prize. One couple acted as if they'd fallen in love during the dance. A 'minister' came from the audience to marry them. Such a farce!" Freda mocked.

"How long did it last?" Mary wondered as she set another huckleberry pie on the table.

Freda cut Ben a piece. "We left after a few hours 'cause I nearly froze, but I heard the winners danced for over nine hundred hours! While we watched, one man and woman became partners after their original partners crumpled."

"Probably have to keep it cool for the dancers," Ben commented before he took a bite of pie. "Drama! Drama! That's what brings in the money. Funny how people like to witness other's misery."

"Rummy!" Peggy threw her hand down with a triumphant look. Her opponents frowned and counted the points against them.

Eleven-year-old Jean held up her calculations. "They danced for thirty-seven and a half days!"

Mary examined Jean's paper. "Good division, Honey. My goodness! No wonder they collapsed!" She turned to her son-in-law and sighed, "Ben, any leads on Marshal Conniff's killer yet? So sad. Such a handsome boy."

"Mom, you know he can't discuss an ongoing investigation!" Freda scolded.

Mary dealt the next hand. "But why would someone shoot that nice young man at the creamery?"

"With butter prices so high, this isn't the first creamery that's been robbed." Ben stated. "Thieves can fence it through shady restaurants or stores. I'm afraid if this Depression doesn't ease up, robberies will continue to rise."

Jean piped up. "Good thing we make our own butter!"

"Ben, not in front of the children," Mary warned in a whisper.

Peggy shot Jean a scowl. *Quiet, you! I want the adults to forget children are listening.*

Freda changed the subject, "Are Rose and Henry back from their honeymoon yet?"

"Haven't heard. Won't those two have beautiful children, though?" Mary mused.

Freda rolled her eyes, "Mom, they barely got married."

"Only takes nine months. Hey, maybe I can help with the delivery."

Ben set down a five-card run. "Now you've got the cart before the horse."

Freda spied the king of hearts she needed in Ben's run. "So that's why I couldn't get the card I wanted!" She drew another card and asked, "Where's Peg tonight?"

"She's catering Turners' fiftieth wedding party. That's why I have her girls." Mary winked at her beloved granddaughters. "Why don't you turn the radio on, Jean? It's almost time for the Will Rogers Program." She steered the girls' attention away from adult conversation.

Jean retired to the parlor and stretched out on the rug next to the big Zenith. She turned the knob in the center of the radio. Static crackled until she found the station. She sat next to the mesh front covering the speakers.

Will's political jokes often went over Jean's head.

"A fanatic is always the fellow that is on the opposite side.

There is nothing as easy as denouncing ... It don't take much to see that something is wrong but it does take some eyesight to see what will put it right again."

Canned laughter filled the spaces between jokes:

Everything is funny, as long as it's happening to somebody else.

I don't make jokes. I just watch the government and report the facts.

Everything is changing in America. People are taking the comedians seriously and the politicians as a joke. Why don't they pass a constitutional amendment prohibiting anybody from learning anything? If it works as well as prohibition did, in five years we will have the smartest people on earth."

He finished with this piece of advice: "Live in such a way that you wouldn't be ashamed to sell the family parrot to the town gossip."[3]

In the kitchen, the card game ended after the grandfather clock announced the time with eleven bongs. "My goodness, I'd better shoo these girls to bed!" Mary declared.

Peggy protested, "But I'm not tired. There's no school tomorrow. One more game, please?"

Mary held firm, "Nope. Time to hit the hay. Your mom will be late cleaning up. I've got her room upstairs ready for you. Jump up and brush those teeth. I'll call Jean."

In the parlor, Jean lounged asleep on a needlepoint pillow. She'd wrapped the crocheted afaghan from the rocker over her feet. Mary squeezed her shoulder. "Wake up, Honey. You're too big for Grandma to carry you."

---

3 https://www.mentalfloss.com/article/59855/18-timeless-will-rogers-quotes-his-135th-birthday

CHAPTER 47

When the temperature dropped, the old porch regulars relocated, circling the wood stove inside Tarbet's store where they gathered every morning for coffee and news. Mary untied the newspaper bundle and handed the top paper to old Tom who let out a whistle and declared, "Well, I'll be . . ." as soon as he shook open the copy of *The Seattle Times.*

"What?" the group chimed in unison.

"'Nother murder." He reached into his shirt pocket for round wire spectacles, opened the bows and perched them on the end of his nose.

"Where now?" Hank stopped rocking, launched a stream of tobacco juice into the spittoon and limped close enough to peer over Tom's shoulder. Tom read to himself.

Impatient for the news, Fred tapped his cane on the wooden floor. "Tom, what's it say?"

"Hold up! I'm finding out." Tom traced the newspaper with his index finger and read the headline:

"KING COUNTY SHERIFF'S DEPUTY, THOMAS MEEHAN, SHOT IN THE FACE ON OLD VALLEY HIGHWAY NORTH OF KENT."

"Some farmer found him dead at three in the morning next to his patrol car."

"What happened? Read it out loud!" Fred reached for the paper.

Tom continued:

"Officers suspect revenge for Meehan's pressure on a 'gambling clique.' Meehan purportedly told people, 'I'm working on a hot one, and when I catch up to the fellows I want, it will be either me or them!' Meehan had been on the job eleven months.

This forenoon Sheriff W. B. Severyns and his Chief Criminal Deputy, O. K. Bodia, ordered a general roundup of all known criminals and persons whose manner of life leaves them open to suspicion. 'It's to be a shakedown, boys,' Severyns told his staff of deputies. 'Turn the heat on everybody who might have had a motive, and who you believe might possibly have killed Meehan, or who might know something of it.'

After careful examination of the crime scene, Sheriff William Severyns reported: 'A gunny sack found at the scene has been traced to one put out by a Spokane poultry feed company which does not sell its product in this area, in fact no farther west than Coulee City. There are organized gangs of chicken thieves who usually operate away from home. Chickens stolen here are sold across the Cascades, or in Oregon, and we know of chickens stolen in Idaho that have been sold here.'" 4

"What's a gunny sack got to do with it?" Fred asked, unable to make the connection.

____

4 https://historylink.org/File/3759

"They think he came upon a chicken thieving ring," Tom replied.

Hank hobbled back to his chair. "Yes, and now they're killing lawmen!"

"And don't furgit, butter thieves been killing, too!" Tom interjected, recalling the recent murder of Marshal Conniff at the Newport Creamery.

Fred poked his cane at Tom. "Anything 'bout the Conniff case in that paper?"

"Give me a minute," Tom groused as he turned the page of the newspaper.

Fred frowned and hung his head. "Knew Conniff's old man. Grew up together. Never thought anything like that'd never happen here in Newport. Back in my day, you never heard of local murders. That stuff only came 'bout in them big cities."

The bell jangled as the front door opened. Peg glanced toward the stove. "Morning, fellas!"

"Morning, Peg!" the group responded, staying focused on Tom and the information from the article.

She traipsed into the back room, hunting for her mother, and found her at a desk, bent over an account book. Mary raised her head when she heard Peg enter. "Good morning! How'd the party go last night?"

Peg plopped onto an empty crate. "Great. All my dough-nuts disappeared, and guests begged for more. Good thing I made extra date cookies, too. Then Mrs. Allen asked me to cater her husband's birthday next month."

"You're becoming quite the businesswoman." Mary looked up from her bookkeeping. "I'm proud of you, dear."

Peg chose an apple from a nearby barrel and took a bite. "With two girls to feed and clothe, every little bit helps."

"You know, I could . . ." Mary began, but Peg cut her off.

"We're doing fine. Girls behave last night?" She wiped the apple's juice from her chin on her shirt sleeve, making Mary cringe.

"Fine. Such good girls. You're doing a fine job raising them. Peggy skunked us all at rummy and almost did at pinochle, too!"

"We play a lot at home. Doesn't take long for the girls to do their schoolwork, so I'm teaching them embroidery and knitting. They've picked it up fast. I'll have Peggy bring over some of her pillowcases to show you."

The store bell jangled again. Peg hopped up. "I'll get it, Mom. You're in the middle of something."

By the time she recognized the man, it was too late. *If I go into the back room, it will be awkward.* She froze.

Charlie moved to the ring of men around the stove and put his hands to the warmth. "How ya doing there, Charlie?" Hank welcomed him by sliding another chair next to the stove. Charlie sat.

Here's my chance. Peg retreated.

"Isn't that right, Peg?" Tom called, sensing her desire to withdraw.

Drat! Shouldn't have hesitated! She pretended to be straightening the fabric on a nearby shelf. "What's that?"

"Jus' saying that Ben will figure it out." Hank's head bobbed in agreement.

"Figure what out, Tom?" Peg's heart raced, even though Charlie's back faced her. *What's wrong with me? I hate feeling like this. It's over. We're both married. Why do I care what Charlie thinks of me?* Charlie turned her way, his eyes lit with cautious hope.

"Who killed the Conniff boy," Tom answered.

His answer jolted Peg from her thoughts. "The marshal was a grown man, Tom, not a boy. I'm sure Uncle Ben's working on it." She excused herself. "Got to run. Have a good day," she called and disappeared into the back.

Mary glanced up from her bookkeeping. "That didn't take long. Who came in? What did they want?"

"Another to join the newspaper bunch. Better check on the girls." Peg darted out the back door.

Curiosity drew Mary from her chair to see who'd joined the men. She spotted a bright red head. *Oh, that explains it.* Charlie's head swiveled expectantly. His wounded face pierced her heart. "Charlie, how are you?" *I want to hug that sadness out of you.*

He stared over Mary's shoulder, asking "Peg left?"

"Yes, she couldn't stay," Mary made an excuse. "It's good to see you, Charlic."

He held out a grocery list. "Just home for a visit. Mom needs me to pick up a few things."

Peg hustled home with doubts trespassing her thoughts. *What's Charlie doing back? Got to get over this fear, get my emotions under control. After all, we live in a small town and our daughters are friends. I can't turn back time.* She took a deep breath. *But if I'm honest, I'd like to. Why didn't I just give Charlie time to adjust to civilian life? When he told me to leave, I shouldn't have. I shouldn't have deserted him.* She chastised herself, but it didn't help. *I didn't know what to do and still don't.* An image from last week flashed into her mind. After spotting Charlie and Belle coming into the school on parent-teacher day, she'd hurried her girls out the back door. *Will I ever feel comfortable around Charlie again?*

CHAPTER 48

The prison squatted low and mean. Razor wire curled atop a twelve-foot fence. The guard tower loomed over the complex. When Charlie pulled into the visitor parking, his palms began to sweat. *Will she even talk to me? What if she won't?* He gathered an envelope containing drawings and a letter from Belle. After months of no response to her letters, Belle didn't believe they'd ever reached her mother, so she asked Charlie to hand-deliver some.

Charlie slammed the door of the farm truck, sending dust and straw floating through the air. He hurried away, so none would land on his hat and freshly pressed suit. The low winter sun crawled toward frosted trees in the west. A pall of shadows fell on the fields from low hanging clouds. Charlie squared his shoulders and approached the beefy guard who opened the door to a long hallway. Cold from stark white walls seeped into his bones

After getting frisked, Charlie entered the deafening silence of the visiting area. He kept his head down. A masculine-looking woman in her sixties edged over to stare at the visitor. Two young women entered and made lewd comments. Charlie's face turned red. *I hate coming here!* When a woman sat opposite him, Charlie lifted his eyes and peered through the glass at her.

His eyes widened and jaw fell. *Is that Florence?* He squinted and drew closer. Florence resembled a refugee with hollow cheeks and matted hair. *She's aged twenty years.* She noticed Charlie's reaction and drew her lips in tightly. "What ya doing HERE?"

"I brought letters from Belle. She thinks the postoffice loses them as you never reply," he explained nervously.

"I get 'em," she growled. "Told you to tell her I died."

Charlie held the letters up to the glass. "But that's not true, and she misses you."

"Humph, better get used to it. Not coming home." She hesitated, fighting her emotions. "Best if she forgets me." Unsaid words thickened the air.

"She's too old for that," Charlie finally responded.

Florence's grief-stricken eyes betrayed her stoic attitude. She lowered her voice. "Belle knows what I did?"

"Yes, but I told her that you did it to protect her. And that's true."

"Don't want to hurt her. I know what it's like to grow up with a criminal parent. Don't want her to worry, to be teased . . ." Tears filled her eyes as she stood. "Tell her I died," she repeated.

"I won't lie to her, Florence." Charlie signaled the guard, indicating he was ready to leave. On the way down the hall, he stopped. "Would you please deliver these letters to Florence? I promised my daughter I'd get them to her mom."

The guard let Charlie out, then returned and escorted Florence to her cell. That evening, another guard delivered the letters as he made his rounds. Florence threw them on the floor, waited until she heard the footsteps disappear, then sprang from the covers and snatched up the letters. She turned one over as tears dropped onto the envelope.

Dear Mama,

I miss you. When will you be home? I have a new friend named Peggy. She always beats me at jacks. It hurts Grandma to sit on the floor, so I practice with Daddy at night after chores. Do you play jacks? I could send some with Daddy. Please write back to me.

Love,

Belle

Florence clutched the opened letter to her chest and mumbled, "My baby! My baby!" She rocked back and forth. Her nose and eyes ran, soaking the front of her gray prison dress. She crushed the pile of unopened letters in her fist and threw them across the cell. "Damn you, Dad! It's your fault I'm here!" Her throat filled with bitterness as the sexual abuse she endured from her father galloped uninvited through her mind.

CHAPTER 49

Mary searched the books for an answer. For the past week, the till hadn't balanced. It had come up short in varying amounts from a dollar and a quarter to yesterday's till missing forty dollars. When Raymond came to work after school, she flinched as the back door opened.

"Oh, Raymond, you startled me!" She rubbed her temples. "Is it that time already?"

"You feeling okay, Mrs. Tarbet?" the skinny teenager asked as his voice cracked.

"Fine, just having trouble with the accounts. There are several boxes in the storage room that need to be unpacked and restocked on the shelves. If you'd like a cinnamon roll first, help yourself." She pointed at the pan of rolls. Frosting dripped onto the shelf.

"Gee, thanks!" he replied, reaching one.

"Wash your hands," Mary reminded. She rose and stretched. "Guess I'll help you. I'm tired of figures!"

After gobbling down the cinnamon roll, Raymond carried a case of Progresso canned beets into the store. He opened the box and handed Mary a can. She placed it behind a line of beets on the shelf. Before handing her the next can, he studied the label. "What does a man driving a chariot have to do with beets?

"Beets me!" Mary giggled at her own joke.

After opening the next case of food, he showed Mary the label featuring yellow wax beans. "At least this label shows what's inside." He went to the storage room and returned with a five-gallon tin of Quaker rolled oats.

"Bring that over here and dump it into this crock," Mary instructed as she checked off the items from her packing list. Her brow furrowed. *I ordered a few things that aren't here.* "Raymond, check in the back again. We should have a case of Nescafe instant coffee and Nabisco shredded wheat. There should also be another case of condensed milk."

He pivoted and returned to the storage room. After moving several things around, he returned. "Those things aren't back there, Mrs. Tarbet."

"Humm, I'll have to check my orders again. I'm sure I paid for them." Her lips pressed together. Raymond passed by as he swept the floor, then took the garbage to the burn barrel behind the store. "As soon as you fill up that Hi-Plane tobacco display, you can go home." She went to the candy shelf and sacked up one-cent Tootsie rolls. "Here, take these home to your little brothers and sisters." She handed the treats to Raymond.

"Gee, thanks, Mrs. Tarbet. They never get candy 'cause Dad's out of work," he admitted.

"You're welcome, Raymond. You know that the country's in a depression. Your family isn't the only one out of work," Mary's voice showed genuine concern. "I'll finish the spices." She arranged bright yellow cans of Coleman's mustard, then straightened the red Schilling spice tins. When the bell over the door jangled, she turned to see Mrs. Hahn, her arms full of a red-cheeked baby and a toddler in a thin sweater hanging on her skirts, struggling in, her usual round face thin and drawn.

"Hello there," Mary greeted the customer.

Mrs. Hahn shifted the baby to her other arm. "Vere is da canned milk?"

Mary moved to the milk display. "We have four cans left. I ordered more, but I guess it didn't get delivered."

"Zatts enough."

Mary took the cans to the cash register. "Is that all you need?"

The little woman's face crumpled. "Zatts all I haff money for," she confided. "I'll be back when I can."

"Take what you need, and I'll let you put it on account," Mary offered.

Tears fell on Mrs. Hahn's worn apron. "Ziss is vat I vas vondering all da day in my hett, Mrs. Tarbet. I vas ofervelmed wis dis: How can I go to da shtore?"

"Don't worry. We take care of each other in this town." Mary withdrew a horehound and peppermint stick from the glass containers behind the cash register and handed them to the little girl whose eyes grew round. "For you, Honey."

Her mother withdrew a handkerchief from the front of her dress and dabbed her eyes. "Ja, you a fery schpecial mutter. Efery time I tell my Helmut dat."

"Why thank you." When the trio left the store loaded with a large sack of groceries, Mary reached for her own lace-edged hankie. *I need to have Peg get together things her girls have out-grown. Those children are ragged and cold.*

Peg bolted in the front door. "I must have thought you here!" Mary exclaimed.

"Why? What did you need?"

After Mary explained the Hahn's dilemma, Peg's mind churned with ideas. "We could put a sign on an empty barrel in the store that says: Donate food for the needy. The church's ladies' group could tie quilts. Let's place a box at the church for donated clothing. What do you think?"

"Good ideas. With this Depression, I'm afraid we'll be seeing more families in need. We are so blessed to own our home, ranch and store, so we can be self-reliant!"

"Thanks to Dad's and your hard work!" Peg agreed. "Aunt Freda just gave me a box of hand-me-downs for my girls. I'll go through their clothes to find things for the Hahns."

"You have a few minutes?" Mary changed the subject.

Peg shed her coat. "Sure, what's up?"

"Well, that's what I'm trying to figure out. I've been pouring over my books and can't see why they keep coming up short. And the invoices don't match with the groceries in the storeroom."

"Let me try," Peg volunteered.

"Would you? I'll go home to start dinner for you and the girls." Mary shed her apron, careful not to mess up her hair. "I need a break."

"And you call making dinner a break?" Peg teased as she followed Mary to the back.

Mary pulled on her coat and grabbed her purse from the office. "Better than bookwork!"

Peg spotted the cinnamon rolls and took two to the desk. "Don't worry. I'll find your mistake." As she took a big bite of roll, crumbs fell onto the ledger. She brushed them aside and picked up the pencil.

"There's milk in the icebox," Mary suggested. "I'll lock up and be off."

Two hours later, Peg rubbed her temples. *Sheesh, I can't see anything wrong with Mom's math.* The back door's loose doorknob jiggled. *What's that? Mom's back?* She froze and listened closely. Someone entered in the dark. *Mom wouldn't do that.* Peg turned off her lamp. The door opened and footsteps sounded down the hall. She cast her eyes about in the dark. *What can I use for a weapon?* She opened the bottom drawer, hoping that Mary hadn't moved the gun. The cold metal at her fingertips calmed her racing thoughts and rapid heartbeat. *I hope it's loaded.* She peeked around the corner in time to see a shadow steal into the storage room. Edging down the hall, Peg felt for the light switch. She cocked the gun and threw on the light. "Hands up! Hold it right there!"

A terrified Raymond squinted against the light as his hands shot into the air. "Raymond! What are YOU doing here?" Peg declared. "You nearly got shot!" He hung his head and planted his hands in his pockets. His slender shoulders shook, and tears spilled uncontrollably onto his thin shirt.

Peg realized why the books and inventory didn't balance. "Have you been taking food and money from the store?" He hung his head and refused to look at Peg. "Have you?" she pressed. "How could you do that?"

"My family's hungry," he confessed after a long period of shame-filled silence.

Peg lowered the gun but used it to point at a box. "Sit!" He slumped onto it. "Ya know I should call the law, don't you?"

His chin quivered. "Please don't."

"Why not?"

He gulped. "I need to feed my family."

"You can't do that if you're in jail, right?"

His chin dipped as he grabbed his stomach. "I'm going to jail?" *Who will get food and money for Mom and the kids. I can't get locked up! It will break Mom's heart.*

"Nope. We're going to my mom's right now," she grabbed his arm, "and don't think about trying to run, or I WILL put you in jail." She relocked the back door and held her hand out for the key. "Give it!" He produced it from his pocket.

"What will I tell your mother?" she demanded.

"Please don't. Please don't tell!" he begged as Peg marched him down the street. When they arrived, she opened the door and pushed him in. Raymond shrank when he noticed Marshall Ben Fox seated at the kitchen table. Peg suppressed a grin. *Perfect timing.* "Hello, Ben." She winked over Raymond's head.

"Who have you got here?" he asked. Raymond cringed.

"The answer to Mom's puzzle," Peg replied.

"What puzzle?" Mary asked as she came out of the pantry. She noticed the quivering boy. "Hello, Raymond. What's the matter?"

As Peg prodded him forward, he blubbered. Mary held out her arms. "Oh, Honey, what happened?"

"I'm sorry," he stammered. Mary searched Peg's face for an answer.

"Tell her," Peg demanded.

"I . . . did . . . it," he confessed.

"He's the answer to your missing money and groceries," Peg announced. "Caught him sneaking in after hours. Said his family needs the food."

"Is that true, dear?" He hung his head in shame.

Ben cleared his throat and Raymond plunged into Mary's arms. "You want to press charges, Mary?" he asked, sounding as official as he possibly could. Mary shook her head in horror.

"Well, son, it's lucky for you Mrs. Tarbet's so understanding. See ya later, ladies. I got real criminals to catch. Thanks for the pie, Mary." He donned his hat and carried his plate and coffee cup to the sink.

Peg stopped him. "What kind of criminals?"

"Moonshiners and thieves mostly. Thanks to this bad economy, I'm run ragged lately."

Peg's eyes lit. "I could help!"

"No doubt. Just caught your first one. And don't know many that can shoot like you," he admitted.

Mary caught her breath. "Peg, no! Your girls!"

"Gotta keep them safe, Mom. I'm serious, Ben," she persisted.

Mary glowered at Ben. "I'll think about it," he promised, not wanting to upset his mother-in-law.

Happy to have the attention shifted from him, Raymond relaxed a little. Peg's irritation returned to him. "Speaking of thieves . . ."

Mary released the teen from her embrace. "Sit down, Raymond. Are you hungry?" She opened the pie safe. "Of course, you are. You're a teenage boy, aren't you? When my boys lived at home, they could eat . . ."

"Mom," Peg interrupted, "what about the stolen stuff? You'll do him no favors to let it go."

"We'll think of something. Do you want milk with that pie?" She set a glass in front of Raymond.

"Don't you have a younger sister?" Peg asked, searching for a solution to cover the costs of Raymond's theft.

Raymond looked aghast, "She didn't take anything!"

"I know, but she can help you." Peg scooted a chair knee to knee with him. *I've got to help him learn his lesson. Mom'll be too soft.*

"How?"

"I'm thinking that she could take your job and you'd work for free until you've paid my mother back . . . with interest," she added for effect. "What do you think, Mom?" Once Mary accepted the suggestion, Raymond pressed his palms to his eyes, wiped away tears and dove into the pie.

"Mom, I think we should find a guard dog for the store," Peg recommended.

The idea of working for Ben spun inside Peg's head. *If I'm honest, my job at the doctor's office is mundane. I miss the adventure of Alaska. Investigating crime, now that's exciting!* She stopped by Ben's office on the way home from work.

He raised his eyes when the door opened. "Hello, Peg. Catch any more dangerous criminals for me?" he teased.

Peg flopped in the chair across from his desk and planted her feet up on the chair next to it.

"I'm serious, Uncle Ben. If you really have an opening for a deputy, I'd like to apply. You know I can handle firearms and . . ."

The phone rang, interrupting her. "Marshall Fox," he answered. "Yes, Fred. Thanks for the heads-up. Yes, I'll let you know." He drew a notepad close and jotted down a name. "Thanks again, Fred." He replaced the receiver with a frown.

"Something wrong?" Peg wondered.

"Fred from the paper. The Associated Press is running Florence Wilson's story. He warned me I might be getting a call from them because he just did."

"What for?"

"I'm sure they have questions. Must be a slow national news day." He tore the top page from the notebook and reached for his hat.

Peg jumped up. "Where you headed? Can I come?"

Ben checked his watch. "You off work already?"

She followed him out the door. "Yeah, no more appointments and Dr. Phillips is in his office, so he let me leave early. People can't afford doctor bills anymore." She nearly had to run to keep up with his long strides. "What do you think? Hey, maybe I could just help on the weekends. This Depression has affected my catering business."

He stopped abruptly. "Do you need money?"

"Always, but I really need something to occupy my mind, something to look forward to, something exciting."

"Well, come along then," he surrendered. "But let me ask the questions. You stay quiet. Got it?"

"Got it. Where we going? Is it a crime scene? Do I need a gun?"

"No, just following up on a tip. Margaret's been calling to report on her neighbor's drinking again. She keeps reminding me alcohol is still against the law. Watch out! She'll turn her questioning on you eventually. I've never seen such a woman who must know everything about everyone! Still game?"

"Well, my divorce is old news, so I'm not worried. You'll have to admit, though, that she's a good neighborhood watchdog!" Peg laughed. "By the way, I told Mom that we need a dog for the store. Any idea who has one?"

They passed the brawny grocery delivery boy with his arms full. He peered over the top of the box. "Morning, Marshal."

"Morning, Bill." He slowed down to let Peg catch up. "Well, some breeds are better for that than others. I suggest you have a German Shepherd. They make nice family dogs. Not too aggressive with your girls."

Peg hopped over a puddle. "Where would I find one?"

"I'll ask around. Maybe you could get two, breed them and make some money."

They turned the corner. "We could keep the male at the store and the female at home," Peg thought aloud. "Thanks. That might be just the ticket."

Margaret sat in a green metal chair on her porch. When the two came into view, she raised her beak of a nose, rushed down the steps and waved, "Over here, Marshal!"

Ben winked at Peg and whispered, "She's on duty." When they got to the bottom of her stairs, she launched her inquisition. "Peg, why aren't you at work? Did you quit Dr. Phillips? I heard you've moved to town. Doesn't your mom miss you since she's a widow?"

Peg rolled her eyes. "No, I have the afternoon off."

Ben mounted the steps and rescued her. "Margaret, you said you have some information that might interest me?"

"Yes, I do," she reported smugly, ready to give every spicy detail. She raised her eyebrows at Peg.

"Don't worry. She's working with me," Ben informed her.

Peg's mouth dropped. *So I do have a job with him!*

"Well, how's she going to work two jobs?" Margaret huffed. "There's a lot of people out of work!"

"She helps part time. What was it that you needed to tell me?"

"It's the neighbors across the street in the Wilson house. Since Florence's in the pen, you know . . . of course, *you* know that," she winked, "and since Charlie's gone crazy and can't live alone, well, they rented it out, for income I'm sure. Though I don't think they're getting a lot for it in the shape that it's in, and . . ."

"Is it about the house?" Ben prompted while Peg fumed over her comment about Charlie.

"No, it's about the renter. I see him stumbling around the yard. I know he's been drinking, too. Remember, I was the first on the scene after Florence's attack?" She gave a self-satisfied smile before continuing, "So as a neighbor, of course, I went over to check on him. When I got close, I smelled it on him. I asked if he was all right, but he ducked into the house. Didn't even have the decency to answer my question." Her eyes narrowed. "And I was concerned." Peg bit her tongue. *It's a fact that you like sticking your nose in everyone's business!* Ben coughed to suppress a laugh.

She continued, "You know there's been unusual things at that house for as long as I can remember . . . fights, screaming, and now a murder. Well, not THERE, but by those people. I guess when you have a slum house, you get slum people. Anyway, I thought you'd better know he's getting alcohol from somewhere." She took a deep breath.

"Have you seen people coming and going?" Ben asked.

"No, I would have noticed, too. Not that I'm spying, you know, but I do like to sit outside and read after my housework is finished. The only person I've seen is the milkman. I don't know how they get groceries because they haven't been delivered. I've even asked Mrs. Tarbet if he's been to her store, and she said she didn't think so." She turned to Peg. "Have you seen him?"

"Don't know him and don't spend much time at the store anymore." *Ya' ol busybody. You'd be the last person I'd tell. And Charlie's not crazy!*

"I could help you with a stakeout, if you need me to," Margaret whispered.

Ben coughed to hide aversion he couldn't conceal at the thought of Margaret on a stakeout with him. "Call if you see anything unusual, Margaret." He motioned to Peg who bounded down the stairs before her need to tell the woman off surfaced.

When Ben caught up to her, his grin caused his laugh lines to fan out. "How's the new job so far?"

Peg's anger dissipated. "So, I DO have a job! Thank you! What's my first case?"

He walked ahead. "Solve the mystery of Margaret's neighbor."

Peg's brow furrowed. *I need to show Ben how valuable I could be as a deputy. I'll do my own investigation if I can without "Mrs. Nosy" blowing it. Well, why not use her? She'd love to think she's on some secret mission. I'll stop by after work tomorrow.*

Five days later, Peg hoisted a wire carton of glass milk bottles onto the marshal's desk. "You bring cookies to go with this?" he joked.

"Open one," Peg directed with authority.

Ben plucked one from the carrier, pushed the wire clamp back with his thumb, removed the lid, sniffed the bottle and guffawed. "This story is one that Fred will want for the paper. It might even go national!" He rubbed his chin. "But maybe not. We don't want to inspire other moonshiners with the idea. But what a great detective you are! How did you discover this?" He opened the other bottles and tested them. "Oh, this one has milk!"

Should I tell him? Why not? Margaret's probably told the whole town by now. "I used the neighborhood spy. Margaret sat up four nights, watching the house for me. I thought she'd be less conspicuous than me hanging around. Anyhow, no one ever came. She said she only saw the milkman three times a week. I thought it odd that so much milk got delivered. Today, I took today's delivery before the suspect. I opened a couple bottles and found them full of liquor!"

Ben laughed. "Pretty clever to paint the milk bottles white! Well, when there's money to be made . . . Want to pay a visit to the dairy with me?" he asked.

"I'm thinking I'll lie low. I've already had a couple of unpleasant run-ins with moonshiners. I do hate to miss the reaction on the owner's face when you show up toting his product! I've got to help Mom at the store this afternoon, but I'll be by tomorrow to hear the report."

"Good work, Deputy," Ben stood and extended his hand in congratulations of a job well done. "Read 'bout those moonshiners caught in Florida?"

"What about them?"

Ben opened his file cabinet, removed an article and handed it to Peg. "Can you believe that? Moonshiners made 'cow shoes.' Wired cow hooves to the soles of their shoes to throw the law off track and hoofed it through the mountains." Ben chuckled at his own joke.

Peg shook her head and handed the paper back with a bemused smile. "Got another case for me?"

"Not yet. You'll be the first to know."

CHAPTER 50

"Good morning, Son! What have you got there?" Mary pushed the squeaky screen door open. In the east, the sun scribbled bright orange across clouds. A rooster crowed and hens scratched the ground, searching for breakfast.

Two wiggly puppies yipped in Ben's arms. "Guard dogs."

Mary giggled, lifting one by his scruff and holding it close. The pup snuggled in. "You're not very frightening, are you?" She stroked the top of his fuzzy head as she held the door open with her shoulder. "Come in. Peg told me about your idea, and I like it. Since she's a deputy, I worry even more about her and the girls."

"I thought I'd better leave them with you until they're housetrained. Her little girls will spoil a puppy." Ben set the other dog down. It left a puddle on the floor.

Mary raised her eyebrows. "Who's gonna housetrain them?"

"Well, Freda doesn't allow animals in the house and I'm not in the office a lot . . ."

"Oh, you!" Mary cuffed his head. "You know I'm a softy for puppies, but I'll have to take them to the store with me. I suppose they can stay in the back until closing time."

"Thanks, Mom. I knew you'd help. The owner had another buyer, so I had to take them." Ben gave her a bear hug.

Mary threw a rag onto the puddle and swiped at it with her foot. "Have you had your breakfast?"

Ben took the puppy from Mary. "Just a cup of coffee." He picked up the wet rag and scooped the other pup from the floor. "I'll grab the box from my truck for these guys."

Mary couldn't help but think, *The things you do for your kids!* She stoked the fire in the belly of the stove, washed her hands and dug out the frying pan. *But honestly, I think I'll enjoy the company. It's mighty lonely with John gone and Peg and the girls in town.* She sliced a slab of ham, cut the fat off, then cracked three eggs in the skillet.

Ben returned with two pups in an orange crate and set it on the front porch. He shook his finger at them. "You kids, behave, or the marshal will know about it!" They whined and scratched at the side of the box.

"They're hungry!" Mary clucked as she stepped onto the porch and threw ham fat to them. They tore into it, their little tails beating against the wood.

"And I worried the little girls would spoil them," Ben laughed. He followed Mary inside and opened the cupboard. "Which bowl can I use for water?"

"None of those!" she squealed, shutting the cupboard. "There's a metal bowl out in the barn. You can get it after breakfast. You want some pie?" She opened the pie safe and lifted a sticky apple pie from the shelf. "I've got cheese to go with it." She cut two pieces and licked her fingers. "Guess I'll have some, too." After turning the eggs and ham, she brought a pitcher of milk from the icebox.

"Sit down, Mom. I'll dish it up," Ben offered.

"Thanks!" Mary found a seat. Outside, the dogs whined. She rose from her chair. "We should give the puppies some milk, too."

Ben touched his mother's shoulder. "You sit. They can wait until after we eat."

"But how can I eat with those little ones crying?" Mary complained.

Ben wiped milk from his mouth. "Better question is: How will you rest? They're two months old, so I'm afraid you've got a couple more months before they sleep all night."

Mary raised her hands in surrender. "Well, I like to tend animals. The chickens and cats need to be fed, but the hired man takes care of the cattle. They'll be good company." She left her pie and went to the porch. Two little black muzzles worked their way between the wooden slats. A rough pink tongue from the bigger puppy's mouth licked Mary's hand. She picked the small one up and sat in the rocker on the porch. When a cat climbed the front steps, the puppy jumped from her lap and took off after it. Mary gave chase. "Come back, you little stinker!"

"Finish your schoolwork. After dinner, we're going to Grandma's. She has a surprise to show you," Peg promised her daughters.

"What kind of surprise?" Jean asked, always wanting more details.

"You'll find out after dinner." Peggy pushed her sister's books across the kitchen table.

"I want to know if it's worth it!" Jean grumbled. She opened her math book. "I hate long division! Guess what happened at school today, Mom."

Peg removed two pans of rolls from the oven. "What?" She set the hot pans on top of the woodburning stove. "Peggy, will you butter the tops of these?"

"I'll do it!" Jean proclaimed, attempting to escape from her homework.

Peg hung the hot pads on hooks over the oven. "You do your division. Peggy's finished with her homework."

Jean pouted from her chair. "She gets to do everything!"

Peg changed the subject. "What happened at school?"

"I rescued Peggy," Jean declared proudly. Peggy rolled her eyes. Jean noticed. "Well, I did to!"

Peg suppressed a grin as she sat across from Jean with a bowl full of fresh green beans. "Tell me all about it." She snapped ends from the beans.

Jean shut her book. "There's this mean kid . . ."

"What's his name?" Peg interrupted and set two handfuls of green beans in front of Peggy who bent to the task.

"Ernest. He stinks and he hits. Nobody likes him. He has sticking out hair and black fingernails."

"What did he do?" Peg prompted.

"Peggy and I took our roller skates to school, so we could skate all the way home. Ernest hid behind a car. When Peggy got close, he tripped her and ran off laughing. Peggy skinned her knees."

"How did you rescue her?" Peg lifted the hem of Peggy's skirt to inspect her hurt knees.

Jean stuck her chin out. "I chased after him and threw a rock. Plugged him in the back, too!" she reported triumphantly. "I helped Sister wash her knees when we got home."

Peg bit back a smile. *Apple doesn't fall far from the tree with you!* "Get the iodine from the medicine cabinet and a couple of clean rags to put over your scrapes. And you little lady lassie," she pointed at Jean, "open your math book."

"Can't you give me one hint about the surprise?" Jean wheedled.

"I will after your homework is finished," Peg promised. "Now get on with it."

Jean frowned and slapped open the book.

"And no sassy lassie!" Peg warned.

Peggy came with the iodine. "It's going to sting, isn't it?"

"Better than an infection. Come here. Sit here next to me." Peg moved a kitchen chair close and dabbed iodine on the scrapes. Peggy winced but held still and didn't cry. "You're a brave girl. After you put this back . . ." she handed Peg the bottle, "there's a box in my bedroom . . ." Peggy limped off.

Jean's head rose. "Is our surprise in the box?"

"Remember, I told you we'll see it at Grandma's. Back to work."

In her mother's bedroom, Peggy unfolded the flaps of the cardboard box. Inside lay neatly folded dresses. Aunt Freda loved to sew and made her daughter Lucille beautiful clothes. She often sent over slightly used dresses. Even though Lucille was three years younger than Peggy and a year older than Jean, Peggy's petite frame often fit into the younger girl's clothes. And Peggy LOVED clothes. She closed her eyes as she ran her hand over an embroidered satin blouse, then shimmied into a ruffled skirt and twirled. When she drew out a plaid dress with a sailor collar, she set it aside for Jean.

Thirty minutes later, Jean stuck her head in and noticed the pile around Peggy. "What's in the box? Oh, just clothes. Come on. We're going to Grandma's to see the real surprise."

"Oh!" Peggy held up two favorites, a pink dress with a full skirt covered in lace and another with bows down the front and on the sleeves.

Jean frowned. "I hope the surprise at Grandma's is better than clothes."

"I doubt it," Peggy answered.

"Shake a leg!" Peg called from the other room. "We need to be back before bedtime."

Jean dashed out. "Don't dawdle, Peggy!"

Peggy took an armful of clothes to her room, dropped them on her bed and followed.

Jean ran ahead. "Grandma!" she yelled as soon as her feet hit the steps of the porch. Mary jumped and dropped a stitch in her knitting. "Goodness, what's wrong?" she replied when Jean sped to the front room.

"Nothing. Mom told us you have a surprise here. What is it?

The puppy on Mary's lap raised its head.

"A puppy! Is it for me?" Jean dropped to her knees beside the rocker. "Can I hold it?"

All the commotion woke the other puppy asleep on the rug in front of the radio. It yawned and stretched. "TWO puppies!" Jean squealed in delight and turned to Peggy. "There's one for each of us!" Peggy wasn't impressed. Jean crawled to the one on the floor. "Hey there! Come see me." She held her hand out to the curious dog. "Can we take them home?"

Peg chuckled at Jean. "Not yet. They're too little to be left home alone all day. When they're bigger, we'll bring one home."

"Only one? Who gets the other? Peggy needs one, too," Jean protested.

Peggy drew back. "No, I don't."

"Grandma will keep one as a guard dog at the store," Peg told them as Mary handed her the puppy from her lap. "Want to hold one?" She held it out to Peggy.

"No, thanks."

Jean giggled as the puppy licked her face. "What's their names?"

Mary dropped her knitting in the basket next to her chair. "They don't have names yet. I'm waiting for you to name them."

"Really?" Jean bounced from foot to foot. "Are they boys or girls? What are you going to name yours, Peggy?"

Peg lifted one and inspected it. "This one's the boy, so the other's the girl."

"I'll name the girl Daisy," Peggy said. "It's my favorite flower."

"I'll name the boy." Jean took the puppy from her mother and studied him. "I think I'll name you Chief, so you can protect Grandma's store for her!"

She ran around the room, giggling as the puppy nipped at her heels.

Peg lounged on the davenport, enjoying the antics. *I know how much love and companionship a dog is. I miss Miko. Hope Ralph's taking good care of him. Wish I could have brought him back with me, but I'm sure he's happier in Alaska. He's a born musher.*

CHAPTER 51

"Did you hear what happened to Mrs. Block last night?" Mary asked Peggy when she came to pick up the girls.

"No," Peg frowned, trying to place Mrs. Block.

Mary continued, "Well, some stranger knocked on her door. He handed her a bundle and took off. Remember Mrs. Block, the young widow who takes in sewing? She thought the bundle contained work. When she unwrapped the bundle, she found a baby fast asleep! There was a note pinned to the blanket that said:

Dear Madam,

Please take care of this baby. It is two weeks old.

You will be well paid. Please destroy this note.

"Wow!" Peg whistled. "Who gives their baby away?" She walked to the sideboard and pinched a cookie. "She didn't recognize the guy?" she asked between bites. "Will she keep him? Is it a girl or a boy? Why did he want the note destroyed?"

"A girl, but not sure how she'll keep her. She takes in sewing to feed her own kids."

Peg shrugged off her dad's plaid jacket that she'd adopted as her own. "How many does she have?"

"Can't remember if it's two or three." Mary took the jacket and hung it behind the door in its old spot. She swallowed and rubbed the sleeve for a few seconds as her eyes misted.

Peg noticed. *I miss him, too, Mom.* She forced her grief back. "What will happen if she can't keep the baby? Have you talked with Ben? Sounds like a new case for me to work on!"

The back door slammed as Jean charged in. "Hi, Mom! Come see the puppies. They've grown so big! And Chief is bigger than Daisy. I knew he'd make a good guard dog."

I'm so grateful they can come to the ranch and spend time with Mom. "That's great. Next time, don't let the door slam. Where's Peggy?"

"Dunno. There're new kittens in the barn, too. Come see." Jean darted into the yard with the puppies cavorting after.

"Peggy's embroidering in the front room, but don't go in there. She's making a surprise for you," Mary whispered. "Go see the kittens. I've got a pot of stew ready if you and girls can stay and eat with me." Hope edged into her voice.

"Sure, Mom. Thanks for all you do for us." Peg grabbed another cookie and followed Jean down the worn dirt path. Jean tugged at the barn door. "Come on, Mom!"

Peg stopped a minute to relish the majestic sunset gold leafing the mountains. Frogs chorused from the pond as geese honked a descant. She slapped a mosquito from her arm and followed Jean into the dim musty barn. Light slanted through cracks in the walls, showcasing sparkling dust motes whirling through the air. Honey whinnied a greeting. Mama cat rubbed against her legs, purring.

"Over here!" Jean knelt in soft hay next to a pile of kittens. "Grandma said I could take one home when they are big enough, but I had to ask you. Can I?"

Peg moved next to her. "Yes, we can leave a cat home alone, and it will be good insurance against mice."

"Yay! I want this one." Jean lifted a black and white spotted kitten and cuddled it.

Peg rose and brushed hay from her knees. "OK, let's go wash. Grandma invited us for dinner and I'm starving." Jean gently placed the kitten back and scampered after her mother.

"Look who's here!" Peg announced when she spotted Mud's rusty red truck with his Springer Spaniel lounging on the running board. She ran to the back door and flung it open, "Mud!" His face had grown tired and thin. Peg gave him a hug. "I've been worried about you."

He squeezed his eyes shut and swallowed. "Sure am missing my Marion. Just doesn't seem right. She was only twenty-eight."

Peg took his hands. "I know. How long you two married?"

"Almost six years."

And no children. At least I have my girls.

He cleared his throat and hung up his hat, exposing a white forehead that contrasted with his tanned face. "Well, I hear you're the new deputy sheriff." He hooked his arm around Peg's shoulders. "A female deputy! That's unheard of. The criminals are in for it now!" Jean ran in. Mud patted her head. "How's my little Mexican jumping bean? Where's Peggy?"

Peggy heard his voice and appeared. "Hi, Mud."

Mud's eyes danced above a lopsided smile. "My, what a beauty you are. You're so grown up." He held his arms open for a hug and enfolded Peggy.

"Sit down, everyone. Soup's on." Mary hustled to the stove.

"Wash up, girls." Peg followed them to the sink. "I gave Jean permission to bring a kitten home when it's big enough."

"You have kittens?" Mud asked. "Save one for me."

"What are you doing up there in Montana to keep yourself out of trouble?" Peg teased.

"Spending a lot of time in my garden. I'll bring vegetables next time I come down. I grow way more than I can use."

Mary set the pot of vegetable beef soup on the table. "Why don't you bottle them?"

"I still have so much Marion bottled last fall before she passed." His voice cracked.

"I'm thinking of growing a kitchen garden in town," Peg changed the subject before they all got weepy. "Any garden advice for me?"

Mud took a big swig of milk. "Here's one trick I learned: When sowing onion seeds, mix in radish seeds. They germinate quicker than onions. Without radishes, the onion rows can't be seen for weeks. And remember to save your wood ashes for fertilizer."

"Good idea. How can I get rid of cutworms?"

"Mix one-pound Paris green with twenty pounds bran and one to two pints of molasses. But be sure to keep this away from chickens," he warned as he buttered a roll.

"Don't have chickens. I get eggs from Mom."

"Dear, you can have vegetables, too," Mary offered.

"I want the girls to learn to garden. Besides, I like to step out the door and pick right from the vine. But that cutworm recipe makes more than I'll need."

Mud tipped his soup bowl and slurped the last of the broth. "I'll bring you some next time I come."

Mary perked up. "When will that be?"

"Don't know. Maybe you and Mom better mix up a batch and share it. By the way, Mom, have you gotten one of those new Social Security checks yet?"

"No, I don't need it. Save it for people who do."

"That's not how it works. They won't get more if you don't draw it."

"Well, how much is it anyway?"

Mud wiped his chin with the back of his hand. "Seventeen-fifty."

Peg's head tilted. "Say, Mom, if you don't need it, why not collect it and give the money to someone who does?"

Mary's eyes widened. "Maybe I will."

CHAPTER 52

To combat the cold, Peg folded a wool quilt over the cracked leather seat of the train. She settled her girls and tucked a blanket around their legs. After squeezing into the seat across from them, she dug in her large bag and produced a new box of crayons and a coloring book. She handed the crayons to Peggy who tugged off her mittens, opened the box and ran her finger along the tops of the crayons, relishing the sharp tips. Jean took the coloring book, thumbed through it and tore out a page with a galloping horse saying, "Hand me the black one."

Peggy carefully plucked it from the box. She watched, hoping Jean wouldn't break it. "Don't push so hard," she warned, earning a scowl from her sister.

Peg stretched stout legs ending in white nurse's shoes under the girls's seat. *In these shoes, I can tromp through the city.* "Be careful, Jean." She handed the book to Peggy. "What do you want to color?"

Peggy chose a vase of flowers with a butterfly hovering in the background. She neatly outlined each object and colored it in. "I'm giving this to Grandma," she whispered to her mother as she meticulously signed her name.

"She'll love it," her mother winked.

Jean's head shot up. "Who'll love what?"

Peg yawned and tipped her head on the back of the seat. She closed her eyes. "Just never you mind."

With Christmas ten days away, few seats on the train remained empty. Excited shoppers flocked to the big city of Spokane in quest of the finest gifts and activities. Peg planned to meet her good friend Rose under the big clock of the Crescent Department Store where she worked. *Can't wait to see Rose. Seems a long time since their wedding. Wonder if they'll return after Henry finishes his engineering studies, but what would he do in Newport?*

Using her mitten, Peggy rubbed a peephole in the frosty window and peered out. Snow covered a small island in the Pend Oreille River and crept out along the edges. Patches of ice floated by in freezing water.

Peg dozed the rest of the ninety-minute trip. After rising at four each morning to prepare food for her boarders, working at the doctor's office, then coming home to feed everyone supper, she'd learned to take advantage of any moment to sleep.

"Mom, we're here!" Peggy tapped her mother's shoulder. Peg blinked. She sat up and touched the bodice of her dress, fingering the money she'd pinned inside. "Come on, girls. Gather your things. Let's go." *I wish I could afford to take them to the tearoom for lunch, but we'll grab an egg sandwich at the lunch counter.*

As they rounded the corner of Wall Street and Main, the creamy terra cotta Crescent Department Store with seven stories took Peggy's breath. She ran ahead to The Arcade on the first floor. Each white and gold trimmed window revealed a magical scene.

In the first window, a family gathered around an elaborate Christmas tree surrounded by gaily wrapped presents. The mannequin father stood under a golden mirror in black silk pajamas while the mother, dressed in a flowered bathrobe, looked on at the joyful scene. A boy mannequin in striped flannel pajamas stood by a shiny red bike with a toy dog and metal drum at his feet. His little sister held a Shirley Temple doll. The fireplace in the background flickered with lights, hiding beneath red cellophane. Peggy and Jean stood mesmerized.

"Come on, Sister!" Jean nudged Peggy to the next display. "It's Santa!" A live Santa sat next to his overflowing sled and waved at passersby. A line of children stretched into the store. "Can we see him? "Jean begged.

"Let's finish checking out the other windows first," Peg suggested. "He'll still be there when we're finished." The next display featured a winter mountain with children sledding and skiing. One mannequin sat on his bottom with his skis in the air. "He fell," Jean giggled before she jogged to the next scene.

In Santa's workshop, two elves with pointed ears and shoes bent over a workbench surrounded by shelves of toys. Three kewpie dolls waved from the seat of a wooden rocking horse. Colorful blocks rose into a skyscraper. Yoyos, bags of marbles, wooden farm and zoo animals, lead soldiers, and race cars filled shelves. The Betty Boop and paper dolls tugged at Peggy's heartstrings. Jean pressed her nose to the window, spellbound by a red steam shovel that worked a pile of sand. Nearby, Mickey Mouse kept company with Pinocchio in a little red wagon.

"Let's go, girls. There's one more." Peg took Jean's hand. A hushed crowd gazed in awe outside the last exhibition, revealing a nativity scene. Three elegant wise men held precious gifts. Next to the straw-filled manger, one worshiped the babe and bowed beside his camel. Mary and Joseph smiled softly. Two sheep and a donkey rested in the background. A kneeling shepherd touched his heart. Another shepherd held a baby lamb. A lit star hanging from the ceiling bathed the whole scene in gold as an angel flew from the ceiling. "This is the best one," Peggy whispered.

"Time to go," Peg broke the silence. "We have an hour until we meet Rose for lunch. Let's get you in that Santa line."

They climbed four steps to the entrance flanked by sparkling Christmas trees and opened heavy gold doors under two entwined crescent moons hugging a star, the store's logo. The design repeated in the rod iron railing around each floor of this shrine to elegance. On the first floor, rich mahogany walls complemented glass cabinets displaying goods. Peg checked the store's gigantic clock with four faces hanging from the ceiling: eleven o'clock. "Maybe the line's gone down. Rose will be on her lunch hour, so we can't be late."

After thirty minutes in line, the girls' turn to visit Santa finally came. Jean danced over and jumped on his lap. Peggy hesitated, then inched closer. A weary Santa peered over his frosted glasses. "And what do you want for Christmas?" he uttered for the hundredth time. Peg moved closer to listen.

Jean studied his beard. "Is that real? I want a horse, new roller skates and a dart board."

Santa chuckled. "Are you a tomboy?"

"No! I'm a girl." Jean bristled.

He beckoned to Peggy. "What would you like from Santa, pretty girl?"

Peggy hugged herself as she pictured wishes in her mind's eye. "A new dress and a doll with real hair and shoes, not painted on, one I can sew clothes for."

"You be good girls, and I'll see what I can do," he promised and gave them a peppermint stick which Peg commandeered and immediately hid in her purse.

"No candy until after lunch. Come along." She herded the girls back to the big clock.

Rose swept in wearing a cream two-piece dress with a slim skirt and crossover drop sleeve jacket. A small red flower on the wide dark brown belt called attention to her slim waist. The mink fur collar and matching hat screamed sophistication. When Rose removed her matching brown gloves, Peggy asked in complete awe, "Where did you get your outfit?"

"I fear we're underdressed," Peg admitted.

"Nonsense. Since I work in ladies' clothing, I need to dress up, and they give me a good discount. You're all fine!" Rose patted Jean's head. "What time's your reservation?"

Peg's eyes widened. "Reservation?"

"Yes, the Tea Room's packed this time of year."

"Oh, I thought we'd just eat at the lunch counter today."

"Too bad. The girls would love it, but we'll let them see it, and next time I'll make a reservation. My treat." Rose's high heels click clacked through the boys' department. "Have you shopped here before, girls?" They shook their heads. She led the way up a ramp to the soda fountain. "Well, you're in for a treat. After lunch, I'll give you the grand tour." Her face fell when she spotted the line. "Wait here. I know someone. Since I work here, they'll squeeze us in, so I won't be late after lunch." She handed her gloves to Peggy, "Hold these, will you?" and disappeared into the back. Peggy slid one hand inside a buttery glove and felt the luxury of the fabric.

Two minutes later, Rose returned, chatting with the hostess. "She can fit us in if the girls sit at the counter." When Peg hesitated, Rose flapped her hand. "They'll be fine. We'll sit in a booth close by."

The girls climbed onto the stools as Rose and Peg sat in a nearby booth. Peg kept an eye on her daughters. "Quit that twirling and read your menus. How about an egg salad sandwich? It's one of their specials." *And inexpensive. I need every penny for their gifts.*

"Order whatever you want. I'll buy," Rose proclaimed.

Did I say my worries aloud? "Oh no, Rose. I'll pay for us."

"No, it will be my Christmas present!" Rose insisted.

Gratitude filled Peg's heart. *What a good friend!* "Thanks, Rose. I'll make you and Henry a good home-cooked meal when you come to Newport."

"We'd love that. I'm afraid I've never learned to cook well. Always had a built-in cook: my mom and meals at the lumber camp. Maybe we can stay a few days and you can show me a few things to cook for dinner."

"Sure. I'm making dinner every night for the people who board with us anyway." Peg changed the subject. "How's the job?"

"Love it!" Rose gushed. "I think everyone who works here does. You can't believe the benefits." A blond waitress with a southern accent took their orders.

"What kind of benefits?" Peg asked.

Rose removed her hat and set it beside her on the seat. She smoothed her hair. "We're treated like family here. You should see the employees' restroom. It has a phonograph, records, games, books and magazines. I've made so many friends. We have sick benefits and discounts. There's even an onsite hospital that's free to employees."

Peg thought of her long workdays. *At least we have free visits at the doctor's office.* "A discount would be nice."

Rose's face brightened. "Put your purchases on my charge account. That way you can get my discount and pay me!"

"Thanks! But I don't want to charge anything."

"But if you paid for it today, it wouldn't be charging, would it?"

"That's very generous of you, Rose, but I don't think I will. I'm not buying much anyway."

"Suit yourself." Rose opened her handbag and brought out a gold filigree cigarette case.

"You smoke now?" Peg asked, somewhat shocked but remembered Rose's need for attention.

"Not that often. I hear from my friends that it's a good way to keep your weight down."

"Would you mind waiting until we're gone?" Peg asked apologetically. "I don't want the girls to get any ideas." Rose slid it back into her bag and removed her compact.

The cheerful young waitress brought their sandwiches. Rose powdered her nose. "Tell me all about Newport. How's your family?"

"They're all good. Mud's still struggling with his wife's death, but he's coping. I want to hear about your life. It's more exciting."

"Let me tell you about the store first in case we don't have time to explore it all. I work on the second floor in ready-to-wear. It's painted French gray with touches of gold. There's a baby shop, women's lingerie and the newest hats displayed in all the alcoves. I got this hat and collar on sale in the fur shop. When you buy furs, they allow you to store them during the hot months in the basement vault that keeps them at twenty degrees. In the men's wing, they have a special dressing room for surgical cases. You know, after the war . . . "

"They think of everything!" Peggy interrupted. She'd swiveled her stool to face the women and never touched her food.

"Yes," Rose continued, "there's even a playground on the roof."

"Can we go?" Jean begged.

"It's not open during winter, but if you come in the summer, you can," Rose explained.

"What's on the other floors?" Peggy begged for more.

Charmed by Peggy's fascination, Rose went on. "The third floor has gifts, bedding, rugs, drapes, furniture, luggage and things for the house. The new Davenport Hotel had the store furnish everything there! But the best part is the women's restroom. You can have your hair done, complexion treated or go into the silence room to rest."

"We'll go there next," Peg promised. "Now, if you want Rose to show you around, you need to finish your lunch."

Dazzled by the descriptions, Peggy asked, "What about floors four, five and six?

Rose took a sip of water and held her hand up to stop Peg's protest. "I'll be quick. The fourth floor has dishes, crystal, pottery, china. They stand out against the black enamel walls. The fifth floor has the mail order department, pianos and a free indoor golf range. They've given one side to the Eastern Washington Historical Society."

"A person could spend days here," Peg marveled in amazement.

"That's what they hope. The longer you stay, the more you'll spend."

Peggy jumped from her stool and hopped into the booth next to her mother. "And the sixth floor?"

"That's a surprise. After you finish your lunch, we'll go there." Peg nudged her daughter back toward the counter. She leaned across the table and whispered to Rose. "Can you take them, so I can purchase their Christmas?"

"Be happy to. It's fun to watch them so enthralled."

Peg whispered behind her hand. "I need to get Peggy a new dress, but what's the return policy?"

"No worries! There's a legend about a man who brought back four shirts twenty years after he purchased them and got refunded the full price!"

"She's never had a new store-bought dress. I redo hand-me-downs," Peg confided.

Jean popped over. "Can we go?"

"Let Rose eat. We've kept her too busy with questions!" Peg explained.

Rose motioned the waitress over. "Will you wrap this up for me?" She handed her the plate as she reassured Peg. "I'll eat it on my next break. Come along, girls." She replaced her hat and gloves and slipped her purse over her wrist. "We'll start on my floor. I'll ask my manager for a few more minutes. I'm sure he'll agree since I'm the top saleswoman.

And no man could ever tell you no, Peg thought. "Where should we meet?"

"How about the sixth floor? There's a continual fashion show in the auditorium and these shoes are killing me."

Peg glanced from her nurse's shoes to Rose's high heels but held her tongue. *I would never trade my shoes for impractical high fashion.* She scurried off to find the gifts on her list.

After taking the girls to the restroom, Rose got permission for a longer lunch and led the girls up to the sixth floor. "We'll start here." They lingered at the entrance to the Tea Room. Potted plants and wicker furniture created an outdoor feeling. They stepped in to see tables covered with linen tablecloths and set with fine china, silver and crystal. Fashion models, displaying the latest styles, paraded through the tables. In a nearby nursery, uniformed nurses tended shoppers' children.

"Come this way," Rose beckoned. They passed shoe repair, picture framing, stationery engraving and walked into the needlework area. "I know your mother and grandmother do handwork."

"I do, too!" Peggy and Jean both chimed.

They passed girls taking knitting and crocheting classes. "Why don't they just learn at home?" Jean asked.

"Not everyone's as talented as your mother," Rose replied. "Come over here. I love seeing all the different buttons. They offer made-to-order buttons."

"Grandma lets us string buttons from her box," Jean reported.

Peg found the perfect dress for Peggy. Even better, the tag said forty percent off. She knew her daughter would love the lace bodice and lifted the fabric to inspect the tulle underskirt. *There's a lot of goods in this dress.* She put the pink chiffon creation under her arm and took it to the register. The clerk placed it carefully in a box lined with tissue paper. Peg scanned the area. She turned her back to extract the money pinned inside her dress. Nothing. She patted her chest and tried not to panic. *Where is it? How will I buy Christmas? What will I do now?* Her heart dropped. *I've saved all year and it's gone!*

The clerk cleared her throat. "May I help the next customer, please?"

Peg blushed. "Yes, would you hold this for a few minutes? I seem to have misplaced my money. I'll retrace my steps." She fled back to the lunch counter, eyes glued to the floor with every step. Nothing. A husky young man with a bucket and mop wiped up footprints. She stopped to inquire, "Did you find any money on the floor a few minutes ago?"

He shook his head, but tried to help, "You could try the lost and found on the first floor."

"Thanks!" Peg sprinted down the stairs. Three people waited in front of her. She tapped her foot. *I hope she holds that dress. It's the only one in Peggy's size!* She finally got to the front of the line. "Hello, I seem to have misplaced my money. Has anyone turned some folded dollar bills in?

The frazzled clerk didn't look up. "No."

"Are you sure? Can you please check again?"

"Nothing to check. I think I'd know. I've been here since we opened."

My misfortune has become someone's fortune. May as well go home. There's no reason to keep shopping now. She plodded up the stairs to the sixth floor.

Rose noticed her crestfallen face. "What happened?"

"I pinned my money to my slip, but it's gone," a dejected Peg reported.

"Oh no! Did you go back and search for it?"

"'Fraid so. I even checked the lost and found."

"Charge what you need to me," Rose suggested. "I know you're good for it and I have thirty days to pay off the account."

"No, I'll figure something out. She fell into the chair next to Jean and closed her eyes in an effort to mask her disappointment.

After a few minutes, she swallowed her sorrow and touched Peggy's arm who sat entranced by another fashion show. "We need to leave after this one," she whispered.

The emcee described the next dress. "Our model Roxanne looks so elegant in a tea dress that is dressy enough for semi-formal occasions. The ivory crochet lace draws the eyes to the flattering V neck. Notice how the charming peplum mirrors the capelet collar. The narrow belt emphasizes our model's petite waistline. You'll be the talk of town in this dress."

Peg rolled her eyes.

CHAPTER 53

"How'd the girls enjoy the trip?" Dr. Phillips asked when Peg arrived at work the next day.

"They loved it. Rose met us for lunch and gave us the grand tour of The Crescent. What a store! They have a children's playground inside with a slide, seesaw, rocking horses and a merry-go-round. They've thought of everything!"

"Good thing you went yesterday. Heard there's a big storm headed this way tonight." He picked up the clipboard from Mrs. Simms and headed to the examination room.

After the doctor left, Mrs. Simms noticed a change in Peg's demeanor. "Things go okay on the trip?"

"They did until I lost my Christmas money," Peg confessed. "I sure wish I hadn't let Peggy open that box of hand-me-downs from Freda. I could have remade a dress for her."

"Need a loan?" the nurse asked.

"No. Thanks, anyway." Peg plodded to the back room.

As soon as Peg exited the main office, Mrs. Simms had an idea. She picked up the phone.

Mrs. Block entered the waiting room, holding the baby abandoned on her doorstep. Her two preschool children trailed behind. She held the door open. "Come in, kids. We're letting the heat out." Their chubby cheeks, pink with cold, gave Mrs. Simms an unusual desire to pinch them.

"Good morning, Shirley. How's the baby doing? Any word from her parents?"

Mrs. Block grabbed the two-year-old's collar as he tried to climb to the top of the counter. "No word. But the bank called to let me know about the deposit last Tuesday. One hundred dollars! Can you believe that? A baby doesn't need that much."

Mrs. Simms pressed her lips together. "Your time's worth something, too, you know. Someone trusts you to take good care of his little girl."

"Well, I've fallen in love with her." She carefully removed a hand-knit cap, exposing dark curls. "We all have. But the money sure helps make ends meet 'round our house. Don't think I could have brought little Jimmy to the doctor without it."

Sucking his thumb, her five-year-old son slumped over a chair in the waiting room. His flushed face made the nurse suspect fever. "Bring him back and we'll check his temperature." Mrs. Simms opened the hall door and took the baby while the mother collected her two boys, one lively and one lethargic. Peg helped the sick boy onto the examination table. Dr. Phillips washed his hands, then rolled his stool over to the boy.

"Good morning, Shirley. How's the baby?" he asked as Peg shook down the thermometer and placed it in the sick boy's mouth.

"She's fine. But Jimmy here has a fever and just isn't himself."

"Well, let's see what we can find out," Peg stated as she removed the thermometer and held it for the doctor to see. One hundred and three degrees! "He has a fever all right. OK, Little Man, let me check your throat." Peg handed the doctor a tongue depressor. He took a little flashlight from the pocket of his white coat. "Open your mouth and say, Aw." The little boy whimpered. "How long has he been sick?"

"Since Saturday. He doesn't want to play, eat or drink. He says his head and ears hurt." The doctor listened to his heart. The boy cried out as he felt along his jaw and down his neck. He patted Jimmy's hand and rolled his stool back. "Well, we have a classic case of mumps here."

"Mumps! Isn't he kinda young for that?"

"No, they often occur in children." He felt below Jimmy's ears. "His parotid glands here are swollen."

"Are my other kids at risk?"

"Maybe. The incubation period's two to three weeks. Watch for symptoms like Jimmy's. It's best to isolate him. Mumps is a virus spread by respiratory droplets, so wash your hands often. Give him plenty of fluids and only soft foods. Place warm or cool compresses on his face, whichever will make him feel better. The disease runs its course in ten days."

Dr. Phillips washed his hands again. The two-year-old ran to the examining stool and began pushing it about. The doctor patted his head. "This guy seems fine, but while you're here, let's examine the baby. Peg, will you bring her back?"

Peg returned to the front office to find Mrs. Simms rocking and humming to the little girl. "It's mumps."

"I wondered. His face seemed puffy." She gave her attention to the baby who cooed. "Aren't you the sweetest thing?"

Peg held her arms out. "Doctor wants to check her over." She brought her back to her mother. "What did you name her?"

"Celestia. She's a gift from heaven."

"That's fitting. Ever find out who the parents are?"

"Not a clue."

I'd get to the bank and find out who's depositing money for Mrs. Block. Surely, Ben's thought of that.

After work, Peg stopped by the sheriff's office. "Ben, can you access bank records?"

"Not without a warrant from a judge. Why?"

"Mrs. Block said someone put a hundred dollars in her bank account. That's how we can find out who the baby's father is!"

"It's not a crime to deposit money in someone's account."

"Can you ask at the bank?"

Ben pushed some papers into his top drawer and locked it. "That's confidential. The bank won't tell you about an account you don't own."

Peg's brow furrowed. "How can we find out?"

"We can't. Some things are best left alone."

"But what if someone shows up and tries to take the baby back? Mrs. Block would be devastated!"

CHAPTER 54

Jean peeked out the window the next morning and squealed, "Yes! Where's my boots?" Last night's storm brought a foot of fresh snow that twinkled in the sun. "Come on, Sister! Get your snow clothes!"

As Jean grabbed her wool coat, her red mittens trailed from a crocheted chain that ran between the sleeves to keep them from getting lost. "Where's my hat? Where's the sled? Ready yet?"

Peg caught her by the shoulders. "Hold 'er, Newt! Breakfast first."

Jean gobbled her oatmeal while Peggy sipped some apple juice. "Let's go, Peggy!"

"It's not gonna melt. Hold yer horses." Peggy patted her mouth with a napkin.

"After you do the dishes, you can go to the hill by Blocks's house. Sleds are in the shed." Peg took the leftover cereal off the stove. "Don't forget to feed the chickens. Here, give them this oatmeal." She handed Jean the pot.

Jean scowled.

When the girls approached the sledding hill, children's laughter and screams spilled through the air. "Wait." Peggy grabbed the back of Jean's coat. "Did you see that massive icicle?" She pointed at the back porch of the Blocks's house.

Jean took off at a trot. "Let's sword fight!" she shouted over her shoulder. A giant icicle hung almost to the ground. Jean broke it off and hit the icicle clinging to the eave. It landed in the soft snow with a muffled thud.

Mrs. Block opened the back door to investigate. At her frown, Peggy drew back. She stepped between her little sister and Mrs. Block. "Sorry! Come on, Jean."

"Careful there, girls. One might land on your head." Mrs. Block hugged herself against the cold as two little boys' heads peeked out the door beside her. "No, Jimmy!" She caught hold of the little boy's pajamas. "You're still sick. Shut the door."

While the girls sledded, Peg took the opportunity to run errands. When she passed the library, she stepped in. *I doubt they have anything, but it's worth a try.* The smell of musty books stuffed into the library's few shelves filled the room. She stepped to the desk. "Do you have any books on foundlings?"

Mrs. Steckler pushed her glasses up her nose and peered up at Peg. "Say again?"

"Foundlings, children abandoned on doorsteps, left at churches and hospitals."

Mrs. Steckler's old fashioned shoes clopped over the wooden floor, past the hand lettered "Quiet, please!" sign next to the card catalog. "What subject would that be listed under?" she muttered. After flipping through the cards for a few minutes, she shook her head. "You'll have to try the library in Spokane."

Playing in the snow set Peggy thinking of Alaska. *Are we ever going back? Will I ever see Dad again?* She'd resolved to ask her mother when she got home but waited until after dinner dishes.

"Mom?"

Peg finished squeezing water from the mop. "Yes, dear?"

"Are we ever going to go back to Alaska?"

Peg froze. *I dreaded this, and I still don't know how to answer.* "Why? Do you miss it?"

"A little. But will we ever see Dad again?"

"I guess that depends on him. It's a long way and I don't know if he can leave work."

Peggy mulled that over as she dried the plates and placed them in the cupboard. She poured the water out of the dishpan, wiped off the cupboard, then asked, "What's a grass widow?"

Peg dropped the mop. "Why?"

"Today while sledding, I heard Pearl's mother say you're a grass widow."

Might as well let her know. "A grass widow is a woman who is separated or divorced from her husband. Are kids teasing you?"

"Which one are you?"

Jean piped up, "Chester told us that we didn't have a dad, but I told him, 'Everyone does, Dummy!'"

Peg pushed the mop bucket back. "Come into the front room." The girls followed. Peg sat and patted the davenport. "Come sit by me, Peggy." Jean climbed onto her lap. "What do you remember about Alaska?"

"I remember lots of fish!" Jean exclaimed. "Remember when I caught that big one and Dad helped me reel it in? Did you take a picture?" She craned her neck to see her mother's face.

"I sure do. When I get some extra money, I'll have the film developed, and we'll see if I have that photo."

Peggy cringed. "I hated touching fish but loved riding in the sled with Kid."

Her comment brought a memory to Peg. "When you were a toddler, we made a big woven willow basket to carry you in.

Kid tied it on the sled in front of me and you squealed with excitement when we took off. You know, I think the fishermen enjoyed you almost as much as we did. When you turned four, one of them told you if you put salt on a sea gull's tail, you could catch one. I found that out when I found my broken saltshaker."

Peggy giggled, "I remember that! I never could come close enough to shake salt on one, so I threw the shaker at it."

"I miss fishing," Jean admitted.

"We'll go when it warms up. I promise. I miss eating fresh fish, but the best meat we ate came from Dahl sheep." Peg closed her eyes. "I remember when our Norwegian friend Helmar shot a sheep way up on the mountain. He climbed up, tied the feet of the sheep together, shoved his arms through and skied down with it on his back!"

"But I do like playing with my cousins here," Jean changed the subject.

Thank you, Jean. "At your age, I loved being with my cousins, too! Our favorites were the Rauchs. We saw them often because they lived a mile away. Sometimes, we got to ride the train to see Uncle Will Long and his family in Ferdinand, Idaho. They lived on a large wheat ranch near the Nez Perce Indian Reservation. Mud and I always worried about getting scalped when we visited.

Uncle Will had a huge arrowhead collection that he'd picked up while plowing his fields. We enjoyed listening to other uncles, John Long and Jesse Bracher, tell war stories about fighting the Indians in the Nez Perce War."

"Tell us a war story!" Jean begged.

"Why did we fight them?" Peggy asked.

"Well, it's complicated, but they raided and killed settlers in the Wallowa Valley."

"Did our uncles kill some Indians?" Jean persisted.

Peg hesitated, "You know, I don't remember. Too long ago."

"Could we go visit and ask them to tell us the stories?" Peggy suggested.

"No, Honey. They died years ago." *I miss those carefree days.*

CHAPTER 55

A short wiry stranger with a wide boxer's nose strode into Kelly's Bar and Grill. He paused to study the ornate tin plate ceiling, then hopped onto a bar stool. The curious regulars watched. Vernon, who saw an opportunity for a free drink, crept over and eased next to the stranger. He greeted him with "You're not from 'round here" and a toothless grin.

"Nope."

"Where ya from?"

"All over."

The old man licked his lips. "Me too, until I landed a job at a lumber mill here. Whaddya do?"

The stranger took a swig and warmed to his tale. "Used to do a bit in the ring down in Los Angeles until I met my match." He stared into the distance, recalling the scene. "Nearly busted a gut."

"What happened?"

"He knocked me out. Rising star, he was. Yes, siree, Little Pancho, younger brother of Pancho Villa, Flyweight World Champion. Some guy gave me a bum steer on a match against him and I bet all my savings. Later, I watched him slay a boxer named Small Montana. Now, that was a fight!"

"You still box?"

"Sometimes. Got a boxing place here?"

"Nope. But sometimes there's matches at Fid's Opera House."

"They fill up?"

"Sure thing!" Vernon eyed his drink. "Maybe you could sponsor an exposition."

He rubbed his chin. "Hum, maybe I could. Sell tickets. Earn some money. I can whip anyone in my weight class."

In the corner, the regulars snickered among themselves. "Hard to find a man that small," one proclaimed in a stage whisper.

The boxer's face turned red. He tensed and whipped around. "I can take any one of you!" He jumped from the stool with raised fists.

Curtis, a giant of a man, came from behind the bar and stood in front of him. "Clear out," he calmly demanded. When Sheriff Ben Fox walked in, the boxer noticed his badge, glanced back and forth between the sheriff and Curtis and slunk out with his tail between his legs.

"Know that little fella?" the sheriff asked.

Vernon's shoulders sagged. "Braggart with a real temper."

"Napoleon complex," Curtis added.

Vernon studied the situation and gulped the rest of the boxer's drink.

Sheriff Fox sat next to Vernon. "Get his name?"

"Nope," he burped loudly.

Ben turned to Curtis who busied himself restocking bottles. "Curtis, have you seen any other strangers here lately?"

"Couple came in yesterday."

He pulled a little notebook from his front pocket. "Can you give me a description?"

The boxer grimaced, swallowed hard and tramped down the street into the Tarbet store. Mary heard the bell and came from the back room. "Hello, may I help you?" Chief growled, being disturbed from his nap.

"Maybe."

"Do you know where the Block family lives?"

A chill ran down Mary's spine. She grabbed Chief by the collar. "Not far from here. Can I help you with something?"

"Just the directions, please." Chief broke away and sniffed at his ankles. He reached down and continued petting the dog's head. Chief rolled onto his back, exposing his stomach. The stranger rubbed the dog.

Mary searched for receipt paper in the cash register to draw him a map.

The mystery of the Block baby kept nibbling at Peg's thoughts. Ben's advice "Some things are best left alone" wasn't helping. *Why can't I quit worrying about it? I guess I don't want someone to take that baby back. I'll stop by on my way home.*

Peg knocked. Mrs. Block shot a furtive glance out the window. Peg knocked again. "Mrs. Block? It's me, Peg," she called. The door cracked open. Mrs. Block's tear-stained face peeked out. "What's going on? What happened? Why are you crying?"

She shooed her two little boys into their room to play. "A man came by," she whispered.

Peg took her hand. "What did he want?"

Her lips quivered. "Money."

"Money? Why?"

She broke down. "He claimed he knew Celestia's parents and . . . wanted money . . . not to tell them where their baby is. Do you think he'll come back? She's my baby, right?" She wailed. Her wretched expression broke Peg's heart. Mrs. Block fell to her knees and sobbed, "I'll die if they take her!"

Peg put her hand on her shoulder and thought aloud. "That will probably be up to a judge, but they did abandon her." *I think, but I'll do whatever it takes to keep that baby here.*

"But why . . . why . . . does someone pay for her keep?" Mrs. Block wondered.

"I don't know, Mrs. Block, but I aim to find out. Don't open the door to anyone. I'm headed to the sheriff's office. Do you want me to take the baby with me?"

"Yes, please, keep her safe." Peg followed the woman to her bedroom where she lifted the sleeping baby from her crib and placed her in Peg's arms. "Wait a minute." She dashed to the kitchen with tears dripping from her chin, brought a bottle and caught Peg's arm. "What if her parents show up?"

"She won't be here. They'll have to prove that they're her parents. Try not to worry. I'll keep her with me. Can you pack diapers, too?"

Mrs. Block's head bowed as her shoulders trembled. She wrapped her arms around herself. When she looked up, desperation showed in her eyes. "Do you think he'll come back? I don't know what to do."

Peg had an idea. "Why not pack up the boys and come with me? My mom has lots of room. I'll bet you could stay there until this gets sorted out."

"You think so?" A wave of relief poured over her and some of the panic faded from her eyes. "Oh, thank you! Just let me gather a few things."

Peg hustled the Block family in the back door of the house and led them into the kitchen. "Do you boys want a cookie? Wait here with your mom for a minute."

Mary heard voices and rose from her chair by the fire. Peg met her, motioned Mary to the hall and explained Mrs. Block's situation. As Mary listened, her eyebrows knit and eyes widened, then narrowed. "Of course, she can stay with me. You know I had a bad feeling about that man when he asked for directions to her house," she confessed, "but I couldn't think of a reason not to give them to him. I'm so sorry!"

Peg whipped around. "You saw him?"

Mary backpedaled. "Well, yes, if it's the same man who came into the store today."

"Can you describe him?"

"Small fellow with a bigger nose, like it had been broken. He didn't buy anything. Just asked for directions to the Blocks," Mary reported meekly.

Mrs. Block overheard and started weeping again.

"Lock the doors, Mom. I'm going to talk to Ben." Peg lifted a rifle resting on the elk horns by the back door and handed it to her mother. "Keep this ready." Mary grabbed the gun and shooed Peg on her way.

Peg trotted off. *I'd better check on my girls first.*

Peggy peeled potatoes at the sink. Jean set out seven bowls, glasses and sets of silverware on the worn kitchen table. "Do you ever get tired of company?" she asked her sister.

"The boarders help Mom pay the rent."

"I know. That's not what I asked," Jean fired back.

"Sometimes, I wish it was only us for dinner, but I remember how hard Mom works."

Jean dropped a fork. "But that ol' maid Miss Pratt isn't even supposed to eat with us. She gets on everyone's nerves the way she goes on about her students."

"She's probably lonely," Peggy guessed. "Come peel these carrots. We need to start the stew."

Peg threw the door open. "Oh, good. You're here and dinner's about ready. I've got to run over to talk with Ben." She grabbed one of the carrots and nibbled. "Do you have your homework done?"

"Not yet," Jean hated to admit.

"Do it while dinner cooks and I'll play pinochle with you after," Peg promised.

Peggy threw the potato peels into the compost bucket. "Why do you have to talk to Ben?"

"Nothing you need to worry about. Please help Jean with her math if she needs it." Peg went into her bedroom, slid the pistol from her nightstand into her coat pocket and trotted off.

Sheriff Fox's stomach rumbled. He glanced up at the clock and began to clean off his desk. When the office door opened, he paused as Peg huffed in. "Hello, Peg."

"Ben, do you know who that stranger in town is?"

"What stranger are you talking about? Grab a chair, sit down and catch your breath."

Peg dropped onto a chair. "A man came into the store. He asked Mom where the Blocks live. She drew him a map! He demanded money from Mrs. Block and threatened to tell the baby's parents where to find her if she didn't comply. Peg's hands shot into the air. Then she grabbed her heart and cried, 'Do you think he's after the baby?'"

The sheriff scratched the stubble on his face. "I'll bet he's after money. There's no proof he even knows the baby's parents. But I can arrest him for attempted blackmail."

"Will you? I'm just so worried for Mrs. Block." Peg shuddered. If someone tried to take away one of my girls . . ." She fingered the gun in her pocket.

CHAPTER 56

Christmas is next week and I'm not ready, Peg worried as she walked to work. *If only I hadn't lost my money in Spokane. I may have to borrow some from Mom, but I hate to do that!* She drew her coat tighter to her chest. *I so wanted that dress I saw at The Crescent Department Store for Peg.* A graveyard of old bikes and cars lay hidden in the snow behind the junkyard fence. *I wonder if there's a bike in there I could fix up for Jean.* The morning sun kindled a flame behind the mountain. By the time Peg arrived, the peaks burst on fire.

Mrs. Simms peered over the counter as the bell over the door jingled. Her lips pressed together and the corners of her mouth twitched up when she saw Peg. An old man with a craggy appearance sat in the waiting room along with Mrs. Block, her son Jimmy and baby Celestia.

Jimmy gave Peg a toothy grin. "Well, Jimmy, you must be feeling better!" Peg crouched next to him.

"I am!" he replied.

"And how's your sister?" Mrs. Block drew the blanket back to reveal a contented baby.

"She's good," he answered as he held his finger out for the baby to grab.

Peg knew the dark circles under Mrs. Block's drawn face stemmed from a lack of sleep. The baby lost interest in Jimmy's finger and focused on a mole on her mother's arm. "We'll talk in the back," Peg whispered.

Mrs. Simms opened the door to the hall. "We're ready for you, Mrs. Block. Peg, stop by my office before you go home."

Mrs. Block gathered her children and followed Peg to the examination room.

"Climb up here, Jimmy." Peg patted the examination table and asked Mrs. Block, "Are you getting any rest? Where's little Tommy?"

"Your sweet mother's watching him. Thanks for taking us there. I feel so much better not being alone."

"I felt so bad when I heard Mr. Block didn't come back from the war. That must have been hard for you." Peg patted her back with compassion.

Tears welled in Mrs. Block's eyes. "I don't think I can lose someone else. She's helped fill that hollow place for the boys and me. If they take this baby . . ."

"Ben and I are working on that," Peg replied confidently. *But we've made no progress and I can't promise you we can help you keep that baby!*

Dr. Phillips opened the door. "Well then, let's have a look at you. Can you open your mouth for me?" While he examined the boy, Peg's mind raced. *Maybe I need to talk to a lawyer. I'll see if Ben found out anything about the man who tried blackmail. I'll ask Dad about finding out who's putting money in the bank. Hold on . . . Dad's gone.*

"Right, Peg?" Dr. Phillips waited for an answer.

Peg jerked back. "What's that?"

"Just telling Jimmy that he's right as rain. And he won't get mumps again." He patted the top of the boy's head and helped him jump down from the table. "How's that little girl?"

"But I can't pay for another exam today," Mrs. Block protested.

"On the house." He reached for the baby. "Peg, will you weigh and measure Jimmy? After that, let him choose a prize."

She reached for his hand. "Come on, Buddy. Let's go see what's in the treasure box."

At five o'clock, Peg kicked off her shoes and plopped into a chair. Her feet hurt. Mrs. Simms's shoes squeaked down the hall. She stuck her head into the room. "I have something for you up front. Don't forget to stop by before you take off."

Peg rubbed her calf. "Need to rest a minute before I trek home. I've been thinking about little Celestia. I'd like to find a way to make sure no one can take her away from Mrs. Block."

"I have a nephew who's a lawyer in Seattle. Do you want his phone number?"

Peg jumped up. "I do!" She followed Mrs. Simms to the front desk and took down the information.

"Wait." Mrs. Simms went to the storage room and returned with a box. "Here, this is for you."

"What is it?" Peg puzzled. She lifted the lid to see the delicate pink dress from The Crescent. "How did you know? How did you get it here?" she choked back tears.

Mrs. Simms glowed. "Let's just say you have friends."

"How much do I owe you?"

"Nothing. I didn't pay for it and you don't have to."

Peg's brow wrinkled. "Rose?"

"There's more under that," Mrs. Simms reported and grinned.

Peg lifted the fancy dress. Underneath were several items: the sailor dress she wanted for Jean, socks, two slips and two pairs of gloves. Her chin quivered.

CHAPTER 57

The whole Tarbet family gathered at the Tarbet homestead for Christmas. An eight-foot Christmas tree Peg had cut from their own land shimmered over a house full of excited children and a kitchen full of tantalizing smells. Mary had baked cookies, pies, cakes and rolls for days. Peg savored each mouthful as she lounged on the braided rug in front of the fireplace. *Cinnamon rolls make me miss Gene. He's been gone for almost six years. At least we have his daughter Betty. I love that she's my Peg's age. I'll tell her all about you, Gene. She'll never forget her dad.*

Gravel crunched and popped. Freda and Ben, arms full of gifts, struggled up the back step. Mary flung the door open. "Merry Christmas! Here, let me take some of those for you." She relieved Freda of two large presents. "See if you can find a spot to light. With twenty grandchildren, we're in a hubbub, but I love it. Do you want a snack to hold you until dinner?"

"When Mud has children, we'll have some real yayhoos around here." Freda set down her last package and patted Mud's shoulder. He answered with a loud sneeze.

"Gesundheit." Mary bustled over. "Poor Mud's fighting a cold. Here, Honey." She fished a handkerchief from her bosom.

Peg heard and loped into the kitchen. "You finally made it!"

Ben removed his hat and beat it against his leg, sending snow crystals into the air. "Sorry, I got held up at the office."

"You have to work on Christmas?" Mary questioned.

"Got a call from Seattle. Guess that little boxer in town who bothered Mrs. Block was discovered dead."

Peg grabbed his arm. "How did they know to call you?"

"Found a paper with Mrs. Block's name and address in his pocket. Guy had a rap sheet. He's a documented drifter who gathered trouble like a hen gathering her chicks."

Mary clucked her tongue. "But what about the baby? Why did he try to blackmail Mrs. Block?"

"Long story," Ben admitted as he sat at the table and took a bite of a gingerbread cookie while the rest of the adults gathered around.

"Well, go on!" Peg urged.

"The baby belongs to the unmarried daughter of a bootlegger named Hollister who sent the boxer to check on the baby and deliver moonshine. Blackmailing the mother's probably what got him killed."

"Why would someone from Seattle choose to bring the baby here to little Newport? And why did he choose Mrs. Block?" Peg wondered aloud.

Mary handed Ben a glass of milk. He took a swig and continued, "Turns out Hollister served with Mr. Block in the war. Block shared the letters from his wife, and Hollister could tell that Mrs. Block was a fine mother."

"Did he know she's a widow?" Freda asked.

Ben's brow wrinkled. "Not sure. Maybe, since he sent money."

"Well, since they're criminals, surely a judge would award custody of the baby to Mrs. Block," Mary commented, expressing a sense of relief.

Ben brushed crumbs from his face. "You'd think, but that'll be up to the courts."

"But since the Twenty-First Amendment got ratified, alcohol is no longer illegal. Can they be prosecuted?" Mud asked.

"I've got the name of a lawyer from Mrs. Simms," Peg suggested.

Mud sat up straight. "How can Mrs. Block afford a lawyer? Ben, do you know who murdered the boxer?"

CHAPTER 58

The sodden soil of spring finally gave birth. White blossoms burst on Indian plum shrubs. Apple orchards buzzed with life. Crocus and tulips resurrected from winter graves. Overhead, Canadian geese honked north in their familiar V formation.

On the front lawn, Peggy set a little wooden table with play dishes. She placed a Shirley Temple doll at the head. Ping, ping, ping. Nearby, Jean hit a ball attached to a paddle with an elastic string. "Here you go, Jean. I'll get the food for our tea party."

"Twenty-seven, twenty-eight, twenty-nine, thirty," Jean counted her hits. When she heard someone approach, she turned expecting Peggy with the food. A man drew near. He smiled. Jean smiled back. Hands full, Peggy pushed open the screen door with her shoulder and eased down the steps, watching her feet so as not to spill the lemonade on the tray.

"Hello there, girls. Your mother home?"

Peggy's head jerked up. She hesitated. *I don't want to admit that we're here alone.* She hugged the tray to her chest. "She's busy. Can I help you?"

"I can wait a few minutes."

Oh no! Peggy set down the tray of food, leaned close to Jean and hissed in her ear, "Don't say anything!" then looked up at the stranger. "Can I take a message? She's napping and told us not to wake her."

Jean stared at her sister with a question on her face. Peggy pinched her arm.

"Well, have a good day," he bowed and swept off his hat, liberating a mass of red curls. "I'll catch her later."

Peggy watched until he got to the corner and grabbed Jean's arm.

"Ouch! You're hurting me! What are you doing?"

"Get in the house!" Peggy dragged her along.

"But I don't want to go in. What about our tea party?" Jean whined, still not understanding.

Peggy forced her up the stairs, shut and locked the front door. She drew the curtains.

"What's going on?" Jean demanded.

Peggy lifted the corner of the curtain, stared and peered down the street. "I'll bring the party inside."

"But I wanted to have it outside!"

"Stay here," Peggy directed as she scurried out the back door to gather the tray and doll. She trotted back to the house and locked the door.

"Who was that man?" Jean asked.

"I don't know, but NEVER tell a man we are here alone. There are bad people out there," Peggy warned.

"What kind of bad people?"

"All kinds. Eat your food while I call Mom."

"It's no fun now," Jean pouted. "You're only two years older than me, you know." Peggy held her tongue. She went to the kitchen and picked up the phone.

"Number, please."

"Dr. Phillips's office."

The operator, who knew everyone in the small town, sensed Peggy's panic and asked, "Is someone sick, Peggy?"

"No, we're fine. I just need to talk to my mom for a minute."

"Just a minute, dear." She plugged the cord into Dr. Phillips's exchange on the switchboard connecting the two.

Brring, Brring. Mrs. Simms swung around in her chair to pick up the other end, "Dr. Phillips's office."

"Mrs. Simms, this is Peggy. I need to talk to my mom."

"She's with a patient. Can I help you?"

Should I tell her? He's gone. Maybe this is silly. "We are fine. Have her call us when she has a minute, please."

"Will do. Enjoy Christmas?"

"Wonderful! I got the most amazing new dress."

"How nice." Mrs. Simms smiled, knowingly. "Well, I'll have her call you."

"Thanks." Peggy replaced the mouthpiece and sagged onto a kitchen chair. "Jean, are you still here?"

In the other room, Jean's eyes rolled and mouth twisted. "Yes, Madam."

Peggy placed her elbows on the table and rested her chin on her clasped hands. *He didn't feel like a bad person. Maybe that story I heard the adults discussing about the dead boxer made me nervous. But "better safe than sorry," Mother always says.*

"Someone's coming!" Jean called.

Peggy's heart skipped a beat. She dashed to the window, "Who?"

Jean pushed the curtain aside and pointed down the street. A man with a military bearing, too far away to be recognized, headed their way. The phone rang.

"Do NOT open the door," Peggy warned as she dashed to the phone. "Hello?"

"Hi, Honey. What's up?" Peg asked.

Someone tried the doorknob, then knocked sharply. Peggy dropped the phone and ran to the door. Peggy's fear spread to Jean who ducked behind the worn overstuffed chair.

"Anyone home?" the man called and knocked again.

The phone receiver swung by its cord in the kitchen. "Peggy? Peggy? Peggy!" her mother yelled.

Peggy peeked under the curtain. The man turned her way. She let out a sob and fell onto the davenport.

"Peggy? What's the matter? Open the door!" Mud demanded, his face a map of grim lines.

Peggy turned the lock, opened the door and fell into his arms.

He stiffened and scanned the room. Seeing nothing amiss, he pushed Peggy back and studied her, "What's going on here?"

Embarrassed, Peggy wiped her cheek with the back of her hand. "We're okay. We were out on the front lawn. A man I don't know stopped and asked for Mother. I got spooked." Jean's head popped out from behind the chair. She edged out.

"Did he tell you his name? Describe him for me."

"Tall, freckles and lots of red hair."

Mud motioned Jean over. She climbed on his lap and hugged him fiercely. "How did you know to come?"

"I'd stopped into the office when you called. Your mom asked me to come by to check on you." He patted her head. "Tell me more about the man. Did he say his name?"

Peggy shook her head. "Wait! Mom's on the phone." She ran back to the kitchen.

"Mom?"

The operator answered. "Peggy, everything okay? When you didn't answer, your mom headed home."

"We're fine. Mud's here with us. Thanks. We spooked ourselves."

"OK, you know I'm always here if you need me," she offered.

"Thank you." Peggy hung up the phone.

Peg stormed in. When she saw Jean on Mud's lap, she let the pistol fall back into her jacket pocket and bent over to catch her breath. Peggy blushed. "I'm sorry, Mom."

"About what?" Peg fell onto the davenport. "What happened?"

Peggy's chin quivered. Jean sprung off Mud's lap. "A man came down the street while we played outside. He asked for you. Peggy lied. Told him you were sleeping."

Relief spread over her mother. "That's good. Have you seen him before? What did he want?"

"He said he'd catch you later," Jean reported.

Mud cleared his throat. "How about I drop the girls at the store with Grandma? I need to pick up a few things."

"Great idea!" Peg responded, "I'll come with you. Let's go." Peg opened the door and caught the back of Mud's shirt. "Need to talk," she whispered. He moved closer. Holding hands, the girls ran ahead. "Stay where we can see you!" Peg commanded. She turned to Mud, "What do you think?"

"From Peggy's description, it may have been Charlie who came by."

Peggy blanched. "What would HE want?"

CHAPTER 59

Charlie sucked his lips in, clasped his hands behind his back and kicked at the dust. *What a stupid idea! I think I scared her girls. I don't even know what I would have said if Peg had been home. I'm still married, at least in name. What am I going to do? I need to see her and talk like we used to.*

After picking up his order at the feed store, he headed to the Tarbet store. As he hit the brakes, the old truck shimmied to a stop. From his shirt pocket, he took out the shopping list from his mother. *Maybe I'll get to see Mary. She makes me feel important.* He opened the door and froze.

Jean turned around when the bell jingled. She plucked her mom's sleeve, "Mama, that's him," she whispered.

Peg turned. *So it was Charlie.* She put her arm around Jean. Her heart thumped.

"Hello, Charlie!" Mary came around the counter and gave him a hug. "Long time, no see." She grabbed his arms, tilted her head back and studied his face, "You're looking good. How's Belle?"

Peg swallowed hard. *Thank you, Mother!*

"I *feel* good," Charlie raised his voice for Peg's benefit. He straightened his back and gave Mary his list. "Mom needs these things, please."

Mary studied the list. "I think we have it all. Give me a minute to gather it for you."

"Grandma, can I help?" Jean asked.

"Of course." She handed Jean the paper. "What is this first word on the list?"

Jean sounded it out, "Line-a-mint?"

"Liniment," Mary corrected. "People rub it on their sore muscles. See that red bottle over there that says Watkins?" Jean hopped over to the shelf.

Charlie cleared his throat. "It's for Dad, not me. He's got arthritis."

Peg forced a smile. "Hi, Charlie. The girls said you stopped by. Did you need something?"

Just you. "Belle wants to know if Peggy can come over sometime after school," Charlie lied.

"She's in the back. Let me check." *And gather my wits.* Peg ducked into the office where Peggy worked on her homework. "Peggy, that man who came by is my old friend, Charlie, Belle's father."

Peggy's eyes widened. "I'm so sorry, Mom."

"You didn't know. You did the right thing." She sat on the desk. "He wants to know if you want to visit Belle after school?"

"Today?" her voice rose.

"No, maybe next week? That is if you want to, or she could come to our house."

"That would be better," Peggy relaxed.

"Didn't you have a good time?"

"It's okay. Can she come here instead?"

"I'll ask him if that works. How's the math coming?" She checked Peggy's work. "Wow! Glad *you* know what you're doing!" She patted Peggy's shoulder, went to the bathroom and shut the door. After checking her hair in the mirror, she gave herself a good pep talk. *What's wrong with you? You're acting like a teenager. It's just Charlie. Go out there and act normal!* She pinched her cheeks.

His back faced her. She stood quietly and studied him. *I do miss Charlie. How would my life be different if . . ."*

He turned around. "What did Peggy say?"

"It's Belle's turn to come to our house, and that would work best for me. That way Jean won't be alone."

"I understand." Charlie shifted his weight to the other foot. "I'll talk with Belle and let you know. Would it be okay if I called?"

Peg panicked. *What does he mean called?*

Charlie sensed her nervousness. "You have a phone? We don't, but I could call from our neighbors. Save me a trip to town," he explained.

Peg let out a breath she didn't realize she held but couldn't get another from air heavy with unsaid words. "Of course," she finally replied. His bright blue eyes shone.

Mary and Jean piled goods next to the cash register. Peg grabbed a sack, happy for something to do with her hands. She shook it open. "I'll ring it up for you."

Jean wiggled in beside her. "Can I do it?"

"Yes." Peg moved to the side and read prices to Jean: "Sugar, forty-nine cents; peanut butter, twenty-three cents; toothpaste, twenty-seven cents; laundry soap, twenty-two cents. This Lux detergent works well." *What a dumb thing to say.* She blushed.

"Mom ran out of her lye soap," Charlie explained. "She said to put it on her tab." Jean announced the total. Peg lifted the record book from below the counter with trembling hands. After flipping to the correct page, she avoided eye contact as she handed Charlie a pen. An electric shock ran up her arm when their hands touched.

Now that Peg stood just an arm's length away, Charlie wondered how she might react if he pulled her close and kissed her right there, something he'd been thinking about for a long time. He signed with short jerky movements. His wet hand smudged the signature.

"Can I stay here and help Grandma at the store?" Jean asked.

Grateful for the interruption, Peg raised her eyebrows at her mother who answered, "Of course, dear."

CHAPTER 60

The passenger door screeched when Charlie tugged it open. He set the bag of groceries on the floor to avoid spilling as he bounced over rutted dirt roads. After the engine turned over, he eased out the clutch and rolled down the dusty window. The fragrance of blooming lilacs filled the cab. As he drove home, fields embroidered with green rows slid past. *How can I see Peg again? Is she divorced? Who can I ask?* Joy crept over his face. *I finally have something to hope for. Maybe Peg and I can get together. How can I find out if she still has feelings for her husband? It's my fault. I shouldn't have let my pride drive her away.*

All the way home, Charlie tapped the steering wheel and hummed a popular Bing Crosby song. "You made me love you. I didn't want to tell you. I want some lovin', that's true. Yes, I do. Indeed, I do. You know I do."

A farmer in a nearby field flicked the reins of his team as they plodded through newly broken earth. *Will's 'bout ready to plant.* He rolled by an apple orchard festooned in pink blossoms. *Soon as the petals drop, I'd better be ready to spray our fruit trees. Sure hope Belle wants to visit Peg's girls. That doctor's right. I'm healing with time. My family and nature help. Wonder how Florence's doing. Since she refuses to answer our letters, maybe we should let her go. People didn't give up on me. Belle pretends to remember her. All those returned letters hurt Belle. She thinks her mother doesn't care. Who can blame her?*

When he drove into the yard, the dog heard the truck and trotted over. "Move, Buddy, so I can get out!" He eased the door open and pet its head. The dog rolled over for a belly rub, too. "OK, off you go!" Charlie nudged him, walked around to the other door and carried in the bag of groceries.

His mother came onto the porch. "Oh, good, you're back. I need to start the laundry. Will you pump me some water and set it on the stove to heat, please?"

"Sure thing," he grinned.

"You're in a good mood."

"Must be the change in the weather. I think winter's finally surrendered. Where's Belle?"

"In the treehouse, as usual." She indicated the big cottonwood standing sentinel over the back yard.

Charlie strolled to the outside pump. His biceps contracted as he pumped the handle and bulged as he filled and carried each washtub. Step, slosh, step, slosh. The water soaked the front of his shirt. After settling both tubs on the woodstove and stoking the fire, he headed to the treehouse.

He paused at the weathered lettering showing through a swaying curtain of waxy leaves. Gray wood peeked through the oxidized red paint warning: "No girls allowed." As he grasped the bottom board nailed to the tree's craggy trunk, deja vu flooded. He remembered pounding it there twenty years earlier. *Magic fills treehouses.* Hand over hand, he climbed. One of the old boards creaked and tipped askew with his weight. He made a mental note to secure it later. When he reached the floor of the treehouse, he pushed up the trap door and stuck his head through. Belle dozed on one of his mother's scrap quilts, red curls covering most of her face. *Sleeping Beauty. You're the best part of my life, not a little girl anymore.*

She opened one eye. "Daddy," she extended her arm from beneath the quilt and reached for him.

"Hey, Freckle Face." He put a finger on her nose. "Sorry to wake you."

She rose from her nest. "That's okay. Come in." She gathered the quilt and pushed her back to the wall.

Charlie placed palms on the floor and heaved himself up. He scrunched over, his knees up to his neck. "Been a long time since I fit here."

"This is fun." Belle giggled.

"Do you know who built this treehouse?"

"Did you, Daddy?"

"Yep, when I was younger than you. Grandpa had leftover lumber from his new barn. He let me use the wood scraps and leftover paint. I spent hours building it, but after I finished, I found it quite boring up here by myself."

"Why didn't you bring a friend or a book?"

He reminisced as he gazed out the window. "My friend Peg came up here a couple times."

"You mean Peggy's mom?"

"Yes."

"Is it true that you two got engaged?"

Who told you that? Charlie winced. *May as well tell her the truth.* He exhaled. "Yes, we were before I went to war. But we broke up after I came home."

Belle moved closer. "Why? When did you meet Mom?"

"We broke up because I had problems from the war. I began dating your mother after that."

"Are you still married to Mom?"

His head jerked up. "Yes, why do you ask?"

Belle lowered her chin and twisted her hair around a finger. "You don't go see her anymore and we don't write her letters."

"That's what SHE wants, but she still loves you. She just thinks it's best this way."

A tear leaked from the corner of Belle's eye. "What's the use of having a mom if I don't ever see or hear from her?"

"It's complicated. Your mother had a very hard childhood. That's something that's difficult to recover from." He changed the subject. "Maybe we should remodel this place, so I can fit in here.

"Could we?" Belle's voice rose.

"Of course, I'll scout around for supplies."

CHAPTER 61

With news of the boxer's death, Mrs. Block felt safe enough to return home. Peg decided to stop by to tell her about the lawyer. She rapped lightly, trying not to wake the baby.

When no one answered, she walked around to the back steps. Mrs. Block peeked out, then opened the door. "Peg! Come in. Sorry it took me so long. Putting Celestia down for her nap." She led her into the front room and tossed a pile of unfolded diapers from the couch back into a laundry basket.

"Here," Peg picked up a diaper, "let's fold while we talk."

"Thanks." Mrs. Block joined in. "You able to contact Mrs. Simms's nephew?"

"Yes, I've made an appointment for us next Friday. Mom will watch the boys for us."

"Thanks!" She stopped folding, "Wait, for US? You're going, too?"

"Yes, I've decided to file for a divorce."

"Oh." Mrs. Block picked up another diaper. *I don't know what to say to that.* "Ever hear who killed that boxer who tried to blackmail me?"

Thanks for not asking me more about it. "Nope. Ben's pretty sure that the mob knocked him off because he messed up. He didn't have orders to threaten you, only to check on the baby."

"How do you know that?"

Peg understood the concern in her voice. "Uncle Ben talked with the grandfather about the baby. Remember his daughter, Celestia's mother, wasn't married? Guess she's barely fourteen. Although she won't name the father, Uncle Ben thinks one of the mobsters took advantage of her."

"That's terrible!"

"For her, yes, but it helps your case for adoption. I think a judge will see that a loving mother who has taken care of Celestia is much better for the baby than a teenager who lives with a mobster."

Mrs. Block sat back and clasped the diaper to her chest. "Oh, I pray so!"

CHAPTER 62

"I hope it's okay if we babysit today until Grandma's done at the store," Peggy told Belle as they walked to their seventh-grade English class.

In the crowded hallway, a young man bumped against Belle. She stepped back. He winked at her. She blushed and turned to Peggy. "That's okay. I love little kids. Out on the farm, we never see any. But we do have the cutest baby animals."

"I'll bet it's lonely out there," Peggy sympathized. She stopped at the door of the history room.

"Sometimes," Belle admitted, "but my dad's helping me fix up his old treehouse, and he spends all the time with me he can."

"What about your grandma?"

"She does too, but there's always work. There's sooo many chores on a farm," she complained, "but it's different when Dad and I work together."

"A treehouse sounds fun. Meet you by the front steps after school?"

"Sure. You can come out when the treehouse is finished, and we can sleep in it."

"Is it safe?" Peggy wondered. "I don't want to roll off."

"You won't. It has walls and a roof. The only way in is a trapdoor, and we can lock that."

"Maybe."

After school, students spilled out the front doors. Peggy and Jean waited for Belle. Peggy put her books down to tie her shoe.

"That's why I like slip-ons," Jean remarked. "Is Belle staying the night?"

"I don't know."

"If she wants, she can have my bed and I'll sleep on the couch," Jean volunteered.

Peggy's voice rose. "Really? That's nice of you. Thanks."

Belle appeared in the front doors flanked by two boys. One whispered in her ear. She giggled. When she noticed Peggy and Jean, she waved and hopped over.

Jean gasped, "Those two aren't nice boys."

Peggy elbowed Jean. "Let's go." Tension followed them home. After the first block, Jean ran ahead.

"What's up with her?" Belle asked.

"Who knows?" Peggy replied, avoiding the uncomfortable truth.

"Maybe it's good to be an only child," Belle speculated.

Peggy jumped to Jean's defense. "She just gave up her bed for you."

Belle raised one eyebrow. "Her bed?"

"She thought you may be spending the night."

"That IS nice," Belle conceded. "Can we have an after-school snack?"

"We often have leftover cookies or cake because Mom caters parties. There are apples in the cellar. They're getting a little old, but still taste good if you peel them."

"Good. I'm starving!" Belle walked faster.

Peggy clutched her books to her chest and scurried along. "Where's your books?"

Belle shrugged. "I don't do homework. That's what school is for."

Peggy's eyes widened. She ran ahead to open the door, happy that Jean had arrived first to unlock it. *Not sure I want Belle to know where we keep the key.*

Belle sauntered in. "Where's your mom?"

"She's usually at work, but today she went with Mrs. Block to Seattle. That's why we're watching the boys."

"On a vacation?"

Peggy set her books on the kitchen table. "No, Mrs. Block is trying to adopt her baby."

"Why does she need to adopt her own baby?"

"It's not hers. She takes in laundry, and someone left the baby in the laundry."

"Really? Who would do that?" Belle gasped. "I wish the baby could have stayed here with us!"

"Me, too. I love babies."

Belle glanced out the window. "So we're here alone?"

"For a few more minutes, Grandma's bringing us Mrs. Block's boys, so she can go down to finish the shift at the store. I thought we'd take them down to the park to play."

"I think we should stay here," Belle suggested.

"Why?" Peggy followed Belle's gaze. The two boys from school had followed them home. "Oh, I see. Go out and tell them to leave, please."

"Why? The kids aren't here yet. It's rude not to talk with visitors."

Peggy stood firm. "They're not coming into the house."

Belle rolled her eyes. "What a bluestocking! Fine. I'll go out and talk with them for a little while."

"I thought you were hungry," Peggy grumbled. Belle flitted down the steps and across the lawn to the boys, waiting on the sidewalk. Peggy got down the cookie tin. "Jean, do you want some cookies and milk?" she called.

Jean finished washing her hands and came from the bathroom into the kitchen. "What kind? Where's Belle?"

Peggy's jaw clenched as she pointed toward the door. Jean moved to the kitchen and put her nose to the glass. "Why are those guys here? What is Belle doing out there? Mom wouldn't approve."

"She's telling them we have to babysit. They'll leave soon." *I hope!*

"But why did they follow you home?"

"Belle probably told them to," Peggy growled.

"Just asking. Don't bite my head off," Jean sulked.

Peggy poured her a glass of milk and set it next to the cookie tin. "Sorry."

"That's okay. Should we take Belle and her friends a cookie, too?"

"No!"

Jean took her snack out on the front porch. Ten minutes later, she saw Grandma nearing with the Block boys in tow. "Grandma!" She scampered to meet them. Belle turned at the commotion and her two boyfriends drifted off. Belle waited on the sidewalk.

"Hello, Belle." Mary smiled. "Peg told me you may come after school to help watch these guys."

"Sure," Belle pouted, dismayed by the boys leaving.

"Come on, guys," Jean held out a hand to each boy and Belle followed. Peggy walked out to meet them.

"Hi, Grandma!" Peggy waved from the porch.

She waved back. "I'll be back in a couple hours to pick up the boys."

"Do you guys want a cookie?" Peggy took down the cookie jar.

"I do!" Belle followed. She caught the screen door and let it bang shut. Peggy winced. "What kind of cookies do you have?"

"Wash your hands first, boys," Peggy ignored Belle as she hustled them into the bathroom.

"What's up with her?" Belle asked Jean.

"She didn't like you bringing those boys over."

Belle rolled her eyes. "I didn't bring them. They stopped by." She took a bite of a big sugar cookie.

"Those James boys are naughty," Jean reported.

"Ha! Who told you that?" Belle smirked.

Jean pursed her lips. "Noone had to tell me. I see what they do at school."

"What's that?"

"They cut class and smart off to the teachers."

"Regular criminals!" Belle snorted. Peggy returned with the boys in tow. "Maybe they're related to Jesse James!" Belle laughed.

"Who?" Peggy asked as she helped the boys climb onto the kitchen chairs.

"The James brothers. Jean thinks they're bad. But Paul told me he thinks you are pretty, Peggy!" Peggy blushed. "And he's the cutest one, too," Belle huffed with disappointment.

CHAPTER 63

Mary spotted an old truck turning into Peg's driveway. "Is that Charlie?" she wondered and flicked the reins on old Dolly to catch up. The buggy jerked along coming to a stop in a cloud of dust next to the truck. Charlie opened his truck door, turned to the noise and grinned up at Mary.

She tugged the reins back. "Hello, Charlie, here to pick up Belle?" He coughed in the settling dust, then moved to the buggy and gave his hand to Mary. She grasped it and jumped down. "It's so nice those girls are friends, don't you think? Reminds me of when you and Peg . . ." She stopped a little embarrassed.

"It *IS* nice. I'm afraid Belle's lonely out on the farm. By the time I get in from the fields, I'm too bushed to do much with her. But we remodeled my old treehouse. She spends her spare time there."

They walked together to the door. Mary opened it. "Yoo hoo! Anyone home?" she called as she entered. The radio blared from the front room. The boys and Jean sat glued to the Lone Ranger program. Peggy and Belle sat on the floor painting their nails. Peggy heard Mary approaching. "Oh, Grandma, we didn't hear you come in."

Belle spotted Charlie, "Dad!"

"Hello, Tinkerbell," he teased, calling her by her pet name, "are you taking care of your lost boys?"

"Did they behave?" Mary asked as she took off her hat.

"Good as gold," Jean reported. "Can we wait 'til the program's over to go to your house?"

Belle shook her hand and blew on her wet nails. "Can Peggy come home with us?" she asked. Peggy's eyes widened. "I thought we could sleep in the treehouse tonight," Belle suggested.

"She sure can," Charlie agreed.

"Oh, wouldn't that be fun, Peggy?" Mary chimed in.

Peggy swallowed. "Can Jean come, too?"

Belle shook her head. "There's only room for two in the treehouse."

"That's fine," Mary agreed. "I could use Jean's help with the boys. Their mom and Peg won't be home until the train comes in tomorrow. Gather your things, Peggy. Charlie's probably anxious to get on the road."

Peggy screwed the lid on the red polish. *But I don't want to go.* "Ready, Peggy?" Belle jumped up. "If we get home before dark, you can see our new lambs."

But I don't like animals.

"Mom, we've got company. Put another plate on," Charlie called as he walked into the kitchen.

"This way, Peggy," Belle pranced down the hall to her bedroom. She yanked blankets from the bed. "Let's set up before dark. I'll find another pillow."

Peggy set her bag on the floor. "Can I use your bathroom first?"

"You can on the way. The outhouse is out back. Can you carry this?" Belle handed her a flashlight, scooped up the blankets and peeked over the top. "Follow me." Peggy trailed behind.

"There's the outhouse." Belle motioned with her head. "See that treehouse straight ahead. Come there when you're finished." She lumbered off under her load. Peg set her bag down and slowly opened the outhouse door. She pulled a face, pinched her nose and entered. Upon exiting, she headed to the outdoor pump.

Belle stuck her head out the treehouse window. "Where're ya going?"

"To wash my hands." Peggy crossed the yard to the outside pump and worked the handle until water gushed forth spraying her shirt. She reached in and rubbed her hands under the stream, pushed the handle down and jumped over the puddle it left. At the bottom of the tree, she paused. *It's a long way up.* She slung her bag over her shoulder and tested the bottom rung. *Don't look down.*

"Come on!" Belle encouraged. The boards hold my dad. They'll hold you."

Peg took a deep breath and eased up. Her legs wobbled. Belle's head appeared in the trap door. "Come on. Just two more." She held her hand down to Peg who clambered in and sagged onto the floor. "You afraid of heights?"

Peggy pushed a lock of hair from her eyes. "Guess so."

After dinner, the girls helped clear the table and do the dishes. "Do you have something we can take to the treehouse to eat later?" Belle asked her grandmother.

Anna disappeared into the pantry and poked two potato doughnuts in a sack. She handed it to Belle along with two rinsed milk bottles. "Fill these at the pump."

"Thank you, Mrs. Wilson," Peg said. Belle took the sack of treats and led the way to their adventure.

Anna watched the girls out the window. "Peggy's such a nice girl. I'm glad she's Belle's friend," she commented to Charlie who agreed, thinking, *That has a lot to do with who her mother is.* He only nodded in agreement, saying, "I'm glad she's Belle's friend, too."

In the treehouse, the girls spread blankets into beds. "I brought some cards," Peggy dug in her bag. "Do you play canasta?"

Belle plumped her pillow and placed it between her and the wall. "You'll have to teach me."

Peggy explained the rules as she shuffled the cards. "It's easy. We play a lot of cards at our house."

"Not us, by the time supper's over, my grandparents and Dad want to relax and listen to the radio. But I don't blame them. They work hard all day."

Peggy dealt the cards. "After we get our homework and chores done, we play cards, make honey taffy or help Mom bake for her catering business."

Belle organized the cards in her hand. "Sounds like more work."

"Not if you want to do it." Peggy put three aces down.

"I understand. When Dad and I work on the treehouse, it's not work. Are aces high or low?" Belle discarded a red three.

"Don't throw that away, "Peg cried. "Remember they're worth one hundred, and if you get all four of them, that's eight hundred points." She dug a notebook and pencil from her bag. "Do you want me to keep score?"

Belle chose another card to discard. "You think of everything. What else do you have in that bag?"

"I brought polish in case we want to paint our toes to match our nails."

"You're always so put together. Where do you buy your clothes?"

The wind rattled a branch against the roof. Peggy glanced up. "My mom likes to sew."

"She makes all your clothes?"

"Mostly remakes. My cousin has pretty clothes that she hands down, and Mom redesigns them for me. When she's finished, they are nothing like the original, except the fabric, of course."

"I wish I had a mother like that," Belle murmured as she thought of her mother living in prison.

Peggy revealed four more eights. "Canasta!" She booked the cards and moved a red five on top. "Clean book. Doesn't your grandma sew?"

"She's too busy, too tired. I've seen her knit at night, but never use a sewing machine except to mend."

"You can come over and use ours," Peg suggested. "I'm sure Mom would show you how, and I could help you learn how to sew simple things."

"Thanks. I'll see if Grandma has any fabric."

"If she doesn't, we probably do." Peggy discarded her last card and yawned.

Belle dropped her cards. "Does that mean you won?"

"We'll know when we count up the cards." A gust of wind made the treehouse sway. Peggy's eyes widened.

"Don't worry. Dad added extra bracing. I hope it pours!" Low clouds began dripping. The girls scooted to the window. Belle turned off the flashlight. Lightning flashed in the distance.

A long low rumble followed. "This is fun!" When rain blew through a big crack, Belle took off her pillowcase and nailed it over the opening. "Let's put our beds together. We'll stay warmer that way." They fell asleep with their backs to each other.

A soft thud woke Peggy. She threw the blanket over her head and scooted closer to Belle's warmth. A knock sounded on the trap door. Peggy froze. Another knock. She tapped Belle's shoulder. "Someone's knocking," she whispered.

"It's just the storm," Belle mumbled. Knock, knock, knock. Both girls sat up. "Who's there?" Belle squeaked.

"Friends," a masculine voice answered. Belle lifted one end of the makeshift curtain. She shone her flashlight on the grinning face of the youngest James brother, Leonard, at the base of the tree. "Paul, is that you?" she called through the floor.

"Yes, let us in."

"Don't open it. We're in our nightgowns!" Peggy demanded and placed her bottom firmly on the trap door.

"Oh, for heaven's sake, it's just a dress," Belle pushed Peggy's shoulder.

"I'm not moving. Talk to them out the window."

Belle threw her hands in the air. "Honestly, you're such a prude." She lifted the curtain and stuck her head out. "Hi."

Paul climbed down. "Peggy with you?"

"Yes."

"Come down and talk to us," Paul suggested as he jumped to the ground. His deep voice sounded enticing to Belle but made Peggy shiver.

Peggy squinted at her watch. "It's four in the morning! What are they doing here? Did you invite them?" she hissed.

"Move," Belle ordered. "You can stay here, but I'm going down."

Peggy reluctantly slid over. Belle disappeared. Peggy scooted on top of the door. *What if they try to come in? I want to go home. This is the last time I stay here! I knew I didn't want to come.* Low laughter and voices floated up. *They're probably talking about me. Do I dare listen?*

Paul patted his pocket for a match and lit a cigarette for everyone. Belle took a drag and began coughing. "Haven't you smoked before?" Leonard asked in disbelief.

"No, that burns!" She tapped her chest "Where would I get one?" she sputtered.

"Any adults in your house?" Paul responded.

Belle gave her cigarette back to Paul. "Mine don't smoke. They never did. Probably didn't want to spend the money."

Peggy crept to the window. Belle flipped on the flashlight, creating a yellow hollow in the dark. She pointed it up. "Peggy, come on down. We're just talking."

And smoking, Peg thought.

"Why doesn't she like me?" Paul asked loud enough for Peggy to hear.

"Oh, she does. She thinks you're cute," Belle smirked, waiting for a reaction from Peggy.

Peggy gasped. *I never said that! Even though I do think he's cute, I'd never tell anyone.*

Leonard threw his cigarette down and ground it out with his heel.

"Hey," Paul protested, "why'd ya waste most of it?"

"Had 'nough." He took Belle's hand. "Let's go for a walk and let those two work it out." He led her toward the barn.

Charlie's dog began barking. "Let me go," Belle whispered desperately. "Do you want my dad to come out and see you?"

The porch light flicked on. "Get!" Belle scrambled back up the tree. The boys sprinted to the protection of a stand of trees.

Charlie stepped onto the porch. He scanned the area. "Settle down, boy." He hunched over to rub the dog's ears. "You see something? A racoon maybe?"

Peggy covered her mouth. Belle scuttled back under the covers. "Shhh!"

CHAPTER 64

As the overcast Seattle skies began weeping, Peg stepped from the train station into fog mingled with coal smoke and hailed a cab. Mrs. Block ducked into the back seat. Peg handed her the baby and dug in her pocket for the address.

An Irish cab driver scooted out. "Ha-ware-yuh? Want yer bags in the boot?

"No thanks," Peg answered. "Fourth Avenue and Denny Way, please." Peg crawled in the back beside Mrs. Block.

"Right. You'll be goin' together, then?"

"Yes." Peg adjusted her bag on her lap and directed him from the back seat, "Take us to the intersection, please."

"Can't be a walkin' with a baby. I'll drop ya on the footpath 'cross the street."

Peg traced a rivelet on the window with her finger. *I wonder how Ralph will react when he receives these divorce papers. Surely, he'll see it's for the best? What if he refuses?*

"Do you see that!" Mrs. Block broke into her thoughts and pointed at a statue of a somber Native American in the middle of the intersection. Wrapped in a blanket, he raised his arm in greeting.

"That's Chief Seattle. City's named for em," the chatty cabdriver reported over the clacking of a passing streetcar. The ruckus woke Celestia. Her mother gave her a bottle. "Chief Seattle got baptized Catholic, like me," the driver continued. "What's the number again?" He slowed the cab and scanned the buildings.

"One fifty-eight," Peg replied. She and Mrs. Block gathered their things and prepared to hop out.

Peg read aloud: "One fifty-eight. Hanford, Waterman and Burke Attorneys at Law." The cabby spotted it and steered the cab to the curb.

Mrs. Block dug in her purse and handed over money for the fare. Peg shook her head. "I can get it."

"No, I want to. You've made all the arrangements and took the day off." She continued reaching over the seat, giving cash to the driver.

He hopped out, opened the door and helped the ladies. "Cheers! Want your change?"

"Keep it," Mrs. Block chimed, relieved to have arrived at their destination.

Peg stared up at the building's imposing facade. Concern flitted over Mrs. Block's face as fear rode on her shoulders. Peg took her arm. "Come on. Remember the lawyer is Mrs. Waterman's, I mean Simms's, nephew. He knows we're coming and what we want." Mrs. Block exhaled and squared her shoulders. Peg shoved open the heavy door into a marble clad lobby. Two elevators rested under arched doorways. Both had gold signs. One read "This car up," and the other "This car down." Off to their left, a staircase curved to the second floor. Peg approached a directory between the elevators and found the location of the office they needed. "Fourth floor. Let's take the elevator," she suggested and pushed the button.

Mrs. Block hugged her baby tighter and stepped in. When the car moved, she caught her breath. "Never been on an elevator before," she confessed. Little Celestia giggled. Mrs. Block smiled. "Guess she likes it." The elevator rose and jerked to a stop. The doors opened.

Peg led the way down the hall to the door with the firm's name painted in gold script. An attractive secretary in her twenties stopped typing. "Good morning."

"Good morning. Peg Sparks. We have an appointment to see Mr. Waterman."

"Have a seat. I'll let him know you are here."

While they waited, Mrs. Block plucked a rattle from her bag. The baby reached for it and Peg reached for the baby. Mrs. Block twisted her hands in her lap. "Will you do the talking?" she asked in a whisper, trying to maintain her composure.

Peg squeezed her hand. "Sure, but he'll have questions I can't answer."

"I can answer questions."

The receptionist's telephone rang. "Yes, I'll bring them back." She rose. "Follow me, please."

They trailed down the hall to a corner office where the door read:

Alfred Waterman, Attorney at Law.

The receptionist opened the door.

"Come in," a paunchy, balding man greeted them as he came around his desk. His cigar bounced as he talked. "My aunt told me to expect you. You're interested in adopting a baby?" Seeing the bundle on Mrs. Block's lap, he crushed the smelly cigar.

"And I need advice on obtaining a divorce," Peg added. But first, she explained the circumstances surrounding the baby.

As Mr. Waterman clarified a few things with Mrs. Block, he jotted down notes. "Considering the condition of the baby's parents, the adoption should go through with no trouble." He gave Mrs. Block a reassuring nod. "We'll draw up the paperwork. Will you have Sheriff Fox give me a call, so we can contact the parents?"

Mrs. Block let out a sigh. "Of course," she replied in a voice she didn't recognize as her own.

"Mrs. Sparks," he turned to Peg, "can you tell me why you're seeking a divorce? But before you do, just know that unless you are a victim of cruelty, adultery or abandonment, it won't be as easy as Mrs. Block's case."

"I guess abandonment," Peg confessed aloud. "I did leave him in Alaska, but we haven't heard from him since. He hasn't answered any letters or sent us any money."

"Do you believe he will cooperate?"

Peg shrugged her shoulders.

He fingered his mustache and turned the page of his notebook. "How can I contact him?"

Peg's forehead wrinkled as she tilted her head. "Send it to Ralph Sparks in care of the Salty Dawg Saloon, Homer, Alaska. If he's not there, someone from that establishment will know where to forward it."

CHAPTER 65

Charlie gave Peggy a ride home after breakfast. "You girls have a good time last night?" he asked as he opened the door for Peggy.

She gathered her bag and fled without answering. *And I'll never go back!*

Peg heard the old truck and opened the front door. "Thanks, Charlie!" she called. Charlie followed Peggy up to the front porch and stood with a shy smile at the bottom of the steps.

He cleared his throat. "Thanks for letting her come. Belle loves company. I'm afraid all she's got at the farm is us old people," he stated apologetically.

"Charlie, we're not old yet," Peg protested.

"I'm trying not to be," he admitted awkwardly. "Hey, how about we take the girls to Natatorium Park next weekend? It'd give Belle something to do." *And me, too.*

"I bet they'd love that. Let me check my schedule and I'll get back with you." *Are you asking me on a date? We're both still married.*

"Sure, I'll call you Friday and firm it up." Charlie touched the rim of his hat. "See you Saturday, I hope."

Peg shut the door and leaned against it. *I do want to go with him.* Do I still love *him?* She struggled to regain her composure. *Why does Charlie make me so nervous?*

Jean finished wiping a plate and set it in the cupboard. "Mom, what's a natatorium?"

"An indoor swimming pool. It's an amusement park in Spokane. Been a long time since I've been there." She returned to the sink and dunked a dirty skillet into the soapy water.

"Oh, can we go? Can we?" Jean begged in excited anticipation. "I've got some babysitting money saved."

"We'll see. Go make your bed and feed the chickens, please."

"But Peggy got to spend the night with her friend. Why can't she feed the chickens?" Jean protested.

"Just never you mind. She's got her own chores. Now, off you go." *Something's amiss with Peggy. I need to talk to her alone.*

After Jean went outside, Peg went into the girls' bedroom. "Well, have fun? Did you sleep in the treehouse?"

Peggy stood at the dresser, unpacking her bag. She turned and forced a smile. "Yes, the treehouse is neat."

"What else did you do?" Peg sat on the edge of the bed and patted a place next to her. "I loved that treehouse, too. Do you want to go again?"

Peggy sat next to her. *I don't want to be a tattle tale and get Belle in trouble.* "I don't think so," she hedged.

"Why not? What happened?" *She's not telling me something.*

Peggy stared at her shoes. "Nothing. It's a little uncomfortable staying with strangers."

"I wouldn't let you stay with *strangers*. Why, I've known the Wilsons my whole life. Did they treat you well?"

"Yes, they're nice, but I prefer being here."

Funny homebody. Not social like me. Peg rose. "That's fine. Belle can come here. Her dad invited us to Natatorium Park next weekend. Does that sound fun?"

"Could we go with just our family instead?"

"Well, we don't own a car, so we'd have to borrow one and pay for gas. That's why this is such an opportunity. A couple of you kids will have to ride in the back of Charlie's truck, but I think you'd have fun. *And I think I want to go.*

"OK," Peggy conceded. "But will you not tell Charlie until Friday night that we're going?"

Something's going on here. "Why?" Peg stood in the doorway, trying to figure out her daughter's hesitation.

Peggy twisted a lock of her hair. *Should I tell her?* "I'm afraid Belle will invite some of her other friends."

"And you don't want her to?" *The more the merrier for me.* "Are you afraid they'll leave you out?"

"No, I don't like big crowds and Belle would invite a lot of people." *I don't want the James brothers there.*

"I understand. I haven't told Charlie that we'll go yet anyway." *But I think I will.* "Put your things away. I need you in the kitchen to help me bake for the Duncan's anniversary party Saturday night. If we're going, we'll have to get all that food ready, so we can drop it off on our way out of town."

Peg got the biggest mixing bowl out, scraped in butter and two cups of sugar. *I guess I do want to go Saturday. Been a while since I've taken a day off. And I know the girls will have fun. Or do I just want to be around Charlie again?* She picked up the whisk and beat the mixture harder than needed.

CHAPTER 66

Friday night, Peg sat next to the radio mending socks. The girls camped out on the rug with a big bowl of popcorn between them. Jean turned the radio dial until it picked up the program.

"The Pepsodent Company brings you Abbott and Costello!"

Organ music filled the room followed by an advertisement:

"Colds and flu are on the rampage! So much so that in one of our largest cities recently, policemen were stationed in all theater lobbies to keep snifflers, sneezers, and coughers from spreading flu and pneumonia. The police had orders to clear lobbies of all crowds to protect the public health.

"Take warning! Start taking this precautionary measure against colds at once. Gargle daily with Pepsodent Antiseptic. It kills surface germs in 10 seconds and at the same time soothes sore throats, resulting from the common cold. In fact, tests show that people who gargled regularly with Pepsodent Antiseptic caught fewer colds and got rid of colds twice as fast. You too may expect these results, but don't wait. Start the Pepsodent Antiseptic habit in your home at once. Because Pepsodent kills germs, even when you dilute it with two parts of water. It lasts three times as long and makes your money go three times as far. To help keep colds away, gargle with Pepsodent Antiseptic every day.[5]

"We now join Abbott and Costello at a baseball game."

---

[5] https://www.genericradio.com/show/MTExMzc3MjYwNQ1

ABBOTT: "I say Who's on first, What's on second, I Don't Know's on third."

COSTELLO: "You gonna be the coach, too?"

ABBOTT: "Yes."

COSTELLO: "And you don't know the fellows' names?"

ABBOTT: " Well, I should."

COSTELLO: "Well, then, who's on first?"

ABBOTT: "Yes."

COSTELLO: "I mean the fellow's name."

ABBOTT: "Who."

COSTELLO: "The guy on first."

ABBOTT: "Who."

COSTELLO: "The first baseman."

ABBOTT: "Who."

COSTELLO: "The first baseman."

ABBOTT: "Who."

ABBOTT: "Who is on first!

COSTELLO: "I'm asking you who's on first."

ABBOTT: "That's the man's name.

COSTELLO: "That's who's name?"[6]

The program stopped. Peg dropped the sock she'd mended and listened.

"We interrupt this broadcast with a special report from our European correspondent, Eric Sevareid:

This morning, September 1, 1939, war began in Europe with the German Offensive in Poland that violates a nonaggression pact made with Poland in January of 1934. German forces bombarded Poland on land and from the air. Germany

---

6 https://www.americanrhetoric.com/speeches/abbott&costellowhosonfirst.htm

gave Poland no ultimatum which constitutes direct aggression. Poland has invoked its treaty with Great Britain. France has declared martial law.

Here in Britain, both Houses of Parliament met tonight, and local authorities have activated the air raid warning system. The king has mobilized the army and airforce."

"Are we at war?" Jean gasped.

Peggy shushed her. "Not us, Europe."

The radio went on to describe Germany's brutal invasion. The details upset the girls. Peg rose and turned off the radio. "There'll be nothing but news."

"Will our uncles go to war?" Peggy fretted.

"Maybe, but don't worry. We're not in it." *Yet . . . And I hope we don't!*

Peggy picked up her book and resumed reading. Her mother fished another holey sock from the mending basket. A few minutes later, Peggy asked, "Mom, what's a de-bu-tante?"

"A what? Let me see." Peggy brought her the book and put her finger on the word. "Oh, debutante, a high society girl that gets dressed up fancy and tries to find a husband at a dance."

"Like Cinderella?"

"Yes, I guess it is."

Jean plopped on the floor in front of her mother. "Is that how you met our dad?"

Peg snorted. "No, he's a friend of the family." She headed back to the kitchen. *I don't want to discuss this!*

Peggy joined in, "Wait, Mom. I've always wondered why you married someone over thirty years older than you."

"For the adventure of Alaska!" she confessed. *And except for having you girls, the marriage was a huge mistake.*

The phone rang, giving Peg the perfect reason to end the conversation. She flapped her hand at the girls, shooing them off to bed and scurried into the kitchen, her heart flip-flopping. "Hello?"

"Hi, Peg. It's Charlie. Can you girls go with Belle and me tomorrow?" Hope made his voice rise.

"Yes, but we'll need to make a stop at the Duncans before we leave. I have cookies to drop off for their anniversary party."

Charlie's eyes widened. "No problem! See you at eight?"

"We'll be ready. Thanks for taking us, Charlie."

"Believe me, it's my pleasure."

Peg hung up the phone. *What am I getting myself into? Ralph's not even signed the divorce papers yet.*

Charlie replaced the handset and started humming the refrain from a popular tune of the day: "Blue skies shinin' on me. Nothin' but blue skies do I see."

His mother closed her eyes. *What are these kids doing? Sure hope Charlie's not going to get hurt, just as he's starting to heal.*

CHAPTER 67

The next morning, Peg rose at six to pack for the park and box the cookies for the Duncans. As she plunged her hands into the dish water, she heard Charlie drive up. She checked the clock above the kitchen table: seven-thirty. *What's he doing here so soon?* "Move it girls! Charlie and Belle are here." She dried her hands on her apron and opened the front door. "You're early. Give us a couple minutes!"

Jean bopped out of her room. "I'm ready."

Peg handed her two boxes of cookies. "Take these. Be careful not to break any. Set them on the front seat." She held the door for Jean, then went to check on Peggy who stood in front of the mirror styling her hair. "Don't worry about that. By the time you ride in the back of the truck, you'll have to redo it. Bring the hand mirror and a brush. Did you girls pack your swimming suits and towels? Hurry!"

"It's only seven-thirty," Peggy complained.

"I know, but I don't want to keep them waiting."

Charlie gripped and ungripped the steering wheel. *I should have listened to Belle.* She'd complained about leaving home early and snoozed in a pile of quilts atop an old mattress in the back of the truck. *Hope I didn't upset Peg. I should have waited around the corner until eight.*

"Come on, Sis. You can primp after we get there!" Peg stared at the ceiling and shook her head. *That girl cares too much about her hair!* She finally shooed her out, balanced two more boxes of cookies with her bag and locked the door. Peggy stood next to the truck, feeling awkward. *Now what?* Peg set the cookies next to the others and glanced over at Charlie. His infectious smile wiped away her irritation. "Hop in, Peggy." He pointed at the bed of the truck.

Her brow furrowed. "But there's no room and I'll arrive looking like I slept in my clothes."

"Then hop in the middle. You can hold the cookies." Peg moved the boxes.

Charlie pinched his lips together. *I wanted ALL the kids in the back.*

Peg climbed in. "Remember we have to drop these at Duncans?"

"I remember." He put the vehicle in gear.

They rode in silence to the two-story Victorian house four streets over. Peg alighted and held her arms out for the boxes.

"Here, let me help you." Charlie opened his door.

I don't want to irritate him by making him wait for me again. "No, thanks. I've got it."

He eased his door shut and sagged against the seat, disappointed she'd cut his chivalry short.

Mrs. Duncan's horse-faced daughter, Joan, opened the door and squinted over Peg's shoulder to spot Charlie waiting in the truck. "So, you won't be here tonight?" She waited for an explanation.

Nosy blabbermouth. "No, my mom will be coming, but I had previous plans."

Mrs. Duncan came to the porch, opened her purse and gave Peg cash for the cookies. *Thank goodness!* "Thanks. I appreciate your business." *This will come in handy today.*

"Everyone appreciates your cookies!" Mrs. Duncan responded.

Music and lights from the carousel lured them to the park. Each person chose a brightly painted animal. Charlie jumped onto the saddle of a reindeer standing erect, proud of its mighty horns. Peggy chose a prancing filly, and Jean climbed onto the galloping horse with mane and tail flying. Peg mounted a roaring lion. Belle chose a tiger with bared teeth. She tilted her head back, laughed loudly and gave it a slap on its behind.

After the carousel stopped, Belle alighted. "Come on! There's the roller coaster."

"You kids, go ahead. They make me sick." Charlie grabbed Peg's hand. "Follow me. Meet us at six at the concessions for dinner," he instructed the girls. Peg handed Peggy a fist of bills as Charlie led her to the end of the line at the shooting gallery. He read the sign: "TEN SHOTS FOR TEN CENTS."

Peg pursed her lips. "Still think you can outshoot me, do you?"

"You never know." Charlie waggled his eyebrows. "Hey, I got a lot of practice in the army." Peg winced at the reference. She placed her elbows on the counter, shut one eye and squeezed the trigger. Plink, plink, plink, plink, plink! Five bottles tipped over. Again, she concentrated. Ping, Ping, Ping, Ping, Ping! Five metal targets flipped down. With a gloating grin, Peg raised her hands above her head.

Charlie chuckled. He stepped to the counter, took aim and hit them all except for his last shot. "Did you do that on purpose?" Peg challenged. Charlie answered with a questioning smile.

The attendant gave a low whistle. "Great job! What prize do you want?"

Peg studied the wall of stuffed animals. Her eyes lit when she noticed a malamute pup. "That one!" When he handed it to her, she buried her face in its fur.

"What will you name it?" Charlie asked.

Her voice dropped, "Miko."

After an afternoon of rides, they met the girls for dinner. The sun slipped behind the mountains as snatches of music drifted their way. Charlie took Peg's elbow and led her toward the dance area. "I have a surprise for you." Peg's eyes widened. "Benny Goodman and his swing band are playing tonight."

Peg caught her breath. "Really?"

"Can we stay, Dad? Please, can we?" Belle closed her eyes to the dreamy melody and spun in a slow circle with her arms out.

"It must have been moonglow, way up in the blue.

It must have been moonglow that led me straight to you.

I still hear you sayin', 'Dear one, hold me fast.'

And I keep on prayin', 'Oh Lord, please let this last.'

We seemed to float right through the air.

Heavenly songs seemed to come from everywhere.

And now when there's moonglow, way up in the blue,

I'll always remember, that moonglow gave me you.

It must have been moonglow, way up in the blue.

It must have been moonglow that led me straight to you.

I still hear you sayin', 'Sweet child, hold me fast.'

And I keep on prayin', 'Oh Lord, please let this last.'

We seemed to float right through the air.

Heavenly songs seemed to come from everywhere.

And now when there's moonglow, way up in the blue,

I'll always remember, that moonglow gave me you."

Charlie ran a finger down Peg's cheek. Her pulse kicked up. Memories stabbed her heart. He raised an eyebrow at her.

She squeezed his hand as she remembered their kisses in the meadow, nights of stargazing, months of loneliness and worry while Charlie fought in the war. *Oh, why did I ever let you go? I hope it's not too late for us.*

"We can stay," he told Belle. A smile teased the corners of his mouth. Peg pressed her lips tight to contain the joyful feelings of her heart.

CHAPTER 68

Mrs. Simms passed Peg in the hall. "You have a call."

Peg went to the front desk. "Hello?"

She immediately recognized her mother's voice as she spoke with a sense of urgency. "Hi, Honey. There's a letter here at the store for you from Alaska. It looks important. Stop by after work and pick it up, will you?

Is Ralph contesting the divorce? What will I do if he refuses? Surely after five years of separation, he doesn't want me back. I can't give up Charlie now! A finger of ice traveled down her spine. "Where's it postmarked?"

Mary squinted at the small writing. "Hum . . . Sitka?" She guessed. "Know anyone there?"

Peg grabbed onto a nearby chair. "I don't. But maybe one of my friends moved. Remember how lonely Uncle Gene was when we visited him in Homer? *Something must be wrong!* Seems he had a brother there. No name on the return address?"

Mary inspected the envelope and read, "Sitka Pioneer Home. What's that?"

"Don't know. Open it and read it to me!"

"I'd feel more comfortable with Fred bringing it to you. He's coming into town. Save you a trip."

"Good idea. Thanks, Mom." *What could it be? Is Uncle Gene in a rest home? I don't know anyone in Sitka! Maybe it's from*

Ralph's lawyer. Peg worried and returned to take Mrs. Hall's blood pressure. At the end of a long day, she gathered her things and flung open the door to the reception area.

Mrs. Simms heard the door and paused. "Don't forget your letter, Peg." She handed it to Peg and waited for her reaction. "Fred just dropped it off a few minutes ago. News from Alaska?"

"Thanks." Peg returned to the office, grabbed the letter and hurried out. She didn't want an audience and waited until she reached the end of the block to stop and study the envelope. *Sitka Pioneer Home? What would they want with me?* She tore off the end and unfolded the letter.

January 21, 1939

Dear Mrs. Sparks:

We regret to inform you that your husband, Ralph Sparks, passed away today. Enclosed find a copy of his death certificate.

Please accept our condolences,

Staff of Sitka Pioneer Home

Peg took a step back, blinked and reread the letter. She swallowed hard and squeezed her eyes shut, then covered her mouth with a trembling hand. She stumbled to a nearby telephone pole and leaned against it as her mind raced. *He's dead? What happened? Did he get the papers? He's dead? Did he take his own life after seeing the divorce papers?* She studied each word in the letter again. Turning the envelope over, she saw another paper inside and shook it out. *There's a death certificate.* She froze and tears welled in her eyes. She folded one arm over her stomach and read:

> Certificate of Death Territory of Alaska
> Office of Registrar of Vital Statistics
> Full Name: Ralph Sparks
> Place of Death: Sitka Pioneer Home
> Date of Birth: May 5, 1887
> Age: 71 years, 8 mos. 17 days
> Occupation: fishing
> Birthplace: Michigan

Peg skimmed the document, then attempted to decipher the doctor's handwriting for cause of death.

> Cause of Death: Chronic valvular heart disease
> Place of Burial: Sitka, Alaska
> Date of Burial: Jan. 23, 1939
> Usual Residence: Seldovia, Alaska

She turned the document over.

> Height: 5 ft. 10 in.
> Weight: 165 lbs.
> Complexion: Light
> Color of hair: Gray

Her mind raced. *He lost weight. I never noticed symptoms of heart disease, but a lot can change in five years. He must have left the island after I did. Did he ever get Peggy's letters? Is that why he never answered them? How will the girls take this news? So, it was his heart. I can't believe he didn't drink himself to death.* She plodded home in a fog. *I guess I don't need a divorce now.*

CHAPTER 69

The Wilsons sat down to supper around the worn kitchen table. Anna placed a platter of ham and scalloped potatoes in front of Charlie. Lost in his thoughts, he traced his finger over the initials he'd carved into the surface as a young boy. *Yesterday at the park felt like a dream. Maybe I should file for a divorce.*

Anna tried to start a conversation with her granddaughter. "Belle, tell us about school today."

Belle shrugged, "The usual" and slathered a hot roll with butter.

"Two more days until school's out," Anna persisted. "Aren't they having anything for the end of the year?"

"Yes, we had an assembly today." Belle realized her grandmother wasn't giving up.

"Tell us about it."

"People got awards. 'Howard the Coward' won a scholarship to Washington State."

Anna clucked her tongue in disapproval. "Howard who?" she scowled.

Belle rolled her eyes. "Howard Hastings. Oh, and Peggy Sparks won best dressed." She licked her knife, which earned her another frown of disapproval. "I don't know why SHE won.

She admitted to me most of her clothes are makeovers from her cousin's dresses."

"Her mother's an excellent seamstress. She should be commended," Anna commented.

At the mention of Peg's name, Charlie's fork clattered to the floor. "Excuse me," he whispered. "What did you say about Peg?"

"I said she's an excellent seamstress," Anna repeated.

Absorbed in his own thoughts, Charlie picked up his fork and rolled the handle repeatedly between his thumb and fingers. *I miss Peg. What excuse can I use to see her soon?* "Belle, I'm going to town tomorrow. Would you like to go and visit Peggy?"

Belle saw through the invitation. "No, go visit them yourself." She pouted. "Why don't you ever take me to see MY mother?"

Anna's head jerked up. Charlie stiffened replying, "Because you've never asked to. Besides, children aren't allowed to visit prison."

Belle folded her arms across her chest. "I'm almost fifteen. And I'm not a child!"

"Tell you what. I'll visit your mom Saturday to see what the rules are," Charlie promised. "If it's allowed and your mother wants to see you, we'll both go." *I need to tell her I'm filing for divorce anyway.*

Charlie took a seat in the visiting room amid solemn faces talking in undertones. *I hope Florence will agree to talk to me.* An iron door clanked and reverberated down the long hall.

Charlie jumped up, glad to see it was Florence who entered. *She looks better, happier and cleaner than last time. Her hair is combed and her countenance curious. Maybe the chip has fallen from her shoulder.* But her demeanor changed quickly when she spotted Charlie.

"Hello, Florence, how are things?"

She growled from her chair, "It's a doggie dog world here."

"I think you mean a dog-eat-dog world."

"Whatever. I'm biting my time."

Charlie suppressed a chuckle but decided not to correct that one. "You're adjusting."

"Had to. Knew I wouldn't get off Scotch free," she grumbled.

Charlie cleared his throat and took a deep breath. "Florence, I'm filing for divorce. I'm tired of living alone." He prepared himself for her onslaught of verbal attacks.

"Go ahead," she responded in a flat voice and shrugged half-heartedly.

He blinked rapidly and processed what he thought he heard. *Did she give up? It can't be this easy!* Grappling to find the right words, he took a step back and gulped, "You promise?"

"Why would I care?" she retorted in a voice devoid of emotion.

"Well, I have another request," he added, still reeling from Florence's previous comment.

"Now what?" she snapped, more impatient than anything else.

"Belle wants to come for a visit. You'll be amazed what a beautiful young lady she's become. I'm so proud of her."

Florence wiped away a tear. "I think of her every day," she confessed. "I don't know if I want her to see me here. She's better off without me in her life."

Charlie reached for her hand. She recoiled at his touch. He pressed on. "No, she's not. You're not a bad person. You're here because you love her. You wanted to protect her. She's old enough to understand that now." He lifted her chin. "If she starts to visit you on a regular basis, Florence, that will give you something to look forward to." Charlie motioned across the room where a mother wearing a prison dress chuckled as she played with her toddler. "Look, Florence, you're not the only one. The people in Newport understand your situation more than you realize. They know you did what you did to protect Belle. Think how grateful Belle is for not having to go through what you did." He took another breath. "And the truth is she needs a mother to talk to. Mom tries, but it's not the same. Besides, she's so busy with the farm that after dinner, she's sleeping in her rocker when Belle's anxious to visit."

A spark of hope pushed aside her overwhelming regret. Her tears fell, and she admitted between jagged sobs, "I would like to see her. I've missed my baby girl. It's been so hard without her." Then she stopped to ask the question that had always kept her from having Belle visit. "Do you really think she can forgive me?"

"I'm sure of it. I have."

CHAPTER 70

The phone rang. Peg picked it up. "Got it. I'll head 'em off." She slammed the receiver and yelled to the girls. "Get upstairs, NOW! Peggy, lock the door and don't open it for anyone but me!" She put her hands on her daughter's shoulders and locked eyes. "You understand? No one!"

Peggy's eyes widened. "What's wrong?"

"Uncle Ben needs help." She snatched the rifle from the gun rack and darted off.

Jean peeked around the doorway. "Where's Mom going?" At the end of the block, a black car peeled around the corner.

Peggy bolted the door. "Follow me!" she commanded, grabbing Jean's hand and taking the stairs two at a time. She crept to the window facing the road and lifted the bottom of the curtain. Uncle Ben's police car sped by. Their mother took off in the opposite direction. Jean stooped under her sister's arm and peered out. The black car passed by again, followed a minute later by Uncle Ben. "They're chasing some bad guys," Peggy's voice trembled.

Jean grabbed her sister's arm. "Will they hurt Mom?"

"No, they don't know she's after them." Peggy hoped she sounded more confident than she felt. The next time the black car appeared, a shot rang out and the car careened across the neighbor's yard. Peg followed and ducked behind the big elm. She fired at the other tire. The car veered to the side. A man jumped out of the driver's side and high-tailed it down the street.

"Hold it right there!" Peg shouted and fired into the air. He dropped to the ground. Uncle Ben screeched to a stop and sprang from his car. "Stay back," he called to Peg. She edged next to a hissing tire and searched inside for another person. No one.

The girls stood riveted to the scene. "Mama!" Jean cried and gripped the windowsill.

"She's okay. Uncle Ben's handcuffing the man," Peggy explained. Jean bolted toward the stairs. Peggy grabbed her by the arm. "Stay here! Mom'll come back in a few minutes. She hugged Jean to her side and lifted the curtain again. Uncle Ben led the culprit to his car and locked him in the back seat. Peg conferred with the sheriff. They returned to the disabled car, and Ben grabbed a bag from the back. When Peg glanced in the direction of her home, the girls immediately dropped the curtain.

"What's going on?" Jean demanded.

"They got him. Mom's talking with Uncle Ben."

Peg emptied the ammunition from the gun and hid it in her pocket. She climbed the neighbor's stairs and knocked at the door. No answer. She knocked again. *Wonder if they're not home or if they're too afraid to come to the door.*

"It's your neighbor, Peg," she called. "You can come out now. We've captured the criminal." Still no answer. She shrugged and crossed the street.

Peggy saw her coming, raced down the stairs and opened the door. "Didn't I tell you NOT to open that door?" her mother repeated sternly.

"But I saw you coming," Peggy blubbered as she wrapped her arms around Peg's waist. "I'm happy you're safe."

Peg enfolded her in her arms. "It's fine. We're safe. Where's Jean?" At the sound of her name, Jean bounded onto the porch into her mother's arms and cried, "We were scared you might get shot."

"But I didn't. Let's go back in the house." The screen door clacked behind them.

"Are there more bad guys?" Jean whimpered.

"No, darling, just one dumb one, and we caught him. Guess he couldn't find his way out of town." She laughed.

"What did he do?" Peggy asked.

"Robbed the bank, but no one got hurt, and Uncle Ben got the money back."

The old-timers at Tarbet's store relished local scandals to chew on. "Now pipe down, all you, if'n you want me to read the paper!" Frank drew a pair of smudged glasses from his flannel shirt pocket, wiped them with a handkerchief and cleared his throat.

Tom tapped his toes and scowled. "Well, go on!"

Frank moved the newspaper closer and read, "Edward W. 'Eddie' Bentz, a career criminal from Tacoma, waltzed into the First National Bank last Thursday and handed the teller, Opal Green, a note demanding money while an unidentified man served as a lookout at the front door. She complied. After taking the money, Bentz ordered everyone to lie on the floor and to stay down. As soon as he left, Opal rang the sheriff.

Thanks to the quick thinking of Peg Sparks, Bentz is in custody in the Newport Jail. Sheriff Ben Fox alerted Deputy Sparks that the black Chevrolet sedan took off down her street. She ran around the block in pursuit. In the heat of the chase, Bentz couldn't find the street out of town and circled the block twice before Sparks shot two tires of the getaway car. When Bentz sprang from the disabled car, Sparks held him at gunpoint until Sheriff Fox arrived. Bentz's accomplice was not found in the car. Anyone who happened to see a man about five-foot three, wearing a black suit and fedora, in the vicinity of the bank between two and two-thirty Thursday afternoon, please call the sheriff's office immediately."

"Well, Mary, Peg's done it again!" Tom chortled as he lowered the paper. "Better not mess with that gal."

"I wish she wouldn't. She's got two girls depending on her," Mary interjected as she continued concentrating on cutting a piece of fabric.

Tom's oversized belly shook with his hearty laugh. "Wouldn't Peg and Mrs. Gardiner make a team, though?"

"Why?" Mary put down the scissors.

"Remember how Mrs. Gardiner scared off those intruders last year? Keeps a revolver by her bed 'cause her husband travels a lot. Said she heard men outside her window and fired five shots right through the screen! She heard a man swear and take off running."

Frank chuckled adding, "Yep. With her, it's one strike and you're out!"[7]

---

7 History of Newport Washington, Tony and Suzanne Bamonte: p. 66

CHAPTER 71

Florence's words, "Go ahead," swirled through Charlie's mind all the way home. He turned onto the final stretch. Thu-thump, thu thump. The washboard road echoed, "Go ahead! Go ahead!" *I DO need to move on, go forward and for the first time in a long time, I feel like doing that. How will Peg react when I tell her I'm filing for divorce? What about Belle? She wants a relationship with her mother. Hopefully, that won't drive her away from me.*

By the time the old truck jerked to a stop in a cloud of dust, he'd made up his mind. Anxious to share the news with his mother, he jogged to the house, found the kitchen deserted and rushed through the back door. Scanning the yard, he noticed his mother's straw hat dip behind a row of corn in the garden. *Will she support me?* He hesitated, then lifted his chin and vaulted down the steps. "Mom?"

Anna stood, pushed her hat back and wiped her brow. She heaved the vegetables to one hip and trudged to the edge of the garden. Charlie stepped over a row. "Here, let me take that."

Grateful for help, Anna handed over the brimming five-gallon bucket of peas. She read the good news in his beaming face. "Well, your visit must have gone well. You remind me of a cat with feathers on its whiskers."

He released his breath. "Yeah, it did."

"Take that bucket to the porch. You can help shell these while you tell me all about it." She stopped at the pump to rinse the dirt from her hands.

Charlie set the bucket on the porch and pushed faded wicker chairs across uneven boards into the shade. He moved a nearby wash tub close for the shells and brought out a dishpan from the kitchen. Popping open the crisp pods, he ran his nail inside and threw peas into his mouth, savoring the starchy sweet crunch. *The first taste of summer.* His foot tapped the porch in a happy beat.

Using the handrail, Anna climbed the porch steps to sit next to him. She bowed her head and wiped her face with her apron. *So good to see my boy happy again. Thank you, God.* She filled her lap with peas and began snapping. "How's Florence?"

Charlie gave a catlike stretch. "About the same."

Then why's he so happy? "Any news?"

He grinned. "She's agreed to a divorce." A chickadee from a nearby lilac bush sang, "Hey, Sweetie! Hey, Sweetie!"

Charlie swung open the door to the doctor's office. Mrs. Simms paused her paperwork. "Hello, Charlie. Feeling ill?"

He gave a thumbs-up. "Feel wonderful. Peg in? Thought I'd drop by to take her to lunch."

Mrs. Simms turned her back and suppressed a giggle. *I can diagnose that illness. He's lovesick!* "Hang on. I'll find her for you." She stepped lightly to the back room where Peg opened a brown paper bag. "Don't eat that!" Mrs. Simms demanded, sounding very official.

Peg inspected the sandwich. "Why not? I just made it this morning and kept it in the icebox."

"There's a handsome man who's in the waiting room and he wants to take you to lunch." She bit back a smile.

Peg dropped the sandwich and brushed crumbs from her skirt. "Who?"

"Come see for yourself." Mrs. Simms led the way. She ducked into the office and pretended not to listen.

"Charlie?" Peg touched her hair. "Are you taking me to lunch?"

He bit his lip. "Yes, Mr. Scott's holding two of the lunch specials, but we'll need to move along.

"Two, huh? Pretty confident I'd say yes, aren't you?" *It feels easy to slip back into teasing Charlie. I can feel myself letting my guard down.* "Be back in an hour," she called to Mrs. Simms.

"Take your time. Only one appointment this afternoon," she grinned like she'd orchestrated the whole thing. *Isn't love wonderful?*

Mr. Scott ushered them to the corner table which held a vase of daisies. "My favorite flower!" Peg noticed. *What's going on?* She rubbed her arm nervously as customers began filling the dining room. *Is he going to embarrass me?*

"I remembered," Charlie confessed. Not trusting her emotions, she chose to sit with her back to the crowd. Charlie took a seat across the table and whispered, "I have good news."

What's he up to? Is everyone watching us? Charlie, be careful. "I like good . . ."

Charlie interrupted. "I talked with Florence yesterday."

Peg's voice trembled. "She's getting out?"

"No, she agreed to a divorce." Charlie tensed for her reaction as Mr. Scott appeared. He set glasses of water on the table. "Two regulars on the way."

Peg sat up straight and cleared her throat, "Thank you and a lemonade, if you have one." Mr. Scott turned to Charlie.

He bit the inside of his cheek. "The same." Mr. Scott made a note and moved to a nearby table. Charlie gazed into Peg's eyes. "Well?"

Her face began to flame. "Well?" *I don't know what to say! This is too public.*

"You know what this means, don't you?" He covered her hand with his.

Noise rose as a group of train passengers entered the dining area, drawing her focus away from Charlie and over her shoulder. She shifted her weight, "What?"

"After YOU get a divorce," Charlie began.

Now Peg interrupted him, "I'm not getting a divorce." Charlie's Adam's apple bobbed with a thick swallow. She paused for effect, "I don't need one. Ralph's dead."

He blinked and drew back. "What? When? How?"

"I got a letter with condolences and a death certificate from the Pioneer Home in Sitka last week." She tried to read his reaction while he digested the information.

"Why didn't you tell me?" Charlie asked with an injured look.

"I didn't want you to think I was angling for something more than friendship. You are still married. I'm not for anyone breaking up a family." She waited minutes for his reply. The meatloaf special arrived; they ate in awkward silence.

When Peg couldn't take the tension any longer, she asked, "Can we get out of here and talk?"

Charlie pushed his plate back. His head tilted slightly to the side as he winked, "I want to do more than talk." He stood and offered his elbow.

Her heart pounded. *Get yourself in hand! People are watching us.* She took his arm, rushed Charlie out the door and ran ahead. He caught up, planted himself in front of her and held out his arms.

An undeniable warmth spread through her body. With tears running down her face, she gave a sigh of relief, pressed her head against his chest and stepped into his love.

Mary Tarbet traveled from Newport, Washington
to visit her granddaughter, Peggy Joy Sparks.
Ishmailof Island, Alaska
Summer 1923

Sundsby, Ralph and Peggy Sparks
Fishing boat Halibut Cove, Alaska about 1924

Peggy and Gladys (Peg) Sparks
Picking wild cranberries
Glacier Spit,
Halibut Cove, Alaska
About 1927

SISTERS
Peggy Joy and Lois Jean Sparks

ABOUT 1928

ABOUT 1930

Acknowledgments

Thanks to all who supported me with kind words, sales and encouraged me to write the second book.

Heartfelt gratitude to:

My editor, friend and cheerleader, Linda Kurtenbach who not only edits, but teaches me about writing.

Martin Publishing for creating covers for my books that make me smile.

My friends in our Utah League of Writers, Rural Writers chapter, for giving me feedback and ideas.

My ancestors whose lives inspire me and make me laugh!

About the Author
Nikki Freestone Sorensen

Nikki Freestone Sorensen, a family history enthusiast and teacher, has been researching and preserving family stories for over forty years.

She finds this African proverb inspiring: "When an old man (or woman) dies, a library burns to the ground."

Nikki believes connecting with ancestors provides us with a sense of identity. We learn new perspectives and gain insights from them. Family stories inspire and strengthen us to meet life's challenges.

For people with a difficult family history, consider the advice of George Bernard Shaw: "If you cannot get rid of the family skeleton, you may as well make it dance."

She recommends visiting the following to help you find and preserve your own family history:

familysearch.org
ancestry.com
storycorps.com
rootstech.org

Nikki would love to hear from you.
Contact her at nikkidear4@gmail.com.

www.ingramcontent.com/pod-product-compliance
Lightning Source LLC
Chambersburg PA
CBHW021246190726
48289CB00005B/1516